OUTSIDE

OUTSIDE

Gustavo Bondoni

GUARDBRIDGE BOOKS
ST ANDREWS, SCOTLAND

Published by Guardbridge Books,
St Andrews, Fife, United Kingdom.

OUTSIDE

ISBN: 978-1-911486-14-5

For Emilia

Chapter 1

His fingers trembled.

The computers had finally decided that the ship was close enough to the planet. They'd been decelerating for two days, and now speeds were low enough that the meteor shields covering the viewports could be retracted. It took him three tries to type the commands correctly because of the butterflies in his stomach, but soon the screech of metal on metal filled the cabin as the thick plates pulled back into their niches above the windows.

Earth was visible ahead of them, its familiar oceans and continents, studied in countless classes easy to identify. Rome Permek couldn't believe that he was there to see it. This was the reason that he'd volunteered for the mission. It was the first time in five hundred years that humans not born in the original solar system saw Earth with the naked eye, with only a half-meter-thick plate of transparent Hulldeck between the planet and the observers. His heart lodged in his throat and tears threatened to escape, forcing him to fight them back as he focused on the captain.

He was sure that, on such an occasion, Ashur Nartiya would take advantage of the unique chance to not only get her name hardwired into the history files as the captain of the expedition, but also to be remembered as the person who delivered the oft-quoted inspirational speech. She looked each member of the bridge crew in the eye before beginning.

"Five hundred years ago, humanity was one." She paused

for effect. "And, thanks to our efforts, it will be one again. We will no longer be divided into two incomplete, unhappy races. The scattered colonists will, once more, have a home, and the people of Earth will once more have a future away from the confines of their single world. The way it's meant to be." She seemed to review the statement in her head and nodded, satisfied with the result. She went on in her usual voice, discarding the oratorical tones of the speech. "I want to thank you for your work so far, and for volunteering for this mission, as well as the months of patience you've put into the trip itself." She nodded to the bridge crew.

Heads bobbed in respect around the control chamber. Everybody knew that the volunteers had numbered in the millions. No person in the Tau Ceti system with even the slightest relevant training had wanted to miss out on this voyage, despite the inconvenience of a few tedious months in space. Interstellar travel, though it had improved over the last five hundred years, was still anything but quick, and boredom had replaced death as the most frequent complaint. Even so, the crew appreciated Nartiya's words. She was big on competence, efficiency, and discipline; compliments and thanks were very rare indeed.

"But now, we've got to get to work. This is where the mission truly begins and where things can get hairy. We have one more week to study the planet before we get close enough that our shielding won't stand up to scrutiny if their technology has advanced at the same rate as ours. After that, we have to make contact. So I'll just shut up and let you get back to it."

She turned back to the viewport, silently contemplating the planet in the distance. The bridge crew took that as a signal to resume their tasks and tore their gazes away from the blue dot and back to their instruments.

Rome knew that the captain wouldn't be fooled. The

entire crew, himself included, was only half-heartedly monitoring their screens. Every few seconds, the rustle of fabric would give notice that someone was surreptitiously attempting to get just one more look at the planet. And then just one more.

But as long as an appearance of discipline was maintained, the captain would be satisfied. The novelty would wear off in a few hours anyway, and the real work could begin.

In the meantime, Rome stole another look and pretended to study his sensors, although, as a binarist, he was unlikely to be needed at this point in the mission. It didn't matter. He could stare at the planet all day.

***

The days went by, and the crew grew ever more restless.

Though nobody had expected the Earthmen to communicate, or even to detect them yet, the complete lack of measurable point-to-point electromagnetic communications within the system had everyone on edge. Even the ring system composed of obviously artificial satellites seemed to be inactive, each component drifting silently in its orbit.

The only communications they'd been able to identify emanated from the surface itself and were evidently short-range transmissions. These were frustrating on two levels: they were weak, making it difficult to pick up a clear signal and, even worse, those signals that had been isolated proved impossible to resolve into either visual or audio communication.

On a ship of that size and nature, no effort was made to keep the situation—except for a few technical details—secret, so it became the favorite topic for crew gossip.

The talk quickly grew alarmist. First, guarded whispers speculated about some catastrophe: war, disease, a meteor impact. Then, more openly, the rumors grew wilder and wilder. Most of the crew seemed convinced that human civilization on Earth had been destroyed in some unexpected cataclysm and that whatever had caused it was waiting to unleash its fury on the *Unity*. It was clear that Nartiya would soon have to do something to get things back under her control.

Rome, for his part, was convinced that there had to be someone down there. "Look," he told Stell, "the energy readings show all the signs of a functioning technological civilization going about its business. Concentrated emissions even point to the existence of population centers and a city-oriented demographic distribution."

Stell snorted. "So where are all the phones? The TV transmissions? Their 3D relay waves?"

"They're probably around. Maybe they use a cable-based system. Massive use of Fiberoptic piping?"

"Oh, come on! That would be completely inefficient, and besides, they have a fleet of communications satellites up that they aren't using. Even you have to admit that it looks pretty bad. I wonder what happened to them."

Rome said nothing, knowing that the other wouldn't budge. They'd been having this same argument with little or no variation for the last three days. It was just a way to let off some steam and ease the tension until they found out something new. Everyone was doing the same thing because what was driving them all nuts was precisely the lack of new information.

He looked out over the windowless dining cabin. The lunch break was coming to an end, and most of the crew on shift had either returned to their posts or had gone to one of the viewports to stare at Earth in the distance, so the large, cream-painted room was nearly empty. He risked talking about one of the few secrets that the brass was trying to keep.

"The short-range communications the signals people found seem to indicate intelligent activity."

Stell eyed him skeptically. "How convenient that you should just happen to know about something nobody else has heard of and that just happens to support your argument," he said, showing that, deep down, he did care about the argument.

"You don't really think that I'd make something like that up, do you?"

"Of course you would. All you want is to find a welcoming committee of Earthlings waiting for us when we land so they can throw their women at you." Another point of discussion was Rome's rampant heterosexuality, which Stell, being a militant asexual, found objectionable and crude. "Just face it. They probably had a big war or invented some new disease and destroyed their own civilization. Hell, if it happened to us on Wolf 349 III, it can certainly happen to a bunch of people cooped up on one single planet! I don't think they're all dead, by any means. But I do think that any survivors we might find will be living in trees."

Rome shook his head. "I'm not making it up. We really have found some signals that are likely of technological source."

"And why would the brass confide in you?"

"Because, as far as anyone can tell, the signals are short-range microwave transmissions of the sort you'd encounter between two physically separated computers, or two banks of the same computer. Binary code. Every binarist on the ship, even junior ones like me, has been trying to decipher them night and day."

Stell was still unconvinced, but seemed willing to suspend disbelief for a few moments, if only to break the monotony. "What I don't understand is why we don't just broadcast a greeting and stop messing around."

"Well, I guess it's because the captain isn't sure just what the hell is going on. We have no information at all regarding the situation on the surface, so we don't know what kind of greeting to expect. We think that our tech is more advanced than theirs, so we're basically confident but, to tell you the truth, nobody wants to find out that their tech is better than ours in the middle of a war against a planetary defense system. The ship is armored, but we really can't survive against that kind of firepower if it has any development behind it."

"I guess it's logical. How long are they planning to wait, though?"

Rome shrugged. "The original plan was to transmit in four days, and I think they'll stick to it. They don't want to risk getting us detected before we're ready to talk to them. I don't think we'll get much of a reception if the natives think we've been spying on them, do you?"

Stell grunted noncommittally, picked up his tray, and stood. "I'm getting back to work."

"I'll be along in five minutes," Rome replied. He'd noticed the pretty brunette engine technician by the Stimdrink dispenser.

Stell turned to look, understood immediately, and gave him a disgusted glare before he walked away.

"Neanderthal," he muttered under his breath, but loud enough to be heard.

Rome just grinned at him.

***

Frustration mixed with eager anticipation as the bridge crew prepared to send their first transmission.

They hadn't been able to pick up a single useful

transmission, even after studying the binary signal for days. The closest analogue to the binary communication they'd found was a model of a sandstorm that had been created using chaos theory. Rome himself had put forward a theory that the transmissions related to an extremely complex simulation, but they still had no idea what it was that the computers were simulating. And even less as to the political and social situation on the surface.

The anticipation had a more obvious source. Everyone on the ship, regardless of rank or specialty, had signed up to be present at this moment, the moment in which the starfaring portion of humanity reestablished contact with the stay-behinds. The unification of the race after five hundred treaty-enforced years.

The blue orb in the viewport was considerably larger, its presence dominating the view in both real and psychological terms.

Captain Nartiya turned to face it. She ordered the comm team to open a channel on as many frequencies as possible. The nature of the initial transmission had been decided in a series of meetings attended by all the senior technical people over the course of the previous week. Basically, since they'd been unable to pinpoint any channel as a dominant or government-controlled emitter, they'd decided to hit as broad a spectrum of frequencies and geographical area as they could, concentrating their efforts on the northern hemisphere, which was where most of the energy emissions seemed to be centered.

The speech had been composed by a team of psychologists and politicians months earlier, before the ship had even left Tau Ceti II. It had been set in stone to keep the captain from being tempted into embellishing it for her own glory. That wasn't the officially cited reason, of course, but everyone knew the score.

The captain pretended to be unaware of this and acted as if she would make it up as she went along. She paused to organize her thoughts, hesitated once, and gave the signal to begin transmission, knowing that the message was not only being transmitted to Earth, but also all over the ship. She was the most decorated ship captain in the entire Tau fleet, but she did have a thing for theatrics.

"Greetings, people of Earth," she said in perfect Hanglish, the last recorded official Earth language. "I am commander Ashur Nartiya of the Human Star Voyager *Unity*, which is currently approaching your planet. I am here to transmit a message of peace from the star-traveling portion of humanity to the descendants of those who chose to remain on Earth.

"According to the terms of the Brooklands-Futa Treaty, it was agreed that there would be no contact between our civilizations for five hundred years, allowing each culture to solidify without interference from the other."

Rome chuckled softly to himself, exchanging a glance with Stell, seated two consoles over. Every child on the Colonized planets was taught the real reason for this treaty: Earth, as a backward, isolated dinosaur, had requested the treaty to keep the more advanced Colonies from dominating their culture. But it probably wouldn't have been diplomatic to say so.

The captain continued. "Those five hundred years have now passed, and we have come to invite you to rejoin the family of humanity.

"In the time that has passed, the Colonized worlds have increased in number from the mere twenty-one at the time of the treaty to forty-seven today. There are also six more missions terraforming suitable planets.

"But it is not enough for us to be many. We wish to be one. For humanity to be whole again. Our Federation consists of many worlds with enormously different cultures. We know how to live with differences, and we can guarantee that your way of life and your sovereignty will be respected.

"We will remain at our current position relative to Earth and await your permission to land to discuss our invitation, which we would be honored to have you, the planet where our race originated, accept.

"Thank you."

She signed off, and a tense silence ensued as the bridge crew settled to wait for a response. At this distance, electromagnetic radiation would take thirty seconds to reach the planet, so the message had a theoretical round trip of one minute. But time also had to be allowed for the Earthmen to craft their reply, and they all knew that it might be hours before a response of any type was forthcoming. But they still relaxed visibly only after the timer had reached one minute with no answer.

After that, subdued chatter began among the crew members as tension slowly but inevitably gave way to tedium, the standard state of mind on any space voyage.

∗∗∗

By the end of the shift, the tedium had become frustration, and as the days went by, frustration became a sensation of near-panic that finally motivated the captain to order the ship to approach the planet and hold a geosynchronous orbit around it.

Rome had already done three shifts at his post since they'd approached although, as a binarist, there was little call for his services unless some systems glitch came up. Since a moving ship had millions of computer-controlled functions, errors were cropping up all the time, and binarists analyzed and corrected them while independent redundant systems took over the workload from the corrupted ones.

A ship in orbit, on the other hand, was just a life-support

chamber in space. And, for some reason, life support systems never seemed to fail.

He was bored. Even the incredible magnificence of the planet dominating the sky had paled after a couple of days, and he'd grown tired of looking at it. In desperation, he'd finally gone back to trying to crack the signals from the transmissions they'd picked up from Earth.

He'd managed to deduce that there were, at least, hundreds of billions of complexly moving particles being controlled by semi-chaotic logic that operated in a slightly more controlled environmental setting, but that was all he could get. The simulation seemed much too complex to unravel entirely unless one had a deeper knowledge of the computer language the Earthlings were using. And, if one spoke to an Earthman, it would be much quicker to ask what the simulation was than to learn the computer languages.

Still, he had nothing better to do, so he spent his shifts honing his theory while, at other stations, the frustration continued to build at the continued Earthling radio silence.

On the third day in orbit, things finally came to a head. Captain Nartiya entered the bridge, face haggard, and began issuing orders.

"Power up the converters," she said. "Redeploy the meteor shielding."

The Engineering Officer raised his head. "Excuse me, ma'am, but are we leaving?" It was the question that every member of the crew had been asking for the past twenty-four hours. But this was the first time anyone had had the courage to ask her directly.

She glared at him. "No," she said. "We're going to land."

The bridge, already silent during the exchange, became sepulchral. The anticipation and curiosity took on a presence that was nearly physical. Rome realized that he was holding his breath.

"And what about planetary defenses?" the engineer, a man named Wellman, asked.

"The brass at Tau Ceti II are convinced that the planet is empty and that what we're picking up are just automated systems going about their business. They've ordered us to land at once."

Rome surprised himself by saying, "The planet isn't empty. There's something going on down there."

The captain gave him a look that was more curious than angry.

"You can tell me all about it later. Right now, we're going to land."

Chapter 2

Emily woke, as she always did, ten minutes before the alarm clock was set to go off. Despite years of experience, she checked the time hoping that, just this once, the glowing numbers would indicate that there was still an hour or, better yet, two, before she had to get up. But no. The implacable reality was 6:50. And Mondays were always the worst.

She sighed softly and turned off the alarm. There was no point in waking Graham. Being a software engineer, he could—and often did—sleep till noon. She fought down the urge to wake him and walked to the shower. Like she did every weekday.

By the time she looked into the mirror, another morning ritual, she was feeling almost human. This particular ritual was new. She'd only been taking the time to look her naked body over in the full-length mirror for the last two months. Ever since her thirtieth birthday.

What she saw wasn't unduly worrying, despite having been up late the previous night mopping the floor with all her friends in a VR gaming free-for-all. She knew her features were attractive enough, in a delicate way, although her face was slightly pale and dusted with freckles and her lips were a little thin. Her shoulder-length strawberry blond hair was thin and straight, serious and professional as opposed to fashionable. Nobody would call her a great beauty, but she knew that she was good-looking enough to get a date anytime she ever needed one.

Her body, likewise, was not a problem. She was thin and of middling height, with breasts small enough that gravity didn't hold any fears. And the rest of her had been kept in shape all her life, partly through her own efforts in the gym, and partly, she suspected, due to lucky genetics. Nothing spectacular, but she couldn't complain.

Emily dressed quickly, checked her electron bag to make sure she wasn't forgetting anything, and made for the exit. The elevator was, of course, waiting for her, and the apartment door slid aside immediately.

She was fully awake and in what she referred to as her 'business' mode. She fumed at the lost thirty seconds as the lift descended the seven hundred meters to ground level and thought, for the umpteenth time, that she needed to get a place closer to the ground. Hell, she could afford it now. And Graham wasn't contributing much to the household economy, so it wouldn't really hurt to kick him out on his ass.

But she wouldn't. She resolved to get rid of him every morning, but he convinced her to keep him every night. She wasn't sure if he was that good or if she was that insecure, but, either way, she wasn't particularly worried. It would pass; it always did.

She walked down the same streets she'd walked down ever since getting her current job. Despite her impatience with the lift, the four-block walk to work was useful. It allowed her to organize her thoughts for the first few hours of each day.

Today's first few hours would be delicate. She had a meeting with the Stuttgart Auto Werke product manager to discuss the new advertising campaign. SAW was United Madison's most important client, logical since they manufactured nearly half of the world's vehicles—land, sea and air. The Chinese were their only competition, and they used the other major ad agency: Fullnet Media.

The early meeting was due to the eight-hour time

difference between Denver and Stuttgart, but the hour was no excuse. Everything had to be perfect. Imperfection, or even a delayed campaign, could conceivably cause SAW to lose the market lead to GV Fukong, and that would, by contract, cut Madison's fees in half. And then would come the layoffs.

The creative and accounts people would already be at the office preparing the virtual meeting room on the Mindnet and uploading the standard commercials and full-immersion net ads.

Her own files could be uploaded in real time. They were just spreadsheets detailing how the media budget would be allocated among the different channels. TV, as always, represented about two-thirds of the spending, with the remainder going to Mindnet and outdoor media. She understood the plan was a conservative one, but this was not a client with whom it was advisable to take risks.

The only thing that worried her was how the product manager on the client side might react to the plan. Lee Taik-Sanchez was a bit of a closet sociologist and was always arguing that a greater percentage should be spent on Mindnet advertising. In his opinion, society was mature enough to use the Mindnet to its fullest capability and that advertising would be more effective there than anywhere else.

Fortunately, there were more than three hundred years of data showing that Mindnet advertising always gave a smaller return on investment than the supposedly outmoded TV ads. The data would be enough to sway his boss, although she knew that Lee himself would remain unconvinced.

By the time she arrived at Madison tower, she felt ready for the meeting: she was calm, she was prepared, and she'd run through all the possible questions in her head and had answers ready. Her part should go off without a hitch.

But trouble found her anyway.

As soon as she stepped into the marble-floored foyer, she

was intercepted by an agitated account executive.

"Miss Plair," the man said, "they sent me down to wait for you since you always arrive at this time. Please come with me."

"What's going on?" Emily asked.

"The other directors are in an emergency meeting. Only you were missing."

"Why? What happened?"

"The Mindnet's down, Miss Plair."

Emily was stunned. She knew that the Mindnet was essentially a series of redundancies piled one on top of the other. It might work sub-optimally at times, but it could never go down. That was impossible, and she said so.

The executive answered, "Well, it's not actually down completely. It's working at maybe forty percent efficiency." That was the lowest number in recorded history. "But that isn't the main problem. The main problem is that we can't get Stuttgart at all."

"Maybe the connection to the Stuttgart office is down."

"We thought of that. We tried other links in the city—even comm links and audio-only emergency systems. We can't get anything. It's as if all of Stuttgart has disappeared off the net."

Emily rolled her eyes. So, it was going to be one of *those* days.

***

Minutes later, everyone in the agency was clustered around the TV set in the conference room, anxiously trying to get any kind of news from Stuttgart. The only channel that seemed to have assigned a crew to the story was MindNewsCast. They were also having trouble getting in touch with Stuttgart, so they were sending a crew there on the ground.

Frustratingly, even the TV feed was coming through on the Mindnet, which was still not working optimally and blanked out every few seconds making the reporter's comments unintelligible. The stress level in the room rose with every passing moment.

Despite the potential for mayhem that a complete Mindnet failure in Stuttgart represented for the agency, Emily could still find the time to smile at the irony. Experts had been predicting the death of conventional television for six hundred years. The argument was that the interactive control available on the old internet, the Supernet that followed and, finally, the current Mindnet would render the old non-interactive, 2-D experience redundant.

Sadly, most hyper-educated young professionals seemed to share this view, which had made being a media planner a living hell for as long as anyone could remember. The main problem was that, although the data clearly showed that more people were watching TV in their free time than operating online, educated people didn't want to believe that the great majority could really be that stupid. After all, watching TV was the equivalent of brain death—there was no mental activity in watching programming that was generated by somebody else.

They insisted that the numbers had to be skewed and that their reality was correct.

Nevertheless, numbers didn't lie, especially when they were backed up by additional research that showed that most people, after a day of pointless toil, preferred entertainment that simply allowed them to turn off their brains. They didn't want to interact with anything. Let someone else do all the work.

Though the delay would mean extra work and heightened stress, Emily found herself smiling as they watched a reporter trying to explain what was going on, even though the reporter himself had absolutely no idea what that was. The static only added to the comedy of the situation.

The final irony was that the reason they couldn't get a good image was that some genius had decided to run the TV feed through the already existing, supposedly infallible, fiber-optic network installed for the Mindnet. The same network that was already critically sub-optimal.

She had to suppress an immature giggle. None of her agitated coworkers would have understood anyway, and her professional credibility demanded certain care.

***

The delay went on through the morning and into the afternoon, making Monday a complete waste.

Even the news from Stuttgart had been patchy all day. It seemed that the closer the news team got to the city, the lower the ratio of clear images to static became.

Finally, the decision had been made to turn off the TV and get back to work, but Emily knew that the silence in the hallways was not the silence of deep productive concentration, but the lack of sound created by dozens of employees scouring the Mindnet for information from the confines of their cubicles.

She didn't even try to stop them. Everybody knew that a critical net failure could affect much more than just a couple of deadlines and business communications, and even the most mule-headed director would be too sensitive to order his or her employees back to work under the prevailing conditions.

At four-thirty, the situation hadn't changed, so Emily decided to release her team and go home. Nothing useful was getting done anyway. Maybe Graham could give her an inkling as to what the hell was going on. Maybe the guy would finally prove that having a programmer living off what you earned was good for something other than a couple of orgasms a night.

Yeah, right, she thought as she shut down her interactive desktop, *and right after that, a flock of pigs will fly by for my amusement, as well.*

She enjoyed the ride to the ground floor. A small part of it was knowing that she was, essentially, goofing off on company time in the middle of an enormous crisis and that nobody would ever question her for it. But mainly, she enjoyed the sensation that something different was happening on a Monday. That by itself was enough to make her ignore the possible consequences.

The wide boulevard that ran in front of the building was paved with stone and had a row of trees growing in the middle. Mechanized traffic was limited to two elevated roads that ran near the building's walls, so pedestrians were flowing in front of her. The density of traffic was about average for a Monday afternoon, but something nagged at her subconscious, telling her there was something unusual. Not wrong, but certainly different.

She speculated that it might be that they all seemed animated and determined, as if they were all going somewhere. Maybe that was what jarred her: the feeling that nobody was simply out for a casual stroll, just smoking a weedsprig.

But that would be perfectly normal for a Monday afternoon in the downtown business area. No, there was something else.

Emily just stood, watching, trying to figure out what it was. The warm spring breeze caressed her face and tousled her hair, but she ignored it, just observing the pedestrians.

It finally hit her. It hadn't been immediately apparent because the traffic wasn't particularly dense, and the people were moving at different speeds, but she managed to see what had been bothering her.

Everyone was moving in the same direction. The entire flow of traffic was headed towards Emily's right. To the south. Purposefully.

She'd seen similar patterns outside rock concerts and lazershow events, but never in this part of Denver. They were miles from the stadium.

Emily shrugged and was about to turn left and head home, against the current, when curiosity got the better of her. These people didn't seem panicked or worried, so it was unlikely that they were moving away from anything, but it did seem that they were eager to get wherever it was they were going. Besides, she really didn't have anything better to do; all she had planned for the rest of the afternoon was to ask Graham about the Mindnet failure, which, she decided, could wait. It was a beautiful brisk day in late spring, perfect for a walk.

She briefly debated whether to ask someone where they were going, but discarded the idea. Despite her aggressive nature in business dealings (her coworkers referred to her as the megabitch) and social skill at parties, she knew that if she tried to simply walk up to a perfect stranger on the street and ask where they were headed, she would feel so self-conscious and embarrassed that she'd probably run away before they managed to answer. And, to make things worse, most of the people on the street were walking along in groups of twos or threes, chatting excitedly as they advanced towards their destination.

Emily simply joined the flow, telling herself that if the final objective was too far distant, she would simply turn around and go home. She enjoyed the walk for its own sake, savoring the sight of the dark green mountains glimpsed between the old brick buildings.

After only four blocks, however, she knew it must be

getting closer. The crowds got thicker, and it looked like everyone in Denver was converging on her position. There was also a subtle but definite change in the atmosphere. The pleasant, unconcerned conversation that had been constant during the walk was developing a more urgent edge as the groups that had gone down one street combined with others that had come down a different route and exchanged rumors.

Being ostracized from all the groups meant that Emily's anticipation was killing her. She put on an impatient burst of speed and pushed through the dense crowds for two more blocks before she finally turned a corner and understood that the tall buildings around her had been blocking an unbelievable view.

The whole southern half of the city was gone.

Well, perhaps gone was not quite accurate, but that was the first impression that came to mind. The reality was that everything was perfectly normal right until the central line of Univac Avenue, the six-lane boulevard that divided North Denver from the Historic Barrios.

But, on the other side of that dividing line was … nothing. A featureless black wall, as tall as the eye could see, ran the length of the boulevard and beyond, from east to west, blocking off the sight of everything behind it.

Thousands of people stood on the visible side of Univac Avenue, just staring at the wall.

Emily did the same. The sheer size of it staggered her, dwarfing the buildings around it and continuing upward until it seemed to curve into the very fabric of reality, becoming one with the sky. She stood immobile, trying to reconcile what she was seeing with her knowledge of physics and structural and architectural rules. Just looking up at that vast expanse of blackness made her dizzy—she was certain that the wall had to collapse onto her, to crush the teeming crowd on the street. There was no way that something so tall could stand under its own power.

She must have stood there, just looking at the thing, for half an hour. Looking and listening to the awed whispers from the crowd around her. It seemed fitting that the people spoke quietly; one loud word would probably bring the whole thing down on top of them.

Finally, Emily's need to stare at the wall was surpassed by another, equally irresistible urge: she had to touch it, she had to understand what the wall was made of, to feel its texture. Was it hot or cold? Smooth or rough?

She searched for an open area along the surface, but realized that thousands of people were already crowded around the base of the structure in front of her. Approach would be impossible.

Emily walked to the right. Five blocks, ten, twenty, looking for a free space along the barrier. It seemed that the whole city had heard of it and was out to see for themselves.

After an hour of walking, she came to Denver's warehouse district, a sparsely populated area where the crowd was much thinner. She headed towards the wall and spotted a gap along the surface.

She rushed in and put her hand against the blackness without hesitation, without pause for thought. The possible consequences of touching the blackness never even crossed her mind.

The texture of the wall came as a complete surprise. Before her mind registered its temperature or its texture, she had to deal with the completely unexpected: her hand had sunk into the wall, disappearing from view.

Panic surged and she pulled it out, half-expecting it to be maimed, or burned, or just gone, eaten by the black nothingness in front of her.

But her hand was fine. She tested the movement of her fingers and looked at them minutely but could find nothing amiss.

She touched the wall again, more carefully this time. It was neither hot nor cold, neither smooth nor rough and, despite standing right next to it, she couldn't make out any detail of the surface. It seemed to be there, solid in front of her, but the eye was unable to see exactly where the wall began and even less able to discern what it was made of.

She pushed harder, watching her hand sink in, maybe two inches into the surface, meeting greater and greater resistance as it penetrated, before finally coming to a complete stop. Emily pushed, putting the entire weight of her body behind it, but couldn't overcome the resistance.

She pushed her shoulder into the wall, but got even less result, maybe one inch. And her head wasn't able to break the surface at all.

The sun was going down, off to her right, and the crowd was dispersing, although some people were just standing in front of the wall, looking at it as if uncertain what to do next.

Southsiders? she thought. But it wasn't any of her business. She decided to get herself home. An idea of what was going on was forming in her head, but she had to talk it over with Graham.

***

The reporter, a woman of about forty, had been on the job since the wall came up, and it showed. Even frequent touch-ups of her makeup couldn't mask the bags that were forming under her eyes or the haggardness of her features.

Emily, in sympathy for another veteran of nightmarish working hours, stopped to listen, curious as to how the media was interpreting this latest Denver phenomenon. How the cataclysmic would be presented to a town used to following a fixed, unmovable routine.

It became immediately apparent that the reporter had already described the wall to her viewers as many times as possible (even the most sensational members of the press can only take "it's huge and it's black" so far), and had even exhausted the speculation as to what was going on. They had finally gone into the "human interest" phase, where they were cynically trying to flog a dead horse by pretending to care about people.

Sometimes, Emily's cynicism surprised even herself.

"…an emergency committee to obtain shelter for the people who live in the Historic Barrio area of the city, who find themselves cut off from their homes by this inexplicable, incomprehensible development," the reporter was saying. "Psychologists from the staff of Denver Unicist will be on hand in the shelters to try to deal with the effects of the uncertainty caused by this event. We have here a man called William Shenken, who is unable to return to his home. Mr. Shenken, what are you planning to do…"

Emily tuned the reporter out and resumed her homeward walk. She hoped Graham knew what was going on. Her own theory was not a happy one, but knew she didn't possess the technical knowledge to form a valid opinion. She wanted Graham to tell her that she was wrong. To tell her that everything would be all right.

That comforting her was a role that would normally have fallen to her mother was something she refused to think about. They hadn't talked much after their last big fight, but that didn't change the fact that her parents were on the other side of that wall.

Chapter 3

Emily fumed. It was vintage Graham.

He could go for days on end without leaving the apartment and was invariably at hand to bug her with his inane chatter as soon as she came back from work, never respecting the fact that she'd repeatedly asked him to give her a few minutes to unwind before bombarding her.

But today, when she actually wanted to talk to him, he was nowhere to be found. The apartment was empty, and there wouldn't be a note—this was Graham we were talking about, after all.

She looked around for it, halfheartedly, anyway, but came away unsurprised. Then she tried to comm him. First standard operation, then audio-only, and finally, in desperation, text-only, but received the same recorded message each time: the lines are saturated, please try again later.

Well, it was her own fault, she thought as she sat and waited. What else could she have expected from a man she'd picked up at a Cyberskill tourney? The fact that she'd become global champion at a game he'd designed had seemed to give them some common ground.

That idea had lasted about a week. When the new wore off, she noted that their personalities were diametrically opposed, and even what she'd thought of as a shared love of competitive simulations had turned out to be another wedge that drove them further apart.

The game he'd designed was called Wolfhunt. It was a full-immersion simulation that required the players connect to the game via brainjack, so it could only be played at authorized community interface centers. Even so, however, the game was so popular that a player had to reserve a jacking post days in advance.

She just had to try it. Having been local champion at a few earlier games, her curiosity had made Wolfhunt inevitable.

She found it brilliant. An inspired combination of mental and reflex challenges, it required intelligence, physical dexterity, and machine sensibility in a beautifully generated, if slightly surreal, science-fantasy worldscape. Players were forced to match their skill and wits against the simulated terrain, the fiendish puzzles, computer-generated enemies, and each other.

She had subsequently given it her full off-hours attention, often playing through the night (especially after discovering that after one in the morning, the interface centers were much less crowded) and her proficiency improved daily. She soon found that nobody online with her locally could come anywhere close to matching her.

She won the local championship in a walk. The regional finals were, surprisingly, even easier. And her showing at the nationals was good enough to qualify for the global championship. The fact that she'd been unable to win the nationals spurred her into adopting an even more extreme training regimen, using her determination as a foil to her lack of sleep.

It had worked, of course. Whenever she went after something with all her heart, she inevitably got what she wanted.

As global champion, she'd been offered the chance to meet the game's designer, Graham Johnson.

Graham had turned out to be a tall, thin guy with longish

blond hair and blue eyes, dressed in Bermuda shorts, sandals, and an old T-shirt. His eyes had sparkled, his wit had sparkled, and his ability in bed had decided her. Fifteen days later, he was living in her house.

But while her brilliance was based on a hard-nosed acceptance of the facts of life—namely that hard work, determination, and perseverance were the keystones to success—he was one of those people who lived on pure talent and worked only if there was an immediately impeding financial crisis that had to be dealt with. There could be no doubt of his brilliance, but Emily felt that it was being wasted by his refusal to apply himself to make it blossom.

Even Wolfhunt, she was soon to learn, was a product of this infuriating philosophy. He told her that his driver in the design of the game wasn't the challenge of creating the greatest simulation the world had ever known, but actually that one day as he was lying on the beach, he'd had this great daydream about a slightly off-kilter fantasy world. The game itself had just been his excuse to share the world with his programmer friends. The friends, of course, had recognized the brilliance and had debugged it, expanded it, and sold it to one of the big game companies from California.

The day she learned that had been the day she decided to leave him.

And yet, here she was, months later, flipping channels on the TV, waiting for him to arrive from wherever it was he'd gotten off to.

Despite her excitement, the sheer length of the day finally got to her, and she dozed off.

***

A noise in the darkness woke her in the middle of the night. Even half-asleep, she knew that it could have only been one possible source.

"Graham, do you have to make so much noise?"

She heard Graham jump. "I'm sorry," he said. "I wasn't expecting to find you sleeping on the couch. You're lucky I couldn't find the light switch."

Emily remembered why she had fallen asleep on the couch; she'd wanted to talk to him. But then she saw the time on the entertainment system's display.

"It's three in the morning," she exclaimed. "Where have you been?"

"Working," he said, self-consciously tugging at a lock of his blond hair.

"Yeah, right," Emily replied. She pulled herself up to her full height and took a deep breath in preparation for tearing his head off, but he held up his hands, forestalling the explosion.

"No, really. I got a call from an old acquaintance in the industry who was in a meeting with the mayor. They called this afternoon before the lines went down. They wanted me to take a look at the black wall, so they took me down there and asked me what I thought about it."

"But why you?" Emily could tell when he was lying. He wasn't, so she softened a little.

"They needed someone who understands the system, and, as you know, I'm a programmer." In response to her less belligerent tone, he went into his charm mode, even going so far as to strike a pose at the word 'programmer'.

"Don't be an ass. Why you specifically?"

"I guess it's because when you have a problem that big, you call in the best."

She rolled her eyes but refrained from expressing her opinion. Even she had to admit that the guy was incredibly talented. If he wasn't so goddamned lazy, he might actually be the best. And not everybody had the privilege of observing his laziness firsthand, so it was conceivable that others might have been fooled by his façade.

Besides, she wanted to know what the hell was going on.

"So, what's your take? Can anyone fix it?"

"I'm not sure. I'm convinced that it isn't a software problem, but nobody wants to believe that."

"If that black thing obscuring southern Denver isn't the biggest software problem ever, then what is it?"

"I think it's hardware," he said grimly.

"How can it be hardware?"

Graham sighed and Emily thought she could guess exactly what he was thinking: that, even though everyone knew how the world worked, the actual technical details of what went on around them were a little difficult to explain to a layman. When one added the complications that the city of Denver itself added to the case, it could be a long while.

His sigh also meant that he knew that Emily wouldn't let him go to sleep until she understood.

She really couldn't have cared less about what he thought. If he could understand it, then she was certainly smart enough to grasp it quickly.

Another sigh. "How much do you know about the way the Mindnet is structured?" he asked.

"Not that much. I know that our physical bodies are plugged into a computer that controls the outside world we view. It keeps the buildings up, the wind blowing. All that kind of stuff. We see and feel the world as if it were a real, physical place, but that's only because of the impulses being fed into our brains. And it works well because we've all been plugged in for centuries."

Graham ran a hand through his hair in frustration. His superior attitude was beginning to get on her nerves. Only curiosity kept her mouth shut.

"It's not quite that simple. In the first place, each

mainframe oversees a specific, clearly defined geographic area. So, if you were to travel to Washington, you'd be under the influence of the Washington unit, and the feedback to your physical body would come through the network from there, regardless of where your body actually is. Bodies are always left inside whatever birthing unit they happened to be born in, which makes the logistics much easier to manage. When your consciousness moves to a different computer's area, a code simply tells it where to route the relevant data.

Emily nodded. She'd heard something about that. "That's why the Southsiders didn't just blink out of existence when their area of the net went down."

"Exactly. But you also have to consider the way the mainframes work. They run three major programs at the same time. The first thing they do is to keep everything running: keep the gravity on, the sky blue, and the buildings up. This includes details like coordinating the weather with the neighboring mainframes; you can't have a storm raging in one place and then a sunny day just one step beyond. It would drive our brains insane."

Emily nodded—she'd been peripherally aware of this but had never really stopped to think about it in detail.

"The second thing they have to do is get the information regarding the interaction of the people with their surroundings to the brains—to the seat of the consciousness of each human moving around inside the base program. This is done because everything has a pre-established set of feedback criteria. So, when I touch this table, it feels the same to me as it does to you, filtered only by the differences between your body and mine.

"And defining the parameters and differences between each simulated body is the third major function, and it's the reason it took so long to get the Mindnet up and running. I don't think anybody really knows how the computers define physical characteristics such as who tends to get fat or be tall or whatever. Perhaps they extrapolate how our bodies would look if they were to live life like we do instead of being vegetative growths in birthing chambers." He paused, waiting to see if she'd understood him. She said nothing, so he continued.

"So that's the base. And that's what we have to analyze to comprehend what happened today."

Emily nodded. Her weariness was gone, and even her irritation at Graham's earlier behavior had faded. Now, she was impatient, wishing he would get to the point once and for all. "What did happen?"

"Well, the official theory is that Denver I, the Southside mainframe, is experiencing a problem with its coordination interface software."

"I didn't understand a word of that."

Graham rolled his eyes, but continued. "The coordination software is what allows the transition from the area controlled by one mainframe to that generated by the next. It's the reason we can see across the zones from one area to another, and why a cloud can cross from one area to the next without seaming or distortion."

"But wouldn't that affect the whole city?"

"Not really. In the first place, only Denver I seems to be having the problem. Supposedly, the people in Denver I are fine—it's just that they're surrounded by an impenetrable black wall and they can't communicate with us through it." Seeing that she hadn't understood, and was about to say so, he hurried to explain. "Not too many people know this, but Denver is the only major city to be divided between two mainframes. The reason for this is that it was the first city whose population decided to migrate completely into a cyberworld environment and have the citizens give up physical life. Eventually, however, so many people moved here to join the cyberworld that the existing computer just wasn't big enough to handle it. Hence Denver II, which is where we are now. This all happened more than five hundred years ago."

"So, this whole thing will blow over as soon as this coordination interface thing is fixed? How long do you think it'll take?" Emily was a bit disappointed. While it might be the single most interesting event that had taken place in her lifetime, it didn't sound like it was anything really important.

And, for some reason, Emily felt that she, and the world in general, needed important things to happen, even if the consequences were disastrous. Otherwise, what was the point?

"The official estimate is two days. It would be even less, but nothing like this has ever happened, so they want to double-check everything before even trying to fix it." Graham shook his head. "But I don't think it's a software problem. I think they're wrong, and it won't be an easy fix at all. I told them that. And then I left when they said I was nuts."

Emily laughed. "Sounds like they know what they're talking about." She could easily imagine Graham telling the city's foremost experts on cybernetic world-management that they were all wrong while he was right. All on the strength of having designed a commercially successful mindlink game.

He seemed about to send her to hell, but became pensive. "Look," he said, "I know what you're thinking. These people are experts, the best we have in Denver and all that, but it doesn't change the fact that the solution they're proposing doesn't fit the technical facts. They're only proposing this because it's what they want to believe."

"Why would you think that? I'd think a group of people who've reached their degree of preeminence in the field would be above that kind of childishness."

"You don't understand…"

She cut him off.

"What don't I understand? That you're brilliant and they're not? Come on!" She laughed again.

"That has nothing to do with it!"

She couldn't believe it: she had finally managed to score, to touch a nerve in his laconic self-control.

He took a deep breath. "I really think that they're trying to convince themselves that it's an interface problem because the alternatives are too ugly to contemplate. But their theory would mean that not only did the primary program fail, but its backup and the backup's backup did too. The odds against that happening are astronomical. We actually calculated them and came up with something like ten to the power of thirty-two against. And then they were all very relieved that it came out as non-zero and announced that we'd had a very unlucky break, but it just doesn't feel right to me."

"It doesn't *feel* right? And here I thought you were motivated by data." Emily knew that she was venting her frustration with the whole relationship into this conversation, but she felt a strong need to push him down a couple of rungs. The man's arrogance had originally been attractive, but now it just grated. The worst part was that he was too arrogant to even give her the satisfaction of taking umbrage at the jabs. He just grinned.

"Look, I know it's an even longer shot, but from the few tests I was able to run, it looked to me like more than just the interface was down. They all told me that my tests were skewed by the lack of interface. But even taking this into account, the results were strange."

He saw Emily's face and suddenly grew serious.

"Look, you have to believe me. I really think we're in deep shit. I really think that Denver I has had some kind of catastrophic hardware failure and that it will leave everyone in the sector blacked out until we can get it back online. And we're wasting time."

Like everybody else, Emily knew that blackouts, the sense of being alive and conscious but unable to move and deprived of all sensory input, were supposed to be psychologically damaging. But she'd never, not once, heard of a single case of it actually happening in the last three hundred years. It was a myth.

"It can't happen," she said.

"Yes, it can," he countered, "and there are worse possibilities. Denver I is in charge of the life-support for all the physical bodies born in its sector, even those who are getting data feed from other computers. So if I'm right and the mainframe is down, the people born in the Denver I area will soon begin to die for no apparent reason. They'll be perfectly fine and then, suddenly, the cyberworld body will still be there but unresponsive because, somewhere in a birthing chamber, the brain will have died."

She looked him over and finally decided. Smiling, she said, "It's late. Why don't you give me a kiss? We'll keep at it tomorrow."

Looking as though he wanted to say something else, he seemed to think better of it and, shrugging, brushed her lips lightly and moved towards the bedroom but was restrained by her arm. She kissed him deep, tongue darting, feeling his dry mouth slowly begin to respond, and pulled him onto the couch on top of her.

His pants were around his ankles before his hands, his magic hands, even began to move.

An hour later, she was at peace once more. At peace with the world and at peace with her decision. He might be unbelievable in bed, but the conversation had shown her that he was just a capricious little boy. Unwilling to work on a team compromise and too willing to cry wolf and frighten everybody. And he thought that 'brilliant' meant that he had to be revered and never had to work at anything.

"Graham, I've been thinking about it, and I want you to move your things out. I don't think it'll work out."

His eyes blazed, but he just nodded, a short, sharp gesture. He was lazy, not stupid.

As he stormed out, she reflected on her peace. She would miss this sensation, for sure, but for now, she was perfectly tranquil, perfectly satisfied with her life, and had no worries in the world.

Just how much she'd learned showed in the fact that she could be this calm even though, thirty years earlier, Emily Cecilia Plair had been born in historic South Denver.

Chapter 4

The buzzer was insistent. Graham flailed around trying to turn it off, nearly dropping to the floor in the process. It amazed him how quickly he'd grown accustomed to Emily's wide bed and to where everything was in relation to it.

Unfortunately, his thrashing managed to do more harm than good. Instead of silencing the buzzer, his fingers hit the full-connection button, causing the vision interface on the wall to light up completely.

A four-foot-high image of Odessa Varzi's face illuminated the room. It was regarding him critically.

"You look like shit," she said.

Graham fumbled frantically with the comm controls again until he found the volume setting and turned it down. Way down.

"Yeah, thanks," he grumbled. "Would it make any difference if I told you that you always look like shit?"

"Of course not," Odessa replied cheerfully. "I don't need to worry about my looks. I'm so rich I can have anyone I want."

That, at least, was mostly true. Odessa owned Cyberdev, one of the main software companies in the world. The company that had bought Wolfhunt from Graham.

He favored her with his patented roughish smile. It wasn't one of his best efforts, but then he'd just woken up. "Not me you can't."

Odessa laughed, a tinkling sound. "I got Wolfhunt, didn't I? And I can't honestly say that there's anything else I might actually want from you that I can't get somewhere else," she said, looking him over from head to toe.

Fifteen years his senior, and a friend of his father to boot, she hadn't let that stop them from playing this game ever since Graham was seventeen. Back then, it had been Odessa who made certain things never went past the verbal stage.

Today, fourteen years later, it was Graham. He simply wasn't attracted to the dark, strong-featured, slightly overweight Odessa. She might be one of his oldest friends, but he certainly didn't want to get mixed up in that way with a woman who was accustomed to having absolutely everything her own way. To make matters worse, she was way too intense. She'd gotten her college degree in advanced cyberdesign at the age of nineteen and founded a company that developed both hardware and software for semi-chaotic simulation programs. After that, she'd spent every waking hour turning that tiny start-up into the colossus it was today.

But that left very little time for relationships and very little inclination to think of other human beings as people as opposed to consumers or users.

"You called me in the middle of the night to tell me that you don't need me for anything?" Graham said.

"It's three in the afternoon."

"Oh." He checked the corner of the vision interface. Odessa was correct.

"Are you all right?" she asked him, although he noted that the concern was reflected in neither her voice nor her features.

"Yeah," he lied. "I just broke up with my girlfriend. Nothing to worry about."

"She threw you out, huh?"

"Thanks for your sympathy." Graham tried to glare at her, but his heart wasn't in it. He was going through the motions of being miserable about getting dumped but, deep down, he knew that he and Emily were oil and water, and he was, as always, better off alone.

After a short silence, Odessa continued. "Look, I didn't call you to talk about your love life, amusing as that might be. We have a problem."

"Who's we?" Graham asked suspiciously. Odessa had been put in charge of the group that had rejected his hypothesis. She'd told him point-blank that the group was not going to waste any more time analyzing his theory regarding a hardware malfunction. It hadn't been her decision, but she'd accepted the majority view. For her part, she hadn't spoken against him, but neither had she lifted a finger in his support.

"The Interface Task Force," Odessa said simply. She knew how he felt about that particular group.

"So now, even the team's name assumes that the problem is in the interface? What a bunch of jerks. Tell you what: when you all finish telling yourselves how clever you are, why don't you solve your own problems?" He covered himself up with the sheets again and moved to disconnect the call.

"Wait!"

Graham's hand paused half way to the switch.

Odessa gritted her teeth. "Look, nothing is working according to our simulations, and we need outside help. You've been in it since the beginning, and you were the only one with a different idea."

"They're smart, they'll figure it out sooner or later."

"Yes, but that might cost lives."

"Not mine. My body's in Manhattan, and that server's fine. I checked."

She looked him over, seemingly undecided whether to try to appeal to his better nature or to try to bully him into acquiescence. Finally, she deflated.

"Look, I told them I'd get you back on board. Could you just do it as a favor to me?"

Graham gave her a sour look, but nodded. "No fair," he said. "Just give me a while to shower, dress, and get down to the office."

She smiled gratefully in a rare display of genuine emotion and signed off, leaving him shaking his head on the way to the bathroom. Strangely enough, all he really wanted was to be able to prove beyond a doubt that he'd been right so he could net-message Emily and gloat.

***

Forty minutes later, he was seated at a table with a monitor in front of him and a brainjack plugged into the base of his skull. He'd promised himself that he wouldn't hurry for these bastards and had begun a leisurely bath. Nevertheless, he found himself thinking about the problem. Absentmindedly, he sped up his bathing process and was out of the bath in five minutes, dressed in ten, and was at the team's commandeered headquarters in half an hour.

They hadn't exactly greeted him with cheers and champagne, but at least he could derive some satisfaction from the respectful nods and the fact that everyone was extremely subdued. The older hands were pretending jaded competence, but even there, Graham could detect what was openly displayed on the faces of the junior programmers. Everyone was really, really, scared.

"Okay, what's the situation?" he asked.

"Here's a summary of the diagnostics." Joe Fan, the leader of the crisis management team by virtue of being the oldest government programmer in the group, handed him a sheet of printfilm. The balding, aquiline man had his collar unbuttoned and was sweating profusely.

Graham scanned the summary, which told him quite a number of things he'd already guessed. The team had run the logical tests for an interface failure. By the dates and times, he could tell that they'd started from the most probable and less serious possibilities and worked their way gradually, ploddingly, up to more catastrophic scenarios. And every single test had given the same result: North Denver was fine; South Denver was unresponsive.

The last test on the sheet had concluded about two hours before his comm rang.

As far as Graham could tell, the battery of tests had been competently selected and correctly executed. It was exactly what he would have done if he suspected an interface glitch. And there, of course, was the problem. As he'd told them in the meeting, they weren't dealing with an interface glitch.

Graham faced him. "Joe, I don't get it. You've eliminated one possibility, and you know what to do next. So why do you need me here?"

Color blossomed on the older programmer's face. "We know what we have to do, and we don't need you here to do it. But we also know that if we'd listened to you in the first place, we wouldn't have spent the past three days looking for something that wasn't there. This is too much of a critical situation for us to get all ego-crazy. I want you on the scene so that we don't miss anything else." Joe gave him a sour look, telegraphing just how much that admission had cost him.

Knowing that that was likely the best apology he was going to get, Graham figured he was entitled to one last jab. "Ah, young Samurai, there's hope for you yet. Enlightenment may still be yours." He grinned at Joe who, surprisingly, didn't tell him to go to hell. They were really worried.

"Let's get to work, then," Graham said. "Can I talk to the whole team?"

Fan nodded. "As far as I'm concerned, you're leading this thing until we get it sorted. Treat the team as your own."

Even if he'd been dropped into the room with no prior

knowledge that very instant, Graham would have known that there was something seriously wrong with the picture. Politicking and power games were central to any public enterprise, and here the top man in the organization was dropping his whole operation into Graham's lap.

Joe turned towards the door, to organize attendance, but before he left, he turned back to face the younger man. "The only thing I'm asking is that you fix this."

"That's all?"

"Yup." Joe went off to gather his team.

***

Graham hated talking in front of large groups of people—it was one of the things that had driven him to programming in the first place. And then from the large gaming companies of his early career to freelance work. Yet here he was, waiting for nearly five hundred people, hastily crammed into the town hall cafeteria waiting for him to give them some hope, or at least a direction. He would have preferred to be somewhere else. Anywhere else.

There was no way out of this one, though. He was smart enough to realize that no matter how talented the group in front of him, they were scared and desperate for someone to look like they actually knew what they were doing to tell them which way was forward.

A hand from somewhere to his right handed him a microphone, which he tapped a couple of times.

"Hello? Can you hear me?" he said, feeling like a complete idiot.

The conversation among the members of his audience slowly died down. Graham waited until he judged that they would be able to hear him and began his speech. He tried to imagine the audience naked, just to calm down.

"Hello, everyone," he began. "I suppose that you've probably heard the news that the problem we're dealing with isn't an interface problem."

Some members of the audience nodded.

"Good," he said, and then realized what that sounded like. "Or, rather, not good at all, but at least we know what we're dealing with." He knew he sounded completely stupid, but at least the plan that had been forming in his head was clear, easy to follow, and should produce preliminary results quickly.

"The mistake we made the first time was that we followed the typical 'mechanic's checklist' approach. We tested for the least serious, easiest-to-fix problems first, gradually working our way up. So we started on the basic interface issues before testing for problems with the base interface program. Only after we'd finished doing that did we realize that we have a more serious problem. And now we have no idea where to go next, where the problem might lie.

"I personally believe that the problem is somewhere in the hardware."

Graham held up a hand, forestalling the rising murmurs in the crowd.

"I know that a hardware problem is even less likely than an interface meltdown. And, to make things worse, I have no idea whether the problem might be in the connections or buried deep inside the mainframe itself. We are, after all, dealing with self-maintaining technology over five hundred years old. It's worked so well and so long that we really don't expect it to fail, and we aren't prepared for it when it does.

"But what I do know is that we can't afford to overlook the possibility of a hardware failure. If the mainframe isn't working at optimal performance, how long will it be before the life-support systems stop keeping the bodies in the birthing chambers alive? How long before the million-and-a-half people based in Denver I just keel over in midstride?

"I propose the following: we need to split up into three groups. I will lead one, Joe will lead another, and Erika," he gestured towards the overweight brunette who had led the design team for Wolfhunt, "will lead the third. We'll need to split programmers, designers, and architects approximately equally among the groups, although I'm not quite sure how much we'll be able to use our skills. I have a suspicion that the answer will come from a cross-field brainstorm, but I'd rather be safe than sorry.

"Two groups will search for hardware problems. Erika's will focus on broken connections, while mine will look for problems within Denver I itself."

A youngish man in a striped shirt seated about halfway down the room raised his hand. "How will we manage to run diagnostics if the connections are down?" he asked.

"Good question, but it assumes too much. One of the few things we do know is that not all the connections are down. Somehow, someway, people based in Denver I are getting their thoughts to their bodies and receiving feedback, so, on a basic level, the communication between I and II is up and running. We need to find out how and use that channel to get back into Denver I. And then we can run our diagnostics."

He paused and saw that more nodding and murmuring had greeted this last piece of information. It wasn't news to them, of course, or at least it shouldn't have been. But they seemed to be so appalled by the sheer magnitude of the disaster that they were forgetting even their most basic knowledge.

"Joe's group exists specifically to avoid repeating the mistake of a few days ago. I might be convinced that the problem is a wires and metal thing, something we'll have to fix with a screwdriver and a welding torch, but that doesn't mean that it's so. In order to cover all our bases, the third team will be looking for major software errors on all three of the major functions based in Denver I."

"We'll share any significant findings with the other groups, and as soon as one of the groups has found the reason for the problem, we'll meet up here again and discuss how to solve it."

He looked over the group. They already looked tired, and they basically had to start over again from ground zero because everything they'd done so far had been useless.

"Okay?"

Weary heads nodded.

"Then let's get to work."

***

Nearly thirty-six hours later, Odessa found him staring into a monitor with the glazed look of someone brain-jacked into a computer. She knew he was trying to simultaneously process the information on the screen and the direct feed being loaded into his retinal nerves, overwritten in his field of view.

She could also tell from his posture that he was probably missing most of it. His chin was resting on one hand, and his eyelids periodically fell to half-mast before he caught them and resumed his former state of half-vigilance.

She stood there, watching silently, for about ten minutes, not wanting to interrupt, but suspecting that he wasn't doing a whole hell of a lot of good anyway and that a little conversation might increase his alertness.

"Graham," she said softly.

He jumped, obviously not expecting anyone to be around at this time of night. He'd ordered the rest of his team to get a few hours of sleep, advice he himself had seen fit to ignore. Others around the complex had done the same, but she doubted he was even aware of it, so deeply immersed in his world of numbers and parameters.

Seeing her, he unconsciously passed his hand through his hair and smiled weakly. "Hi, Odessa. What are you doing up at this hour?"

"I came to seduce you while there were no witnesses present." She smiled at him, an open, engaging smile calculated to let him know that she was only teasing.

He missed it. "I'm working on something important."

"I know," she replied, laughing at him openly now. "I couldn't get to sleep all night, so I came by to see how everyone was doing and see if I could lend a hand. Even if, among all these recently graduated technical geniuses, all I'm qualified to do is make coffee runs. Of course, I'll also get the names of the most talented and steal them for my company, so after this is all over, I'll want a list of who impressed you the most."

He finally showed a little bit of life. He pulled the brainjack out in frustration, blinked a couple of times as he refocused his eyes, and turned towards her.

"For all the good that our technical geniuses are doing, we might as well be illiterate truck drivers," he said.

"No luck?" she asked, walking over and placing her hands on his shoulders. She felt him tense at the touch and chided him. "Don't be an idiot, just relax. I'm as worried about this whole mess as anyone, and I can keep my priorities straight. Tell me what's going on."

He relaxed slightly as she kneaded his shoulders, feeling nearly two days of frustration residing in the muscles of his neck.

"I just don't get it," he began. "We've tried to get into the system through every single documented access route and have had absolutely no replies at all. About twelve hours ago, we even reassigned Erika's team to the task of finding unregistered connections to Denver I. They even found a couple, old UHF connections that hadn't been used in centuries. But we had no luck there, either. It's as if Denver I doesn't even exist!"

He shook his head. She shushed him, kneading harder, trying to get him to relax. He was less than useless in his present state, although, of course, he would never admit it. "Maybe the mainframe is completely down."

"It can't be," Graham replied. "We have twenty programmers here from that area. If the computer was down completely, or all the connections were out, they wouldn't be able to control their bodies here in our little cyberworld. And the worst part about it is that exactly the same thing happened to Stuttgart and Jakarta only a few hours before it happened to us."

"Could it be a virus?" Even though there had never been a virus that had caused a single dollar of damage before being identified and neutralized by automated systems in the entire history of cybercivilization, everyone knew the word. Doomsday agitators had been predicting the end of the world as everyone knew it by way of virus since Denver had first gone fully virtual.

"We're looking at that possibility very hard. But, unless we can get Denver I to talk to us, there's no way to see what's going on in there. If the virus came from outside, it might have left some trace, but even if we can identify it, we still have to get into Denver I to fix it. And besides…"

He was silent for a few moments, moving his head in small circles, to the rhythm of Odessa's fingers.

"Besides what?" she prompted.

"I don't really think it's a software problem. Don't ask me why, I just have a hunch that something is really fucked up, and that we can't even start to imagine what's really going on."

"Shouldn't there be an organization that monitors this kind of thing?"

He chuckled. "There was, but it was a casualty of

government cutbacks. It was the first thing I asked when they originally called me in for this project. When Denver initially became a cybercity, we had a team on the outside making certain that every function of the simulation was working precisely within the parameters. Five hundred experts on retainer. Within a decade, everything was going so well, what with the multiple redundancies and automated maintenance, that they cut down the team to a skeleton crew of just ten members."

"Ten?" Odessa asked, appalled. How could they leave the lives of millions in the hands of just ten people?

"That's just the beginning," he told her. "By that time, most of the rest of the world was going virtual as well, so our outside team was soon encased in their chambers and loaded in. The inmates weren't exactly running the asylum, but we were trying to control it from the inside. Five hundred error-free years later, and after the multiple billions of people who have lived their lives completely inside the cyberworld without a single problem, the task of monitoring the system gradually fell to one person in each metropolitan area and eventually became more of an honorary title than a real task—kind of like British knighthood in the twentieth century."

"And in Denver…" Odessa said, knowing she wasn't going to like the answer.

"In Denver, it is one of the duties of the mayor's office." Graham chuckled.

"Is mayor qualified?"

"The mayor is a graduate of political science. He has no idea what any of this means. Hell, he wasn't even aware that the old records regarding the mainframes were even stored in the public memory. And he thinks that his team of game designers and database programmers is the most suitable answer to a problem of this type. We aren't. Unfortunately, we're probably the best team in the country to deal with something like this."

"So what can we do?" Odessa was worried sick. For the first time, she truly considered the consequences of Graham's team being unable to fix this. Could it be possible that a whole half of the oldest real city on Earth could just disappear?

"There's only one thing I can think of. We'll have to go outside and have a look."

"Outside? You mean…"

"Yeah, baby, that's exactly what I mean," Graham said, finally giving her his roughish grin. He was excited, the bastard! "The real world!"

Chapter 5

The Prophet was on the news. Again.

Emily sighed wearily, wondering for the hundredth time how the guy had managed to become the most famous face in the world in just a week. The talking heads went on and on about the fact that he'd been predicting a worldwide systems meltdown for the past ten years. But that was nothing to write home about—other doomsday predictors had been ignored and even lambasted by the same channels that were giving this one almost unlimited airtime.

Maybe it was the fact that he'd gotten the month of the meltdown nearly correct. He'd predicted late May. The reality was early June. The distinction of having been "close enough" was the only thing that had saved him from complete humiliation and brought him fame and fortune. He wasn't even particularly photogenic. A middle-aged black man with at least some oriental blood and balding at the top, he was also getting fat—a fact that was only slightly disguised by his ever-present embroidered white robe.

The volume was turned low enough that she could hear the irritating drone but not make out any of the words. She walked to the remote with every intention of turning it off but, instead, upped the volume.

"...and we must all return to our original bodies, or humanity itself might just be on the verge of extinction," he was saying.

"Why do you say this?"

"The virus that wiped out half of Denver is so insidious that I've heard our technicians can't even get into the mainframe to shut it down. We have no choice but to accept the fact that everyone there is dead, and only those who were lucky enough to be on the north side of the city or in other mainframes were saved. It's already hit at least three cities on different continents. What makes you think it will be satisfied with that? I know the phrase has been overused in the last millennium, but this one truly is a doomsday virus!"

The reporter interviewing him feigned interest. She was one of the world's best known anchors, despite constantly irritating everyone with her affected, and probably fake, British accent. Emily thought she was probably from India. Or maybe North Carolina. But in either case, she was showing an admirable restraint in not laughing at her impassioned subject. Here was a woman who understood her audience.

"How would you propose to do that? Is it even possible to return?" she asked him.

"There's nothing stopping us. All we have to do is build robots to go down into the basements and disconnect the bodies, one at a time. If we take the time to plan it correctly, there should be no problem with the disconnections. After all, the equipment that keeps us all alive is supposed to keep us in relatively decent shape. The atrophy can probably be dealt with surgically."

"But why would we subject ourselves to the pain that this would bring?" the reporter said, echoing Emily's thoughts. "After all, our world has no disease, no real suffering. Is there anything you can say to make our audience want to sacrifice that?"

"Yes. They all have to take into consideration that if we don't act now, we will all be dead soon. What's happening in Denver and Stuttgart aren't isolated incidents. They are just the beginning of greater disasters looming. In much the same way that I predicted these events, I also predict that, in a few months, the entire Mindnet will go down, leaving all of humanity terrified and lost, waking inside dark, sealed metal boxes. It is unlikely that humanity would survive that awakening."

Emily finally shut off the TV and walked to her window. She could still make it to work on time, if she hurried, but she was debating whether it was worth it. It was partly the fact that her biggest client was still down until someone found a way to get Stuttgart back online, but mainly that since Monday one week before, she'd come to feel that there were more important things in the world than just making certain a customer's thirty-second spot was on air at the right time and in the right slot.

She shook her head and laughed at herself. *Damn*, she thought, *there's always something.*

That her life had finally been shorn of Graham should have been a cause for rejoicing. And, in fact, she did feel as if a great weight had been removed from her shoulders, a weight she'd only become conscious of after it was gone.

The irony was that she couldn't enjoy it because, now, she was worried about the entire future of humanity.

She decided to let the Prophet worry about humanity and called in sick. What she really needed was a walk to clear her head, sans comm units of any kind and, very likely, a large pizza in a little while.

***

The early June sun and pleasant breeze, one of the last remaining vestiges of a cool spring, had helped clear her head, not to mention opening her appetite. She'd walked to the comm to order pizza when she noticed the message-waiting light was on.

All her light-heartedness vanished when she noticed the name on the message tag. She should have known Graham wouldn't leave her alone. He wasn't the type to simply accept the facts and move on. Dreamers never were. She slapped the delete button in irritation and walked into the shower.

Forty-five minutes later, comm-less once more, she was seated at her favorite table at Romano's pizza place, a faux-Italian spot on Elway Boulevard, just a couple of blocks from her house. The dark interior was helping her get back to the state of relaxation she'd had before seeing the message.

She set her reader on the table and began to read while taking a couple of bites of one cheesy, gooey slice of the deep-dish pepperoni, which was to die for, when, completely out of the blue, someone sat in the empty chair on the other side of the table.

Her shock turned quickly to anger when she saw her uninvited guest.

Graham was sweating profusely, blond hair matted against his forehead, and panting like an excited bovine.

"What are you doing here?" she asked, her voice icy.

He grinned at her. The idiotic grin hadn't changed at all.

"I knew I'd find you here," he exclaimed, struggling to keep the volume of his voice down despite his agitation and failing. Half the restaurant turned to look at them.

"Graham," she whispered. "I don't know what you think you're doing, but if you think that just because we're in public I won't want to make a scene, you're sorely mistaken. I still don't want to be with you, and nothing you say is going to change that."

A look of genuine surprise crossed his face.

"That's not it at all. I've been trying to reach you about something else completely," he said. And then he did the grin again. "I know when I'm not wanted!"

Now it was her turn to be surprised. But then she hardened—he was obviously fishing for some excuse, any excuse, to reestablish a relationship with her, hoping it would lead to other things.

"What could you possibly want me for?"

"It's not me. It's the team that's working on Denver I," he said.

Yeah, right. "So why didn't anyone call me?" she said.

The look he gave her seemed to doubt her sanity for having said that, or his own for believing she had. "What do you mean? I've been calling you all morning! I left text and voice messages."

"Yeah, but they took you off the team. So now you've crawled back and agreed to make their phone calls?"

"Huh? No, of course not," he said. "I told you they were wrong, didn't I?"

The way he said it made Emily want to hit him. As if just the fact that he said it made it so. God, how could she ever have wasted her time on this guy?

"So," he continued, "they eventually realized that they'd screwed up and called me back. Actually, it kind of looks like I'm in charge now. Luckily for us, it seems the life-support systems are fine and that nobody's going to die off anytime soon, but we still need to get the rest of the city back online."

"You still haven't told me what any of that has to do with me."

"We need your help."

"Why? I don't know anything at all about computers. From what you told me, every expert west of the Mississippi is on that task force. What could I possibly have to add?"

"We need to go outside the program itself to look at the physical mainframe."

"So?" The only way she could think of to look at the machine itself was to wake up one of the engineers, get his body into a semblance of decent—or at least mobile—physical condition, and have him walk there. She was sure that personal transport (or even public transport) no longer existed on the surface of the planet. She still couldn't understand what possible relationship to her any of this possibly had.

"We need someone to drive the robot!"

"What in the world are you talking about? What robot?"

Graham tried to rein in his excitement. "Since we haven't been able to contact Denver I at all, this morning, we decided that we'd have to go outside to look at it. The main problem with this is that we couldn't even reach Denver I's maintenance module, and we can't send one of Denver II's maintenance bots into the area."

"Why not?"

Graham chuckled. "Because the interface is down," he said.

She gave him a hard look, one that he'd learned meant that if he didn't get on with it, there would be unpleasant consequences.

"As I explained before, each mainframe oversees a certain area. That was originally programmed in to avoid one city damaging another, especially places that had been in different countries when the concept of countries still had meaning. For all practical purposes, our bot could supposedly only go as far as the border."

She waited for him to go on. He had this infuriating tendency to assume that everyone could make intuitive leaps and understand what he was saying even though he seldom took the trouble to explain himself.

"So, we rigged the bot to be driven by remote control. We had to cannibalize the two other robots in storage to do this since the original idea that the bots couldn't be controlled across boundaries was built into the design. Anyway, we think we've got it right, now, but there's a problem: we've only got one robot left."

"And you want me to drive it."

"Bingo! I had a hell of a time convincing Joe that you would be the right person for the job. Even Odessa thought I was being an asshole and that all I wanted was to get you close to us so I could try to make a move now that I was an important person on the team again. God, how pathetic do they think I am?"

Emily decided not to respond to that question.

"Anyway," he went on, "I managed to convince them that, in light of the fact that you're global champion at Wolfhunt, you'd be the best person to drive the robot without breaking it. You've got experience with moving avatars in 3-D simulations, and driving the robot should be somewhat similar. So you're currently the most qualified person in this city to drive the thing."

He paused, as if afraid to say anything else, but finally concluded. "And did I mention it's very important that you don't break it?"

She rolled her eyes at him.

And yet, only that morning, she'd been thinking that her life had no true direction.

"Don't worry. I won't break your robot. Now show me what I have to do. And, if you are lying to me…"

***

He hadn't been lying. If anything, he'd probably downplayed the amount of hostility he'd gotten when he put forward the idea that she'd be a good candidate to drive the robot.

Two anxious-looking technicians, a young man and woman, hovered over her every moment. From their comments and the way they sounded, she assumed that they had been the ones responsible for turning the useless parts of three maintenance robots into one that could cross the invisible boundary between mainframes.

"Now, please be careful," the woman told her. "The joystick is very sensitive to movement. We've already hit one wall, and it might take us days to repair the unit if something breaks that we don't have spares for."

Emily had difficulty imagining what she could possibly bump into. From the feed being sent through the robot's 360-degree field of vision, it was standing in a vast empty warehouse or staging area of some sort. The walls were hundreds of yards away, and the nearest solid objects were the tattered remains of what had once been two humanoid metallic constructs—obviously, the cannibalized maintenance robots. Debris was strewn haphazardly around these now-worthless hulks.

"And you need to know that some of the mods we made make this one a little top-heavy. We had to put an antenna on its head to insure reception, and the equipment we had to make it out of was basically all steel. Strong, but not light or good for the center of gravity. You have to be careful not to tip it over."

Emily smiled at her. "What's your name?" she asked.

The woman, a tall, dark-haired woman who seemed to be about twenty-five, shyly answered, "I'm Kate Lysak."

Her companion, a thin, tall dark-skinned youth chimed in. "Prakash Pendalai," he said.

"Well, Kate and Prakash, I'm Emily, and I want this to succeed as badly as you do. Don't worry about me doing something stupid. Just teach me how to drive this thing and give me any information you think might be useful, and we'll get where we need to go. I know we have to move quickly, but that doesn't mean we have to hurry. If we go slowly and steadily, we'll probably get there faster than if we take unnecessary risks."

God, thought Emily, looking at their anxious faces, *when did they start making engineers so young?* And then, shaking her head, she answered her own question. *Maybe they did it at the same time you got old. You're just thirty, and already you feel like a crone around these people.*

Slightly reassured, or at least resigned, the two walked her through the controls. She had at her disposal a simple joystick control and some ancillaries. The stick controlled horizontal movement—the robot's four legs allowed it to move freely on flat surfaces in any direction she cared to input. The delicacy of control was nowhere near the movement available with brain-jacked simulations, but it would have to do.

"You can also climb ladders," Prakash told her. "All you have to do is press this button." He indicated a small blue button on the console in front of her, next to which had been stuck a small square of printfilm with a hand-drawn ladder on it.

"Check," Emily said.

"This function was included in the original programming, with a few redundancies thrown in, so we thought it might be important. We're guessing that a lot of the movement these bots were designed for is in the vertical."

"Okay, and what are the rest of these buttons for?"

"Those control arm movements. Most of the arm movements are controlled from over there," Kate said, pointing to a workstation a little farther off. "We'll use the full range of motion when we arrive at the mainframe, as that'll let use the fine motor abilities of the short arms. What you can control from here are the long arms, which are basically hydraulic battering rams. This button raises the arms to horizontal position, this one lets you push, and that other one lets you lift. The big red one with the cover is the fist motion. It basically slams the metal ball on the end of the right arm into anything within thirty centimeters of the end of the arm. Very hard."

"That's it?"

"Basically, yes. The original programming included a whole lot of other functions, but we had to take the robot's main processor offline to bypass the blocks that made it impossible to get into Denver I. That's not a problem, though, because we still have access to any subroutines we might need, and uploading them onto the unit if we need them should only take us fifteen minutes or so. Unfortunately, uploading all the functions, one by one, would have taken days."

Graham chose that moment to walk in. Watching him immersed in the management of a large group of people had been a revelation, but seeing his messianic arrogance had just made her remember why he was impossible all over again. In the end, she'd just asked him to point out the people who would be training her and walked off to learn the ropes.

"So," he said, "what do you think?"

"They haven't let me try to move it yet, but, as a first impression, I don't think we'll have any trouble unless the access route is completely blocked."

"Good. When do you think you'll be able to get started?"

"Like I said, I want to practice moving it around a bit first, but an hour should be enough. It isn't too complicated; these kids have done a good job."

Kate smiled up from her console.

"Yeah, I know. That's why I chose them for—"

He was interrupted by one of the mayor's aides. "Excuse me, Mr. Johnson, but Miss Varzi needs to see you. She said it's urgent."

Graham rolled his eyes in irritation. "There's always something," he said to Emily. Then turning to the aide, "Did she say what it was about?"

"Yes, she said that if you proved to be, ahem, difficult, to tell you that something horrible has just come out of the black wall in Stuttgart."

Chapter 6

Michael Chung huddled in a doorway. He knew it was unlikely to do him any good, but there was nowhere else he could really go, nothing else he could do.

The thing—there was no other possible description for that monstrosity—was approaching, stumbling steadily down the dead-end street, the end of which had stymied Michael's attempt to flee. It didn't seem to be aiming at him deliberately. Hell, it didn't seem to be doing *anything* deliberately with the way it zigged and zagged, here gouging a ragged, pixilated hole out of the wall of a building, there bouncing off the black behemoth on the other side. But still it came.

The alley had once been defined on both sides by industrial buildings, but now one side of the alley had, by dint of being in the Stuttgart mainframe area, disappeared, making the alley a darker, deeper place.

And yet, the thing approaching him was perfectly illuminated, seemingly from within. It looked like nothing he'd ever seen before. It wasn't an animal, it wasn't a mechanical construct, and, despite being about four stories tall, it wasn't a building. It most resembled a sheet of green and blue light veined with yellow and red streaks folded in on itself until it looked like some kind of giant misshapen dwarf, bowling along on two legs of severely unequal length.

It seemed to Michael as if each time it bounced into a wall and tore out a chunk of material, it got that tiny bit bigger and just slightly better defined. But he had little time to elaborate on this theory—the thing reached his position and pushed a leg into the wall at the end of the alley. Michael screamed as the blue light went through his body, disintegrating it as it passed. There was no pain, no sensation of anything at all except that there was no longer flesh where there once had been. He watched his body evaporate as if it were made of mist, and then saw nothing more after the leg went through his head.

***

Odessa, Graham, and Emily watched in shocked horror as the TV crew filmed the carnage. Even though it was eight thousand miles away, the images of the rampaging thing had the power to chill them to the core.

"Where is that?" Graham asked.

"The reporters say it's a place called Heilbron, right on the border between the Stuttgart mainframe and the one in Hamburg. Eyewitnesses say that the blue giant just walked out of the wall a couple of hours ago."

They watched the live feed for a few moments in silence before the network cut back to more dramatic footage taken earlier that showed pedestrians, walls, and even an unlucky commuter bus get disintegrated by the passage of the monster.

"What is it?" Emily asked in an awed whisper.

Graham shrugged. "I have no idea, but if we can get the diagnostics from Hamburg, we can probably figure it out quickly enough. It looks like an intentional construct, not just a random error pattern in the simulation. The odds against an error pattern staying together quite that long are astronomical."

"Worse than the odds against Denver's mainframe collapse?" Odessa asked with raised eyebrows.

Graham stuck his tongue out at her. He'd already forgotten his horror of a few minutes earlier and was beginning to see the problem as another challenge to be solved, and solved quickly, before something else caught his fancy.

"I don't know," he mused. "Might be a virus."

As if on cue, the network cut to another live feed. This time the now unmistakable features of the Prophet filled the screen. This time, he was less formally dressed in a pair of jeans and a button-down shirt, but had obviously been prevailed upon to give this interview by some enterprising young journalist because it was much too good an opportunity to pass up. The smug, self-righteous expression on his face seemed to support this as the fire and brimstone act began.

"We are being punished because we took a wrong turn on our path to true civilization," he began. "When the final cities were built and people were relocated into the simulations at gunpoint. Yes, not everyone wanted to come with us, but the powers that were back then decided for them. It seemed that having people who weren't in the cyberworld was deemed too dangerous, so they caught everyone and forced them in, even innocents who were living in the wilderness without ever having encountered modern civilization. Entire ways of life truncated. And for what? A life that isn't a life! One of my holy predecessors predicted the collapse, perhaps he caused it. He put a curse on the men who tried to take him and then jumped off a high cliff to his death. That story never appears in the official histories, of course.

"But the curse didn't come to pass all at once. First, we were warned. Whole sections of our land on many continents have been walled off. We have lost contact with friends, been sundered from loved ones."

He cut off and glared at the camera.

"But did we listen?" he asked rhetorically. "I have been telling you what you must do since the walls first came up, but most of you chose to ignore my pleas. You go on with your lives as if this travesty of a true existence is what God intended for us!"

He paused again. Graham admired the man's showmanship. He wasn't quite sure whether the Prophet believed a single word of what he was saying, or if he was just taking advantage of his fifteen minutes of fame with rhetoric calculated to extend it, but either way, he was one hell of a performer.

"And now," the Prophet boomed, "we are being punished! Punished for our arrogance, punished for living a shadow of the life meant for us. Punished for not heeding the warnings we were given."

The reporter, who'd moved back half a step to allow the Prophet's rant to come through in its full glory, stepped smartly back into the shot.

"Is there anything we can do about it, or is it just too late to save ourselves? That thing in Germany looked pretty tough. Is this what we can expect to be dealing with from now on? Doomsday?"

The Prophet looked at her theatrically, and Graham laughed to himself. The man had to know that his reputation was on the line; if he got this answer wrong, he would never be listened to again.

"Yes, it is Doomsday. The monster that is laying waste to Heilbron as we speak is no less than a manifestation of the Doomsday virus. The end of the world as we have known it for centuries is at hand. Thank God."

The reporter, who'd probably been chosen because she was nearby—she was obviously too green for this assignment—let her anger show.

"What do you mean, thank God? How can the end of the

world possibly be a good thing for anybody?"

"Not the end of the world, child. The end of the world as we know it. There is an enormous difference. A world of difference if you like. You must never forget that this world, all of this around us, exists only in our minds. There is a much greater world outside. A world God created for us is waiting to be reconquered."

The reporter nodded, and continued. "Moving back to events in the U.S., what's your opinion on the taskforce put together to repair the Denver mainframe that went down?"

"I haven't been following their progress. As I've said quite often, what's happening is the will of God, and no matter what they try to do to thwart it, I don't think they can possibly be successful."

"So you believe that their plan to go outside and manually repair the computer is doomed from the start?"

"That's what they're going to try?" he said.

"Yes."

"That's the most ridiculous thing I've ever heard. They'll fail abjectly."

The Prophet turned around and, leaving the journalist standing with her mouth open halfway through her next question, he walked off. The network went back to the live feed from Stuttgart.

"God, what a jerk," Odessa said, shaking her head. "We're breaking our backs trying to get everything back the way it was, and this asshole keeps tearing us down every time one of those stupid reporters puts a mic in his face."

They watched the blue monstrosity in silence again for a little while. It seemed to be doing absolutely nothing, simply contracting and expanding slightly as it stood. It made a ghastly whistling sound. And then was silent again, silent and immobile.

Nevertheless, something about the footage they'd already

seen was bothering Graham. Something that just wasn't quite right about… Well, about something, but he just couldn't quite put a finger on it.

"Odessa," he said, "do you think you could get them to send me the diagnostics of that thing's movements from Hamburg?"

"Of course, we're all working together on this one. It's late afternoon there, and I can get the government easily enough. I've already been working with one engineer, a fellow named Franz Schumacher. He can probably get us a real-time feed."

"Great, but tell him I also want the earlier diags as well as a list of all simulation parameters that were affected by its contact with them." Graham was already moving into problem-solving mode, where anything else was irrelevant.

"Anything else, my liege?" Odessa asked him.

Graham blinked, smiled at her sourly, and replied, "Yeah, make sure there's lots of coffee in the console room. I have a hunch that I'll be needing it."

***

Rome took a deep breath. The air on Earth made him realize just how flat and lifeless the air on Tau Ceti II tasted. Perhaps it was just the humidity rising from the soft forest floor, but he suspected there was life in that air, probably the something to do with the millions of microbes that the biology team was going insane about.

Dr. Unameya had ordered everyone on the *Unity* to get a bio-pathogen booster, which was irritating as he'd had a runny nose ever since. But with the way the air tasted, the thickness he could feel in his mouth and nose, it was probably for the best.

He should have been on the ship, he knew. Should have been working on the mystery of the simulation. Captain

Nartiya was convinced that the huge computer program would, once they got deep enough inside it, reveal what had happened to the missing inhabitants of the planet.

Even after the diaspora, even after the best and brightest minds of the Sol system had headed for the stars, there had still been a vibrant society of billions on Earth. There was no way they could have just disappeared without a trace unless they'd done it on purpose.

But there were no abandoned shipyards, neither here nor in orbit, to indicate that they'd gone anywhere. The number and size of the ships that would have been needed to move a population of that size would have left traces. There were none.

But the ship, crisscrossing the planet for days, had found nothing to indicate that they'd managed to kill themselves, either. The infrastructure was decayed, true, but it was the decay of neglect, not of war. Likewise, the physicists swore that there was no latent radiation that might indicate a nuclear war.

Disease? It had been mooted, but where were the mass graves? They'd been to some of the densely-packed cities in the eastern hemisphere—cities with legendary names: Shanghai, Beijing, Kolkata—and had found no sign of pandemic. The bones of tens of millions were not abandoned in buildings or buried under a few centuries of dust.

It was a mystery, and the captain seemed to think that he had the best chance of solving it.

Rome sighed. The mossy floor under his feet felt heavenly after the steel deck of the *Unity*, but he made an effort and walked away from it. He had a job to do.

***

The Prophet walked very quickly down the stairs, taking

the steps two at a time, and hearing the door slam behind him. The interview had been conducted in the foyer of the apartment building where he lived, modeled after an ancient brick-fronted place that had once, before Denver had converted, been a brewery.

The basement apartment holding his home and office was littered with discarded clothes and pizza boxes. The bedclothes were in disarray following his rude awakening to the sound of someone hanging on his doorbell. He reflected that if he was going to be a media personality, he was going to have to clean up a little and might even have to fork out the cost of a maid.

Well, it didn't really matter. His newfound fame had brought him a little wealth. No panacea, but some pocket money to supplement his meager funds was always appreciated. And besides, it was more important to get support than to make money.

Money would soon be irrelevant since the outside world was not, he imagined, at a state where it would have any meaning. And in this case, you really couldn't take it with you, as the ancient saying went.

The office wasn't much better. Rolled up posters and boxes of flyers made the dark room a minefield, and the Prophet tripped over one or the other every couple of steps as he tried to reach the table lamp.

Light finally flooded the little room, and he could reflect that, for the first time since he'd had his initial revelation, the boxes were half-empty and not covered with dust. The posters were going out faster than he could have them produced. The people might not believe anything they said, but at least they were reading them. At least they were thinking about the issues discussed therein.

It would, after all, take only a small group of true believers to found the newest incarnation of the human race.

But to get there, he had to insure the credibility of his movement. A credibility that was based mainly on the fact that he'd known what was going to happen and the fact that he was the person with the best idea as to what awaited outside. He'd been researching it for nearly a decade.

To have the government fooling around outside, and therefore bringing information to the public which was better—or at least more official—than that which he was offering, would be a disaster.

He hit the comm controls on his desk and was rewarded by a soft humming as a glass screen rolled down from the roof. He coded for Jarrien and got down to the inevitable wait. She was difficult to get out of bed at reasonable hours, so he imagined that at this time of night, it would be impossible. His hand was halfway to the volume control, about to turn the emergency siren on, when the screen blinked on.

Jarrien, who showed no signs of having been asleep, looked him over. "Nice interview," she said. As always, Jarrien's hair was iridescent. How she managed to make her blue hair give off small points of light was something he'd never dared ask her. He imagined that she'd hacked into the simulation code—a felony punishable by termination all over the planet. But she'd been the only programmer willing to work with him, and, as time went on, he became aware that she was, by far, one of the best. So he could live with a little major crime on the side.

"So you heard?" he said.

"Yup. They'll probably be using a maintenance robot to get out there. Probably modified, unless there's some security bypass they know about that I don't, which I really doubt." She giggled, her pale, freckled face looking even younger than her twenty-three years. And then, shaking her head. "They never did have any imagination."

"We need to move up the timetable," he told her.

"How soon?"

"Tonight."

"Typical. You don't pay me, you treat me like you think I'm insane, and you ask for the impossible. I don't know why I bother with you."

The Prophet wasn't certain about that either, but all he said was, "All right, when can we move?"

"Tonight, of course. I was just pulling your chain," Jarrien laughed.

The Prophet nodded. "Good," he said.

***

Graham sat alone in a darkened control room, trying to isolate himself from the world sufficiently to be able to think. Long experience had taught him that inspiration came when relaxing on a beach, so, as tired as he was, he would have to rely on perspiration. And coffee.

The numbers were spread out on four enormous screens in front of him, and he'd been over them what seemed like a million times, but still couldn't quite put a finger on what he was looking for. He knew something was truly unusual, but for the life of him couldn't pin down what it was.

The progress of the alien object through the simulation fields had an effect similar to that created by an error pattern in the simulation lattice. Basically, random chaotic effects were sometimes generated by the effects of external magnetic fields on the signals in the mainframes, and they were characteristically unstable, lasting for thousandths of a second at most.

And yet, their effects were often very similar to what he'd seen in the diagnostics sent in from Germany. The same unscrambling of the simulations parameters, the same 'holes' in the pattern. The main difference seemed to lie in the fact that, since this manifestation was a much longer-lasting example of the breed, the damage was much deeper. Hence the jagged holes in the walls of the buildings and the floor.

If I were to program a large-scale virus, this is the way it would act, Graham thought. There really wasn't anything unusual about the effects. Hell, they'd programmed similar bugs in controlled subsimulations in college. The obvious answer was that someone had programmed it and set it loose. Open and shut. All that remained was to find out who.

But he still wasn't convinced. Something didn't fit. His head dropped into his waiting hands as he tried to dig whatever it was that was bothering him out of his subconscious.

Odessa found him in this position and had to shake him to get him to respond.

"What?" he asked, startled.

"Sorry to wake you. I was going to let you sleep till the rest of the team got back, but I think this might be too important to let slide. The thing's gone."

"What do you mean, gone?"

"One second it was right there, being filmed by every network except the porn people, and the next, it wasn't. Just disappeared."

"Have you got the feed?"

"Yeah, and Hamburg's sending us the data," said Odessa, punching an access code so that they could watch the video.

The blue thing on the screen was standing exactly where it had been when Graham left. It just stood there for a couple of minutes, and then suddenly wavered and disappeared. Had it not been for the fact that Graham was watching the screen like a hawk, he would almost definitely have missed it.

"Play it back," he said.

They watched the recording innumerable times. Graham compared it with the data that had arrived from the site. It seemed to agree with the feed: the thing had been stable one moment, unstable about half a second, then absent.

And then Graham sat up straight in his chair. "That's it!" he exclaimed.

Odessa, who was dozing in the chair next to him, came awake with a start. Graham hugged her and spun her around in the air.

"Careful," she told him. "Ten more seconds of this, and you'll lose your temporary immunity. Now what's going on?"

"I figured it out!" Graham replied.

"What, what happened to the ugly?"

"No, not that, I figured out what was bugging me about the earlier recordings. Look." Graham set the player back a few hours to a point where the big blue monster from Stuttgart had only recently emerged and was still moving. It bashed a couple of buildings, disintegrated a surprised pedestrian, and bowled through an intersection, taking out a bus and about seven people standing at a stop.

"There!" Graham said triumphantly, pointing at the screen. "See?"

"What? We already knew that the thing had damaged a lot of stuff. There's nothing particularly new about it."

"Not the stuff, the people!" Graham said.

"Who cares about the people? They're backed up. Even if they get completely disintegrated, they'll just reappear in about five seconds or so."

"So, where are they?" Graham said, playing the tape again. He'd assumed the same thing, of course. People didn't just die in the cyberworld. That had been part of the original attraction. Your body, of course, was hooked up in a bunker somewhere, perfectly safe, while you enjoyed life without too many risks in the wide, if not exactly real, world.

Odessa paled. "Oh my god," she said. "They're not coming back."

"Exactly." Graham was rifling through the data stream printouts, following the path of one specific pedestrian. The data group that represented it became entangled with the chaotic matter of the virus, or whatever it was, and then just vanished. It never reappeared, no matter how much he searched. That particular string was gone.

"Impossible," he muttered.

"What's impossible?" Emily asked. She'd entered unnoticed while he was absorbed in investigating the fate of the pedestrian.

"This." He handed her the dog-eared printouts. "Any people who came into contact with the thing just disappeared, their data streams cut off as if the body had died of old age."

"Oh, boy, that's not good," Emily said.

"I know. We need to find out what the hell is going on, not to mention find a way to reboot the victims. Now we not only have the people behind the black walls to rescue, but also the victims of the virus. We're getting deeper every minute."

"There's another reason: another one of those blue things just appeared."

"Where? Shanghai?"

"Nope. At the Denver I wall, about twenty blocks away."

Chapter 7

When had daybreak happened?

Graham ran into the street, and Emily shielded her eyes against the glare as she aided Odessa in trying to stop him from doing something they considered even dumber than leaving the building, which they thought was already really idiotic.

But scream though they might, there was no stopping him. Pausing only to get updates from the base as to the position of the monster, his rangy frame easily outran Odessa, and even Emily was hard-pressed to keep him in sight.

He finally stopped, at the intersection of Vine and Ford, allowing her to catch up. Her mouth was half-open, ready to remind him that he was one of the dumbest people on the face of the Earth—or whatever, when the reason for his stopping became apparent. A blue creature like the one in Germany loomed over the warehouse half a block down the street.

It was unmistakably the same type of construct. Blue, veined with green, standing in a pair of shallow pixilated holes where contact with its legs had torn up the simulated pavement. And yet, somehow, it was different from the one in Stuttgart. It seemed more defined, less clumsy as it moved. More purposeful. More solid. And, although Emily knew that she might be imagining it, smaller.

It bellowed, an awful screeching sound, and advanced towards them. It walked and screeched, and they retreated before its mass. But it soon became evident that it had no idea that they were there—it was simply following a predetermined route and not following them at all.

Graham, of course, picked this up immediately and began to throw things at it. There were no rocks on the ground, of course, so he balled sheets of paper and threw them. They disintegrated on contact.

"Pretty colors," Graham said absently. Then, ducking low, he passed between the creature's legs and began to walk away from it, staring at the ground.

Emily waited for the thing to pass, pressed into a recess in the wall that also held a small, prickly pine tree, and then joined him.

"What the fuck do you think you're doing?" she screamed. "This is so typical of you. Always trying to show off, never thinking of anyone else. Do you know what kind of shit we'd be in if you get yourself killed?"

"In answer to your only relevant question," he replied calmly, "I'm trying to find out where that thing came from."

She could have murdered him and kept hurling abuse, but he kept ignoring her, backtracking the thing's footsteps. These were easily identifiable by the ruined pixilated pavement.

They only had to walk back seven blocks before the footsteps disappeared, about twenty feet from the infinite black wall cutting Denver in two.

"Now that's interesting," he muttered.

"What is?"

"The footsteps don't end in the wall, which means that this time it didn't come out of the blackness. It appeared right here."

"Maybe it fell through?"

"There doesn't seem to be any sign of that. There would be a bigger disturbed area on the concrete if it had landed on its side," he replied.

"Maybe it jumped," she retorted, anger rising again.

"Nah, too far."

"Go to hell." She stormed off, in the general direction of Town Hall.

"Now what did I do?" he asked nobody in particular and hurried after her.

***

Two pairs of eyes watched the tiny monitor. It showed a black-and-white picture of wrecked geometrical forms. The rubble in the low-resolution image was difficult to identify—it might have been the remains of a small house or perhaps a column. The concrete floor was cracked and pitted. A quick zoom showed small clumps of grass pushing through the thick layer of cement.

The Prophet gazed upon it rapturously.

"Is it truly the real world?" he asked.

"That's what you signed me up to get you, isn't it? I'm good at what I do, mister." Jarrien sounded amused. "Bit of a dump, don't you think?"

"I would never call it a dump. It is real life in the real world. Of course, it may be a little the worse for wear. How could you expect a cityscape not to be completely demolished after five hundred years of abandonment?"

"Okay, let's just say that it's a little under-maintained, then."

The Prophet ignored her. His eyes were glued to the screen, despite the image showing just another clump of abandoned concrete here, another obviously artificial flatness there.

"Why isn't there more grass in the cracks? This should be completely grown over by now," he said.

"Not really. We're under a roof, in some sort of tunnel,

and not much light can make it through. The grass we saw before was only there because the roof had caved in. That also explains why there was more rubble than here."

"So where are you driving this thing?" he asked nervously.

She laughed. "You sound as if you're afraid our little robot will break the real world. Don't worry. It's not even touching the ground!"

This didn't seem to make him any happier.

"Why not?"

"It's how I designed it. You wanted something that could get us from one place to another without being balked by the rubble? Well, here it is. It's a blimp with a camera and a couple of arms. I spent six months on this, so I'll thank you not to criticize."

"I'm not criticizing, it's just that I was expecting something with wheels or legs."

"Look, I had to build it with what I could get. The maintenance robots would only let me access non-critical supplies. And it's nearly impossible to hack into the robots without at least some of the access codes, and I don't have them. I got the final idea by cross referencing the whole stock of non-critical supplies with robotic drone-building instructions on the Mindnet. And besides, this is better than a walker."

"All right," the Prophet said. He didn't sound convinced, however. "Where are we going, now?"

"Outside."

"You mean we'll be able to see the sun, the real sun? And the sky?"

"We might have to be careful. This thing isn't designed for high winds. I haven't taken it farther than those columns over there," she indicated a blurred area on the monitor, not yet fully recognizable, "so as soon as we pass them, we'll be in uncharted territory."

The Prophet was still jittery, but now awe had taken root as well. Jarrien rolled her eyes.

"We'll be the first humans to see the surface of the Earth in centuries. At least since the last of the military people hunting for stragglers were uploaded into the cyberworld."

"Good for us," she replied. "I promise to get you some screen captures so you can show them to your grandkids. Just kidding. I want to see it, too."

And they both watched as the bobbing camera approached the columns. Beyond them, they could vaguely make out a bright point of light—the mouth of the tunnel.

As they passed the columns, even Jarrien was caught up in the sensation of moment. "Well, from here on out, it's uncharted territory," she told him.

The point of light grew closer, first becoming a blinding blur, and then, as the camera adjusted to the luminosity, a clearly defined tunnel exit—a bit ragged, having long since lost its industrial smoothness of finish to the effects of the untamed elements of the outside world.

The Prophet, straining his eyesight and moving to the edge of his seat, thought he could make out shapes in the blinding brightness ahead. When they crossed the threshold and the screen went completely white, he turned to Jarrien in anguish.

"What happened?"

"Don't worry; it's just recalibrating the light intensity. There were no really good micro-optics available in the spare parts bin I raided, and even the newest were really old. All maintained in perfect order by the robots, but not all that impressive. I think they were built to last more than as cutting-edge instruments. Give it a minute."

He fidgeted and fretted as the whiteness persisted, imagining that a furious God had struck the robot explorer down with lightning, straining his vision to have to see any change on the screen. He imagined he could see shadows in the whiteness, slowly shifting and moving slightly.

As the image returned, he realized that the shadows weren't in his head, but actually existed. They were trees, leaves rustling soundlessly in the breeze. The movement was caused by the effect of the same light wind on the blimp, creating a slight weaving that made the image dance.

"Oh…" the Prophet said. He could feel the tears welling in his eyes.

They explored the surface for an hour, Jarrien learning to control the airship in the slightly windy conditions, the Prophet silently drinking it all in. Here a grass-covered mound of rubble, there a more recognizable form, something that had unmistakably been an office block in other times. The building stood, proud and erect as if the time hadn't passed. It was difficult to see the ravages of time in the low-resolution image. Only the gaping holes where missing windows could be seen gave away the age of the building.

But even though that building had survived, due to chance, better building materials or the will of God, relatively unscathed, the passage of time could be seen everywhere else. Overgrown spaces that had once been roads passed between the overgrown piles of what had once been buildings. A column might be visible here, a toppled wall there, but no sign of human occupation. Centuries of Rocky Mountain winters had not been kind to old Denver.

This was where humanity was meant to be. Men were created to roam the grassy expanses of the wilderness, not to have their bodies cocooned inside a sealed wrap of wiring and machinery, and their minds in the hermetic safety of the cyberworld, a place where death was reversible and suffering nonexistent. The sociologists and psychologists claimed that the simple fact that the world was similar to what the real world had been, and that everyone had to work in order to be economically independent was sufficient to insure that humanity would still strive, still be imbued with the will to live.

But he knew that was bullshit. Man was meant to struggle against an often unpredictable planet, built to survive the cold, to master the elements, to fight reality, not some pointless simulation.

After the second hour, the sensation of subjective eons relentlessly pressing down on them, the Prophet decided that enough was enough. Even though he was, he felt, prepared for the adventure of existing outside, he knew it would take a while to get used to the desolation.

"To disconnect the life support and awaken the bodies, we'll need to take a look. Do you have the map?"

Jarrien closed her eyes, and the jacking port LEDs glowed momentarily. A schematic of old Denver appeared on the screen to their left, with a dot marked 'GZ' and an arrow pointing in the direction of the life-support chambers.

"'GZ'?" the Prophet asked her.

"Graff Zeppelin," she replied.

He looked at her oddly, but she just smiled and said, "An old historical reference, and a bit of a joke. Don't worry about it." She adjusted the altitude of the blimp, which had been going off course in her distraction. "We should take about fifteen minutes to get there."

At full power, the ground seemed to zip quickly under them. It was just an illusion, of course, since the blimp's battery-operated fans were not built for speed, but for efficiency. Nevertheless, they were soon at their destination, a tunnel with a slightly downward slope, the entrance to which looked solid enough and was only partially blocked by tall grass. They could fly over the grass and into the darkened building.

They didn't expect to get too far—the life-support

chambers were probably sealed behind layer after of security locks, pressurized doors, and airtight seals.

But this mission was not meant to liberate the bodies—that would require months, possibly years of study, political consensus, and the building of a facility on the ground for the first reanimates to occupy—it was meant to allow them to begin studying the security, with a view towards breaking in. The motives for this were twofold. One he admitted to Jarrien and his followers openly: only their Movement could be trusted to control the operation, and for that, it was imperative that they have access to deeper and more exact information than any other organization on the planet. The second was a personal desire, something he only admitted to himself in moments of absolute honesty: he wanted to make sure that his own body was safe. Only then would he allow anyone else to step into the grace of God.

Half an hour later, the blimp emerged into the sunlight once more.

It was a pale and shaken Prophet who told Jarrien, "We have to stop them."

A grim, determined expression marked him as a man forever changed. He walked out of Jarrien's lab, intent on getting his followers together. He was at the Zenith of his popularity, and he had to use it to insure the survival of mankind, even if that meant going back on everything he'd ever said before.

***

Emily was not enjoying the attention.

The maintenance robot was not easy to maneuver with the rudimentary controls they'd given her. She was willing to grant that the need to bypass the Mindnet entirely was a large technical obstacle, but someone should have foreseen the need to navigate tall, choking grass, which was getting into every single joint and required frequent pauses to allow the fine-control arms to tear out the vegetation.

From the color and density of the grass, it seemed to be springtime or early summer outside. That meant that the cyberworld had stayed in sync with the outside world. She wondered if that had been managed through sensors or if the time-settings had been programmed in at the beginning and had just, like everything else, worked perfectly until a couple of weeks ago.

Either way, she was thankful for it. She preferred to wade through shoulder-high grass than hip-deep snow.

Especially with everyone looking over her shoulder, trying to be helpful, but succeeding only in managing to make her more nervous than she already was. She knew she should be used to performing in front of noisy, well-meaning crowds. After all, tens of thousands of people had been present for the Wolfhunt finals. But then, she'd been brainjacked and the people hadn't been physically present—she'd been in a sound-deadened glass chamber. All she'd had to do to forget about them was to close her eyes. And she had; people had later commented that she was so peaceful only the movement of her avatar on the public viewers' screens allowed them to know that she wasn't asleep on her game couch.

Here, however, there was only a slightly-padded chair, a couple of rudimentary non-Mindnet controls, a system which required her full eyesight and concentration to operate and, worst of all, Graham.

And as she waited for the techs to finish clearing the joints, she reflected on how much she hated the fact that Graham could still get to her like that. While she knew that she definitely had no real feelings left for him, she was honest enough to admit that she still wanted him to acknowledge that she was worth listening to, instead of always doing whatever he thought was the most interesting thing to do. She wanted him to admit that he needed to grow up once and for all.

The bitter irony of the whole thing was that he seemed to have taken the end of their relationship a lot better than she had. He seemed, in a small measure, at least, to relish his new-found freedom to do whatever he wanted and ignore what she thought, but, probably even more so, seemed to love the challenge presented by the new turn of events. The fact that millions or even billions of people could be irreparably affected by all this seemed to matter to him not one whit. And he could see nothing wrong with that!

"There, you should be able to walk without problems now," Prakash informed her from his position at the workstation that was logged in to the fine-motor arms.

"Yeah," she replied sourly, "for the next ten feet."

Prakash just shrugged and resumed his previous position in the crowd behind her.

Well, thought Emily, *at least this thing is good at dealing with big piles of rock.* There had been lots of that to deal with. The collapse of several buildings and pieces of buildings onto the streets had made the going pretty difficult. And to make things worse, the southern half of Denver had had narrower streets than the north, rebuilt after the last war on a grander plan with wide boulevards and open spaces.

The mainframe was located near the center of the city, where the old 20th and 21st century buildings had been raining concrete, steel, and stone onto the streets for hundreds of years. And the remains of the buildings themselves looked none too sturdy.

Graham, standing at her shoulder, said, "Watch out for the buildings; it would really suck if one of them came down on top of us."

Emily gritted her teeth and ignored him, but the whiteness of her knuckles around the joystick must have been visible to all around her. In her tension, she nearly did crash into a hopelessly rusted steel beam that seemed to be the only thing holding up a section of heavy-looking highway bridge.

"Watch it!" Graham exclaimed.

"Will you shut up!" she exploded at him. "It's hard enough trying to walk this thing over mountains of stone without tipping it over without you people telling me how to do it every five seconds. Look, you brought me in for a reason. Unless one of you really believes he or she can do it better than I am—in which case you're welcome to it—then shut up and let me drive!"

They watched in silence the rest of the way, abstaining from saying anything even when the robot stepped onto a manhole cover that had survived five hundred years of elements, but immediately gave way under the robot's weight. They took a sharp breath when the robot toppled onto its side and let out a sigh of relief when it managed to right itself with the help of the pushing arms, but no words were spoken.

Silence also reigned as the robot began the climb up the final pile of rubble before the bunker housing the mainframe, supposedly built to last forever with the correct maintenance, would come into view. For some reason, this pile was a lot taller and less grown over and stable than the previous ones they'd encountered, and there ensued a tense twenty minutes as she delicately guided the robot up the slope.

After a couple of minor landslides, she found a method that seemed to work. She would plant the robot's weight solidly on the back foot and probe the area where she wanted to take her next step before putting the weight on the front foot and repeating the process.

In the end, sweating and weak from the nerves, she guided

the last step, the one that would take them to the top of the mound, and only then did Graham break the silence.

"Oh, fuck," he said.

She said nothing. This time, he seemed to have summarized the situation brilliantly.

Chapter 8

The crater in front of them was at least a hundred meters across and thirty or forty deep. The mound they'd just climbed was not due just to the natural accumulation of detritus from the adjacent buildings; it was the elevated edge of an enormous explosion.

Emily felt as though the robot were standing on the edge of the caldera of a volcano. They used the zoom controls on the vision circuits to try to get a better look. The bottom of the crater seemed to have an organic quality to it: large pieces lumped together with no sharp edges.

"Seems to have been melted," Odessa said, breaking the silence.

"But what could have melted steel and rock together? What could have caused this?" Emily asked.

"Oh," Graham replied, feigning nonchalance, Emily was sure, just to bug her. "Lots of things. A very big bomb. Or a meteor strike. But I think we have bigger problems. Does anyone remember what we came here to find?"

All eyes turned back to the screen, scanning the crater. There was no sign of the bunker that was supposed to be there.

"How deep was the mainframe buried?" Odessa asked.

They waited as Prakash leafed through the old maps until he came to the cross section. He shook his head. "Not deep enough," he said. "Being the first mainframe, it was only placed about thirty feet underground. Thirty feet of reinforced concrete must have been considered sufficient to deter casual molestation, and everything was backed up pretty frequently onto the mainframe that later grew into Denver II. They weren't guarding it against nuclear strikes. They just wanted any wacko who tried to blow it up with a homemade bomb to be unable to do it."

They all knew that, of course. They'd been living and breathing nothing but Denver mainframe history for the past few days.

"So it's gone."

Prakash rechecked the coordinates on the robot's positioning system.

"Yes."

"Holy shit," Emily breathed. The trembling of her hands on the stick as the implications sank in was being transmitted to the robot. The image blurred with the vibration. "All of Denver I, gone. My house, my friends. What's keeping me alive?" By this time, she was screaming and had let go of the controls. She jumped out of her seat and grabbed the bewildered technician by his shoulders. "What's keeping me alive?" she screeched.

Prakash just shook his head, and Graham came to the rescue. "Our records show that life support was handled by multiple redundant systems in the bunker," he said gently, as he pried her arms away from Prakash. "But obviously, that's not the case. Just calm down," he told her, as she struggled hard to get free. "Think about it for a minute. The Mainframe's been down for a couple of weeks. But you're still up and about. If life support had still been hooked up to D-I, you'd either be awake in the real world somewhere or dead. It's only logical."

"But—" she began, but got no further. Tears welled in her eyes, and she buried her head into Graham's shoulder, quickly soaking the fabric all the way through. She pulled back for a moment to dry her nose on her sleeve. "I'm so scared," she sobbed.

They stood there, thinking somber thoughts, while Emily shuddered softly against Graham's chest until a strange movement on the screen called their attention back to the robot. The image was rocking, swaying and, to all who were watching, seemed to indicate that the robot was about to keel over into the depths of the crater.

Kate was the first to react, quickly grapping the joystick from where Emily had dropped it and, pausing only long enough to make certain the arrow that indicated 'up' was pointing the right way, she used it to take the robot two steps back. Now though it tottered precariously on the slope leading up, it was in no danger of going into the hole.

The violent rocking continued unabated: shudder, then nothing for a few seconds, and then shudder again.

"What's going on?" Odessa asked, peering intently at the screen.

"It looks like something is hitting the robot," Prakash replied.

"Turn us around!" Odessa shouted at Kate.

Kate worked furiously at her buttons. "I'm trying!" she replied. "But I just want to rotate the head. I'm afraid that if I try to move the body, it'll fall. And I wasn't the one who got all the practice time!"

Emily tore herself away from Graham and snatched the joystick from her hands. "I'll do it," she said.

She waited while Kate vacated her seat, sat down, and got her bearings. It took her just a couple of seconds to turn the robot around and find solid footing again. She scanned the area behind her to see what was impacting the robot. There was nothing beside it, so she moved the head to study the ground around the robot's feet. They saw the accustomed rubble and assorted loose debris, but nothing was moving among it.

Suddenly, without warning, the robot jolted again. The blow was not hard enough to topple it, positioned as it was, but everyone in the control room greeted it with gasps and clenched teeth. Emily moved the joystick frantically, trying to bring the unseen assailant into view in order to stop it from striking them again, or, at the very least, avoid the next impact.

She could barely make out a blurred shape in the air off towards one side of the monitor. Emily tracked it with the robot's head as best she could, a procedure which was made more difficult by the fact that the object seemed to be trying to get behind them again. Whatever it was, it was definitely being controlled by some intelligence or another.

"What the hell is it?" Graham asked nobody in particular.

"How the hell should I know?" Odessa replied. "According to everything you've told me, there isn't supposed to be anything out there, is there? So what's that?"

"Looks like some kind of miniature airship." This last came from Prakash, who'd been silently studying the monitor while the rest of them bickered.

Silence reigned as the rest of them considered this affirmation. The picture was jumping around as Emily fought to keep the object in front of her, but, slowly, they seemed to come to the conclusion that the technician was correct. The thing on their screen looked like a short, fat sausage with fins and other protuberances stuck all over it.

"Evidently, there is somebody out there. That airship didn't evolve naturally, and that big hole back there didn't dig itself," Graham said.

At that moment, the blimp swooped towards them, missing by a couple of feet as Emily took evasive action.

"Well it's here," Emily said. "I would appreciate suggestions as to what to do about it."

"Try to catch it," Graham replied.

"I meant intelligent suggestions."

Graham rolled his eyes, although this was lost on Emily because her complete concentration was focused on keeping the airship in sight and trying to stay out of its path. "It is an intelligent suggestion. Listen, that airship has to be lighter than air, which likely means that it's been built from lightweight materials, and unless whoever built it had access to some exotic composites, then it's probably fragile."

"So?"

"So it's at a disadvantage. Our robot may not be the most elegant construct, but it was built to last. The airship had the advantage of surprise and would have succeeded, had it been able to knock us off the pile, but we're in much better shape. All we really have to do is stand on a solid place and let it hit us. If you can grab it or impact it with one of the arms, then better yet. And, if it's built of strong material, then we might be able to get it tangled in the arm."

Emily looked unhappy, but got to work on it immediately. She descended a couple of steps and found a relatively flat area on the debris pile, all while deftly keeping the airship in sight, showing off the coordination that had made her Wolfhunt champion.

As soon as she reached a place she considered solid enough, she moved the joystick more violently, in a jerky pattern.

"What are you doing?" Odessa asked, alarmed.

"Trying to make him think I stumbled." Emily seemed almost on autopilot, her eyes locked onto the screen in front of her.

Sure enough, the airship took that opportunity to strike. It swooped in from the left, aiming to overbalance the seemingly unstable robot. But just as it was about to strike, Emily gave two pulls on the lever and pounded on a button on the console. The first motion caused the robot to straighten, while the button raised the heavy arm.

It was a testament to either Emily's incredible skill and coordination or to her amazing luck that the arm actually struck the airship in midair and sent it tumbling out of control in a downward arc.

But whoever or whatever was in control of the blimp was either equally skilled or equally lucky. Just before the airship impacted against the side of the mountain of rubble, it stabilized suddenly and righted itself. The envelope was dented on one side, and its movements, graceful and fluid before the impact, were noticeably unstable, but it was still aloft. It immediately turned away from them, heading to the north.

"Follow it!" Odessa exclaimed.

Emily had put the robot in motion even before Odessa's reaction, but it soon became apparent that it was no use. The robot had barely descended a few feet by the time the airship disappeared.

"Damn," Emily muttered, tossing the joystick aside in disgust. She stalked out of the room, leaving Graham, Odessa, and the technicians wondering what this latest development meant for the inhabitants of Denver I.

After a few moments of silence, Kate picked up the dangling joystick and, somewhat listlessly, began to guide the robot back to its hangar.

***

Graham fumed. He paced, he swore softly, and Odessa laughed at his antics. She accepted easily the simple truth that was causing him so much heartache: politicians would always keep you cooling your heels in the waiting room, regardless of how important your business might be.

In this case, the fact that it was nearly eight o'clock at night and that the mayor had been called back to his office from a gala cocktail party went a little way towards explaining it, but Graham was completely uncomprehending.

"Damn him!" he exclaimed, loudly enough for Odessa and Joe Fan to hear, but not loudly enough to be picked up by the secretary at the desk guarding the mayor's impressive pair of oaken doors.

Joe Fan was completely silent. Of the three, he was the only one whose day job was on the government payroll. This conference represented his first ever audience with the man who signed his paycheck. Like many public servants, Fan had made a career of quiet competence, trying to avoid notice whenever possible, and being promoted on the basis of seniority and time spent on the job. Now, his pallor and his quick breathing gave a clear idea of just how unhappy he was at having had enormous responsibility and its consequent visibility thrust onto his thin shoulders.

He'd initially tried to make Graham calm down but had been brusquely brushed off. After that, he acted as if he was afraid of the bigger man making a scene—possibly even throwing him down the stairs—and he'd left well enough alone. It was almost impossible to tell if he was scared or relieved when the mayor's secretary announced, in snooty tones, that they could pass.

"It's about time," Graham said, picking his comm off the chair where he'd dropped it and storming past the secretary. Odessa and Joe had to hurry to catch up.

The mayor's office had been redesigned about a hundred years previously and had the slightly kitschy feeling that went with it, but no one had dared to change anything in the intervening years. Design language had not changed much—just enough for some of the details to be slightly jarring. The green curtains were especially dated.

The man himself was not an impressive sight. Fiftyish and balding, he didn't look powerful and commanding. Mainly, he just looked tired.

"Hello, Odessa. Mr. Johnson, Mr. Fan." He shook each of their hands, and then studying Odessa's face, let out a weary sigh. "More bad news?"

Odessa just nodded and motioned for the impatient Graham to speak.

"Sir, we've lost Denver I," he said.

"That's old news, kiddo. I thought you were leading the task force to bring it back online."

"No, no, you don't understand. We've lost the mainframe physically," Graham insisted.

"You're right, I don't understand. Why don't you take it from the top?"

Graham deflated, but nodded.

"A couple of days ago, we realized that we were making almost no progress in our attempts to get Denver I to talk to us. This made us suspect that the mainframe might be physically damaged, which could, with the right tools and schematics, be fixed in short order."

The mayor held up a hand. "How could it have gotten physically damaged? I understand that it's in a bunker with ten-foot-thick concrete walls."

"I'll get to that in a second, and, trust me, you won't like it. Our main problem was how to get out there. To make a long story short, we eventually modified one of Denver II's maintenance robots so that it could get into DI's area and went in to have a look."

A pause in the narrative ensued as Graham plugged his comm into the overhead projector. A screenshot image of the crater appeared.

"This is what we found, sir."

At first the mayor seemed about to ask, angrily, what he

was seeing, but then thought better of it. As comprehension dawned, the anger dissolved and was replaced by a look of deep concern.

"Is that..."

"The crater is located on the precise spot previously occupied by the bunker holding the Denver I mainframe."

"Oh, my God," the mayor said. He studied their faces in silence for a few moments, trying to find any sign that they were joking. "Could there be some mistake?"

"No. We checked everything thoroughly. No mistakes."

"What could have caused something like this?"

Graham shrugged. "We don't know. We couldn't really get too close because our robot would have fallen off the inner slope. Whatever it was caused the area to heat up enough to melt metal and turn sand into glass. A big atomic bomb. Or a meteor strike, maybe."

The mayor walked around his desk and sat down. "How can it be? How can the city even function with half of its computing capacity gone?"

"Because it's Denver," Graham said. Then, seeing that his audience expected something more, he continued. "In the 21st century, a huge, simulated world was created on the older versions of the Mindnet, which weren't really a Mindnet at all, since you couldn't plug into it. By 2100, a company sprang up in Denver that allowed people to connect their brains to the computer simulation to live a life free of disease and most pain, in which economic variables and other threat factors were tightly controlled. This company went bankrupt, but it was deemed by medical experts that the rehabilitation of its customers would be more expensive than keeping the people connected, so the company was taken over by the state of Colorado."

"I know all this," the mayor said testily. "Is it relevant?"

"Yes, because that company's computers were basically Denver I. What happened was, since it was state controlled, the service of 'going under' became a political issue, and it was finally decided that everyone had the right to do so. Immediately, a quarter of Denver's inhabitants exercised that right. And so was born Denver I. But, you see, as everyone else in the world slowly converted, a plan was put together to create a seamless network of functioning computers, one in each major urban area. But Denver I was not designed to be part of this network. Denver I was already there. So they simply interfaced it onto the wider web, but not as a fully integrated member."

"So that's why we're still here."

"Precisely. And I also think that's why the people who were in the birthing chambers under Denver I are still with us. Somewhere along the line, somebody must have decided that it would be safer to connect life-support to the main system instead of leaving it to the older, unintegrated system. Unfortunately, they neglected to document the change, and we haven't been able to track it down, yet. There's a huge amount of data in the network, and we need to sift through all of it to find the control code we're looking for."

The mayor put his elbows on the desk and rested his chin on his hands, seemingly lost in deep thought. "I presume that's exactly what you're going to do now," he said.

"No. Well, I mean, yes, some of us are, but there's more. The other reason we came to see you is that we were attacked by something that seemed to be a tiny robot airship out there. To me, that can only mean a few things," Graham said. He began to count on his fingers. "One, someone else is out there. Two, someone else can get into DII's source code and get something outside but controlled from within. And three, there's an automated defense mechanism set up by someone that uses unarmed blimps to try to dissuade people from visiting. Given that the last is ridiculous, the question I need to answer is whether the first is true. Do you have any information coming to you about that?"

"All the information the government has regarding anything having to do with the mainframes and the outside is in your hands. Frankly, the whole thing just creeps me out. Imagine living in a world of disease and germs. No wonder the people in the 2100s eventually just uploaded everyone. Ugh." The mayor grimaced in disgust, which surprised Graham a bit. While there were still some people who fundamentally hated the outside, most had gotten over that phase and saw the outside world as a curious mystery, a romantic place of moonlit ruins from a simpler time.

"Then I, for one, will be trying to track the hacker in control of that blimp," Graham said. "Whoever they are, they probably have more notion as to what's going on than we do. I'm sure Joe's team will gladly continue working on the problem from the more conventional angle."

Joe nodded eagerly at this affirmation.

"Do whatever it takes people, but fix this," said the mayor. "I've already lost any chance of reelection, and another few days without solutions will get the impeachment talk started. I don't want that, and I can assure you neither do Mr. Fan or Miss Varzi."

Joe Fan turned even paler and swallowed. Odessa just glared at him. The mayor ignored them both and turned his attention back to Graham.

"But somehow, the only person I can't really threaten is the one I think holds the key to the whole thing, so I'll try to appeal to your better nature. I'm starting to believe that a lot of people are going to die if you don't get to the bottom of this mess. Please solve it for us, will you, Mr. Johnson?"

"I'm doing my best, sir."

Chapter 9

Joe pushed his hair from his face and looked back at the screen in frustration. The diagnostics had been running for hours, and, if Graham wasn't talking through his hat, they should have found some trace of the life support systems from Denver I by now. He was starting to believe that they'd been connected to some other mainframe, but how it had been done and maintained for God knew how long without anyone noticing was beyond his powers to ascertain.

A large map of Colorado was draped over his console with big chunks of it hanging off the edge of the desk, from which he'd managed to come to a few conclusions. Other than Denver II, the now defunct DI had been directly connected to only two other mainframes: Colorado Springs and Vail.

As soon as Joe began to suspect that they wouldn't find anything even remotely related to the life support protocols on Denver II, he'd taken a flyer and communicated with Vail, explaining what he was looking for. The answer, unsurprisingly, had been negative: Vail was a tiny machine on which the demands of keeping half of Denver's population alive would have been discovered a long time before.

Now, all he could do was to drill ever deeper into the seemingly infinite stream of data that was Denver II to see if they'd missed anything, or if what they were looking for was simply placed alongside some other protocol that had nothing to do with it and wait for Colorado Springs, a larger mainframe, to send their reply. He knew that Colorado

Springs might take a day or two.

He got up, walked to the coffee machine and stood, thinking about the how the world was structured and what the people who'd been in the area controlled by the Denver I mainframe when it collapsed must have felt. What were they feeling now? Were they locked in darkness, screaming in the complete sensory deprivation of nothing? Or had they woken up in buried, darkened birthing chambers, flaccid and weak, and were even now trying to extricate themselves? Trying to find the surface and live real lives. In terror and pain worse than anything they'd ever known. Suffering from the cold, feeling the weakness of their bodies, the product of years and decades of inactivity.

Joe shuddered and turned back to his console where he was unsurprised to find five messages awaiting his attention. It had just been that kind of week.

He quickly scanned and dismissed four of them. They were from his team, basically hourly reports reporting no progress whatsoever. The fifth was different. It was from Germany, saying that they'd managed to isolate the telltale code disruptions of the apparition they'd had, and they'd used this signature to backtrack and try to locate the point where the virus had entered the Mindnet.

Much to their surprise, and after having assumed that the virus had entered through the wall from the Stuttgart mainframe, they'd found that the entry point was actually a working access port in the Frankfurt mainframe. Deeper analysis had shown that the circuit was easily accessible, physically, from outside the mainframe. Their conclusion was that someone or something had located that access port and put the virus into the system.

Well, at least Joe knew exactly what to do with this one. He forwarded the message to Graham and, carrying his coffee, went over to see how the other man took the news. Knowing him, Joe wouldn't have been surprised if Graham, disregarding all the dire possibilities, reacted with glee at the news that there was outside interference with the mainframe network.

He wasn't disappointed.

***

The fact that the Germans had thought of it first was really galling to Graham, but the challenge itself was irresistible. Where had the virus entered the system, and did the one in Stuttgart have a different source than the one in Denver?

"What have you got?" he asked Prakash, who, after he and Kate had done such a good job with the robots, had been co-opted into Graham's 'unconventional methods' team.

"Well, in the first place, the signature the Germans sent us doesn't seem to match what we saw here in Denver. The footprint the Denver virus left in the simulation was much smaller, less destructive. The regeneration protocols we had to run were massive, but nothing compared to the scale of the Stuttgart sighting."

This hardly came as a surprise to Graham, who'd begun to concoct another theory, and was less and less convinced that they were dealing with viruses every day.

"Can we track it?"

"Yes," Prakash replied. "But I'll need a couple of minutes to recalibrate the algorithms the Germans sent in. They don't have fine enough resolution to follow our footprint. And there's another potential problem, which is that tracking finer disruptions might set us on a false trail. We could run into something else and mistake it for the virus."

"I think we'd have noticed anything that big tearing chunks out of the Mindnet, even if it was smaller than the one in Germany, don't you?"

Prakash shrugged and turned to his code. The green lettering on the screen bathed his face in unhealthy-looking illumination. Graham turned to Kate, who was busy trying to get the maintenance robot into the crater. She'd made it walk halfway around already, but had yet to discover a path down the crater wall that wasn't too steep for the thing.

"Kate, I need your help with something," Graham told her.

She nodded, seemingly grateful to have any excuse to tear her eyes away from the minute study of the jagged edge of the crater.

He continued, "I just sent you the footprints of the virus we saw in Stuttgart and the one we saw here. It seems to have adapted to the simulation programming and is becoming less and less invasive. What I'd like you to do is to look at the parameters and extrapolate how the improvement would have evolved from the last sighting to today, and then I'd like you to look for footprints that match that profile."

"Where should I look?"

"I dunno. Could be anywhere."

"That'll take a while. A long while."

Graham sighed. "I know. Just let me know when you have anything." He turned back to a workstation he'd appropriated for himself. He almost had the blimp. Much to his relief, and after nearly a full day's search, he'd found a radio transmitter setup hacked into an obscure Mindnet path, one of the redundancies in case of moderate system failure.

In a sense, it was a good thing that the whole of human activity on Earth was confined to strictly defined movements and perturbations in the simulation programming. This was the only reason that Graham had any chance whatsoever of locating the hack, and especially this hack, as it was so well put together. He just set the diagnostics, already running at full tilt, the additional task of finding anomalous sub-routines capable of data transmission into non-standard hardware in little-used areas of the Mindnet. He'd been surprised at how quickly the results had turned up.

The transmitter itself was elegant enough to make him whistle. It was merely a subroutine connected onto the circuit that governed the Denver II maintenance robots—simply coded, but effective as hell, giving the hacker complete control of the robots without setting off one single alarm. The blimp had presumably been built by the robots with one of the robot's radio receptors embedded in it, which, in turn, was controlled through the hack itself, leaving the robots completely undisturbed in the future. Which explained why Prakash and Kate hadn't noticed anything unusual in their process of tinkering with the maintenance bots.

Graham shook his head in admiration. Whoever had done this was someone brilliant. Brilliant beyond any other programmer he'd encountered recently, possibly ever. The Mindnet's security, especially as concerned modification of the source simulation code, and even more the hardwired permanent functionality, was nearly impregnable. To have done what this guy had done undetected and unpunished was mind-blowing. A criminal genius.

Graham decided that he wanted to meet the person responsible. For the first time in his life, he felt that another programmer was at his level. He'd met countless people more successful than he was, but, deep inside, he'd always put it down to the fact that they worked long hours in pursuit of that success, while all he did was put together a little code on projects that interested him. But here was someone who'd done something he wasn't certain he could ever have managed. The fact that it was completely illegal made absolutely no difference to him.

The difficult part was done. Now, all he had to do was to backtrack from the communication connector to find where the decisions were being made. It was there that he'd either find his hacker or someone who knew where the hacker could be located.

Pushing back from his console, he turned to the two technicians working on the problem of the virus and asked them, "Are you guys ready yet?"

Prakash said, "I still need a little while." Kate, more expressive, just gave him a steady look and rolled her eyes.

Graham redoubled his search. His quarry's track went one way, then the next, laid various false trails and tried to blend into the legitimate information stream from the Mindnet's normal operation, but unsuccessfully. Graham had it identified, and he wasn't going to let the hacker out of his sights.

Slowly, he peeled back the onion, discarding false trails and deceptions, getting ever closer. Much of the data path was dispersed over Asia, making it look like the epicenter was in Japan. An apartment in Tokyo was the last link in the data track. There. He just had to find out who or what was occupying that apartment, and he would have his hacker.

But something just felt wrong about this match. It had been too easy. Why had the hacker, with obvious access to the global network, chosen to create most of his false path on the very continent he was located? The obvious answer, and what Graham suspected that the hacker had wanted anyone investigating to assume, was that the false trail had been laid in an area with which the quarry was familiar. But that assumption was only valid if you ignored the skill with which this individual had managed to install an illegal exterior transmitter in an American city halfway around the world.

He had no need to be familiar with the surroundings. And going after the apartment in Tokyo would probably lead to the discovery of a very confused-looking Japanese family and all sorts of alarms going off at the hacker's house.

And the back-trail would disappear like smoke on a windy day.

Very delicately, in order to avoid tripping the alarms he suspected, Graham began to observe the entry and exit channels to the data feed in Tokyo. Regular Mindnet channels were not being used to transmit any additional data, so the feed had to be in the simulation control itself, in the programming that controlled the physical aspects of the house and its interaction with the inhabitants and the rest of the simulated 'environment'. A huge amount of computing power went into maintaining the simulation of that two-bedroom apartment, one of millions in the city.

It took him nearly an hour, running non-intrusive diagnostics before he found an anomaly in the layout. One single data stream was completely superfluous, not being part of the primary or backup feeds.

He followed it back over the globe. This one wasn't all that disguised, once found. But then, it didn't really have to be. Only someone with access to the government-controlled diagnostics could have found it, and the government never varied from their standardized checks. Or at least they hadn't for the last few hundred years. They would never have spotted the transmitter, much less this data feed.

Only a maverick with access to the diagnostics would have spotted it, and it was only the hacker's bad luck that Graham had been on hand to play that role.

The data feed finally ended, leaving Graham speechless. The address corresponded to a basement apartment less than a mile away.

"I'll be back in a couple of hours," he told the techs. "Please try to have the results by then."

He ran into the street.

***

When had it become noon? In the confines of the

windowless operations room, Graham and his team were immersed in endless night, completely losing track of the passage of time outside.

The June sun blazed down from the cloudless sky, and Graham shaded his eyes as he bowled down the street, waiting for his vision to adjust to the brightness. He'd already gone two full blocks before being able to see where it was he was going. But this was worth it. This was important.

The address on the datapad took him to a slightly seedy area. Of course, physical crime was a thing of the past, as the threat of violence was not a valid tool within the cyberworld, but still, some areas were less well cared for than others. There would always be places frequented by people who simply cared less about their surroundings, their image, and even their lives, than others.

And, Graham suspected, there would also be those to whom such areas were ideal camouflage—a place to live as one liked beneath the unwanted notice of a hidebound society. He grew ever more certain that he had the right place as he approached.

Fifteen minutes later, he stood before a six-story brick building. One of those typical, almost clichéd late nineteenth century rectangles with slightly recessed windows and fire escapes sprouting down the sides like whiskers. It seemed to have been modernized at some point, but nothing could hide the building's origins.

The front door stood open, but Graham hesitated, uncertain that he wanted to face the person behind it. After all, a person who not only had the ability to get into the base simulation code, but was also willing to do it, could conceivably be a very, very dangerous mind. The simulation controlled every parameter of modern life, from the way things looked to the physics of the area. For all he knew, this guy would turn off the gravity once he saw that he'd been discovered.

But what the hell. He'd come this far, and knew he wouldn't forgive himself if he didn't go ahead with it—for the first time, he'd found someone he could admire, someone whose abilities seemed to be on a par with his own. He walked through the door and down the stairs. To his relief, the interior of the building was relatively well-kempt and acceptably illuminated.

Apartment three was the second door to his right.

Graham took only one second to steel himself before knocking. He waited a few seconds and was about to knock again when the door unexpectedly opened.

"Come in, Graham," a voice said from the dim space beyond. A girl's voice, which surprised him—he'd pictured his villain as a scarred bald man in his late forties.

Graham hesitated, letting his eyes adjust to the gloom.

"Well, are you going to stand there all day? Or are you coming in?"

He went in.

The room was sparsely, but expensively furnished and, much to his relief, seemed clean. There was no clutter on the floor, no unpleasant crunching when he walked. Only the lack of any steady illumination made him uneasy. The blue glow that represented the only light in the room seemed to move about, weaving and bobbing just out of direct sight in the room beyond.

A voice came from that same room. "Can I get you something to drink? I've got some stimcaff in the synth."

"Sure," he replied, cursing his unsteady voice, "stimcaff will be fine." And he chuckled to himself. Here he was sharing a room with quite possibly the most dangerous individual in Denver and what were they talking about? Refreshments.

He decided to remedy the situation. "How do you know my name?" he said.

No response was forthcoming other than the mundane tinkling of the stimcaff mugs in the adjacent room. While he tried to decide what to do, Graham stood immobile in the front room, a living room complete with sofa and entertainment system, he now saw.

The decision was made for him when a girl entered, carrying two mugs of steaming caff.

Graham gaped. Oh, she was pretty enough to justify the reaction, in a wispy, freckly blonde way, but that wasn't it. It wasn't her beauty at all. It was her hair.

The natural strands—blonde?—generated by the simulation program that ruled the appearance of all of their bodies were nowhere to be seen. Instead, her head glowed, emitting light from what seemed to be strands of luminous blue shoulder-length hair. It framed and illuminated her face, but that still wasn't why he gasped.

His shock could, however, be explained by the sheer audacity of anyone who would flaunt such an illegal hacking of the system that framed their society, gave them their air, and, at a more fundamental level, kept their immobile bodies alive, somewhere deep under the city.

There were few crimes of any consequence in this simulated city. Theft was reversible just by describing the object to the authorities, who would simply steal it back. Murder was impossible. There were few crimes that caused any comment. Embezzlement, psychological abuse.

And there was only one crime that the inhabitants wouldn't stand for.

And not only had this girl committed it, she'd committed it openly, and flaunted it. And what for? To have a different hairstyle. Wow.

"Are you going to stare or are you going to drink?" she said.

He started, shook his head and grinned. "Sorry," he said,

sheepishly taking a mug. "I was just wondering where you get your hair done."

She chuckled back at him, "So, you noticed that."

"Pretty hard not to. I thought getting noticed was the whole idea."

"There's noticed and then there's noticed. Almost nobody knows what this hair means. Most of the ones who notice it are women who get frustrated after years of trying, unsuccessfully, to get someone to give them the same look. I can walk by any civil servant in the city without even getting raised eyebrows." She paused, looking him over. "You, of course, are a different matter. Your reputation precedes you."

He struck a pose, not quite recovered from his shock, but damned if he was going to let on. "Of course. How can one not strike fear into the heart of damsels? It might help if they didn't know who you were and that you were coming for them. How'd you do that, anyway?"

She shrugged. "Left an alarm on the pathway from Tokyo to Denver. Not much help in hiding, of course, but nobody would ever suspect it. That told me someone was coming, and I'd had a look at the government team. Only one person could have done the back-track: the world-famous Graham Johnson."

"So you deduced it?"

"Actually, I saw you coming through the window," she admitted.

"I've never seen you before in my life."

"You have, in fact. We met at a gamer's convention a couple of years ago. It was before the hair."

"Oh, that explains it. So, are you going to tell me your name? Or will you get all huffy at me for not remembering it?"

She held out a hand, mock-daintily. "Jarrien," she said.

He took it. "Graham, but I guess you already knew that." He studied her. "And are you going to tell me what you were doing out there with an attack blimp of all things?"

"Of course not," she replied. She pantomimed a couple of keystrokes in the air and vanished with a shimmer.

Graham stood still, finished his stimcaff, and turned back toward the door.

"Damn," he muttered, as he let himself out.

***

On his return to the control center, Graham was immediately confronted by not one, but both of his analysts waving printouts at him.

"I've found where the virus entered our system," Prakash told him.

"And I've found a match to the footprint we were searching for," Kate added, unwilling to be left out.

Graham held out his hands in a protective gesture. "One at a time, please!" he said, and grinned at them. They might originally have been languishing under Joe Fan's lukewarm leadership, he thought, but they were good.

They both began to talk at the same time again, causing Graham to laugh and hold out his arms again.

"All right. Let's take this in logical order. Prakash, your findings should be the older data set, you go first."

"Well, you asked me to find where the big thing you saw entered the Denver II environment. I immediately assumed that it had come in through one of the connections to Denver I. After all, it appeared right next to the huge black wall."

"By all of this, I assume it came in somewhere else."

Prakash started and favored Graham with a sheepish look, knowing full well that his preamble had stolen his own thunder. "No. It came in through a data port on the Denver II mainframe."

"A data port? What's a data port?" Graham had never heard

the term before.

"Actually, I made the term up because I didn't know what else to call it. It's a connection from a mainframe to the outside world, a physical connection."

"You mean that whoever did this did it from outside? From the real world?" Graham made air-quotes around the word 'real'.

"Exactly," Prakash replied, relieved that his information, at least, was of sufficient moment to warrant some surprise.

"But why? I imagine it would be easier just to hack in from the inside."

"Maybe because this way, it's nearly impossible to trace. We have to go outside and find physical traces of whatever did this, and then follow the tracks. Not something our society is ideally equipped to do."

Kate jumped in. "But we can trace the latest version."

Both men turned to her. Graham spoke first. "You mean you've found something giving off the extrapolated footprint?"

"Not exactly. I tried to extrapolate the way the footprint would look today but got too many different potential paths it might have taken. So I did something else—I simply analyzed the three most disruptive patterns being created by the things and tried to find scaled-down versions of the same things anywhere else on the Mindnet."

Graham felt excitement mounting. "And where is it?" he said.

"New York," Kate replied simply.

This was met by silence.

"But that's ridiculous," Prakash said. "If anything like what we saw in Stuttgart or here in Denver was in New York, it'd be all over the news."

"Not necessarily. Here, let me show you." Kate walked over to the monitors. One was showing a street scene, the other a readout from the base simulation program. "What do you see on that screen?" she asked, pointing at the street scene.

"A bunch of people crossing a street—just a feed from a monitor camera somewhere," Graham replied. The scene flickered as the program switched cameras, seemingly following one nondescript man in a green jacket.

"Do you notice anything interesting about that man?" Kate asked.

"Not at all. Why?"

"Because he isn't a man. That's the latest incarnation of the virus."

Prakash snorted. "Yeah, right. Where's the rest of it? That guy's no bigger than I am!"

"And yet, it is. Here, look at the data from the net. Here's the thread tracking the man I showed you."

Graham and Prakash studied the readout for some time in silence, before Graham gave a low whistle. "Wow, whoever did this sure refined the virus quickly," he said. "It shows massive skill, but why would anyone capable of creating something so well made, so nearly undetectable, have given away his presence by making the monstrosities we saw before?"

"I'm much more worried about who has the skill to create something like this and why they would risk breaking so many laws to do it."

Graham thought he knew the answer to the first question. The answer had glowing blue hair and a complete disregard for anything resembling ordered, structured society. As to why, the only way to find out was to keep tracking her, blocking her in until she had nowhere to run. Which was going to be difficult as she'd probably hacked the Mindnet full of escape routes. But the pursuers could be much more open with their hacking since they didn't need to fear discovery by the authorities. Strange as it felt to Graham, they were the authorities.

"Where's the feed coming in?" he asked Kate.

"It seems to be entering through one of Prakash's data ports."

Graham thought for a moment. "Call Emily," he said. "Tell her we need to get to New York today. We'll need to get outside with one of the robots before they can get away again."

Chapter 10

The Prophet was on the news again. He had, by this time, become the background noise to this chaotic period of everyone's lives.

Emily, who'd been granted permission to miss work due to being on loan to the government and consequently had plenty of downtime available for watching the news, had soon learned to ignore him.

Today was no exception. The man was droning on and on, expounding his unrealistic views about life on the planet to anyone who cared to listen. Emily, meanwhile, was studying a set of printouts from the robot explorer's cameras, specifically focusing on the design of the blimp, trying to understand what capabilities the thing had. She knew that Graham had a team of experts doing the same thing, but it didn't worry her. Another pair of eyes could only be a positive thing; besides, she had nothing better to do with her time. She'd been told that her talents were indispensable but had so far had very little to do over the last five days.

As far as she could tell, the little airship could do little but fly and film things. There were no manipulator arms or other appendages on the fuselage save one that looked like a camera. She'd been studying it for over an hour already—enough was enough.

She looked up from one of the prints and focused, for one second, on the Prophet.

"...and that is when the spirit of the planet spoke to me and said that humanity must never return to the surface."

What? Emily thought. This was exactly the opposite of what he'd been saying up until this point. He'd worked the world into a panic about the "virus to end all viruses and the urgent need to return to a 'real' existence on the surface," and now this? What was going on here?

Emily turned the volume up on the monitor. She wanted to make certain that what she heard was what the man actually said.

The reporter, another young woman, was speaking. "But isn't that exactly the opposite of what you've been saying these last few weeks?" she asked.

"Yes." The Prophet hung his head theatrically. "But you must consider that, then, I was merely a man. My opinions were my own, and I had not yet reached enlightenment. I was living in fear. Fear of death, fear of oblivion. In my ignorance, I was afraid that mankind could be wiped out by something as silly as a Mindnet virus." He looked straight at the camera. "But now the voice of the Earth has made me understand. Do you know what awaits outside?"

"You've always told us that the real world is out there."

"Yes. But who does the real world belong to? What was once despoiled by man is now a pristine wilderness, a beautiful preserve of all of nature's wonders. That is what the voice of Gaia has said to me. It pleads that we leave the planet to its rightful owners. And everyone wins."

"How does humanity benefit from giving up our rightful place on the surface?" the reporter asked him.

"Look around!" the Prophet replied. "We have everything sentient beings could possibly want! Comfort, safety, prosperity."

"But haven't you been telling us for months that these were the very things that were making humanity complacent and incapable of any kind of proactivity? And, therefore, susceptible to having even the slightest variation in our environment wipe us out?" She stared into the camera, reading the teleprompt, Emily guessed. "Your words were: 'We must go out to our rightful place, to be tempered in the forge of the cold and cruel nature of the planet's surface. Only then can we survive.'"

The Prophet, unperturbed, responded, "I had not seen the light, then. I was trying to help the race as I saw most fit, but I was wrong. Now I know the truth: humanity must never again walk the surface of the planet."

Emily was distracted from the interview by the comm chime. Odessa. She lowered the volume and answered the call.

"Hello."

"Hi, Emily, sorry to bug you, but we've got a new assignment."

"No bother, I was starting to get really bored."

"Yeah, but this particular assignment means that you need to travel to New York."

"I already told you. This whole leave to be on the government payroll is only a fun assignment if I have something to do. Just tell me when my flight leaves. Should I pack for a long stay?"

"No flight this time. Just get yourself to town hall as soon as you can. Don't bother to pack—we'll get you anything you need."

Emily, slightly puzzled, told Odessa that she'd be right over.

She'd completely forgotten about the Prophet and his inexplicable about-face.

***

Graham actually looked serious when she arrived.

"Look," he said, "I'm sorry about the rush, but there's no time to lose. You need to get to New York immediately. We've found what might be the source of the virus monsters we've been seeing and tracked it to an access port at the Manhattan mainframe. We need you to take one of the Manhattan maintenance robots out there and look around."

"Can't they do it on automatic?"

"Well, they could, but I asked them not to. I have no idea what we'll find there, and I would rather have someone who can pass a Turing test on hand to react to anything unexpected. I trust you with this one."

"When's my flight?" Emily asked, thinking that maybe they'd arranged for a helicopter from the pad on the roof or something—still, a cross-continent flight by helicopter didn't sound very appealing.

"No flight," Graham replied.

"Then how am I supposed to get there?"

"Direct transfer."

"What?"

"I discovered that, in certain extreme cases, we can do an emergency override on the simulation base code itself, which allows us to transfer complete people from one mainframe's area of influence to another's, instantaneously. You'll be in New York before you can blink."

"What?" Emily repeated, remembering why Graham always irritated the hell out of her. He was either laissez-faire to the point of inaction or full of efficient sounding technobabble. No middle point of normality that a real human being could touch base with.

"Think of it as teleport, but without the physical movement."

"But if you don't move me, how will I get to New York?"

"Your body won't move. It'll stay in its birthing chamber under Denver II, wherever those are. Your body in the

Mindnet, this body," he pointed at her, "will move, though. We'll just instantly transfer you to New York. No travel needed."

"Oh, my God. That's sick."

"Not really, you won't feel a thing. I've already inputted your data set, and we're ready to go. Prakash and Kate have already gone and they're perfectly all right," he said. And before she could even lift a finger to stop him, he pressed a button on a console to his left, and she was suddenly standing in another room, equally full of monitoring equipment, which, for Graham's sake, had better be New York.

So typical of him to pull something like this. The bastard.

Kate, seated in front of a monitor, spotted her and waved.

***

Graham stifled a chuckle. Emily was going to be well and truly pissed, but it was worth it just to see the look on her face. He knew that he should be in New York, but couldn't bring himself to go.

Not going was easy to rationalize, of course. The blue-haired hacker was dangerous and had to be found and neutralized. Ideally, her talent would be a very welcome addition to the team—look how, just by extrapolating her disappearance trick, they'd already managed to shave hours off the commute from Denver to New York. Even if she couldn't be brought aboard, he had to find her. She was currently the only person he knew about with the talent to do something like this. He had to find out if she was behind it.

This was all very rational, but he was smart enough not to believe it. He knew that what he really wanted was to spend a little more time with the fascinating woman.

The first thing he did after Emily was gone was to check the program he'd created to track Jarrien's movements through the simulation. No matter how skilled she might be, she had to use the existing structures to move, even if she did so in a way that was completely different from what the builders of the system originally intended.

This was nothing but a source of frustration. The tale told by his program was a sad one, expressed through four columns that stood side-by-side on his screen. The column on the left gave the web coordinates of the position where she'd passed. The two in the middle were times—the middle left marked the time at which she'd passed through the coordinates, and the one on the middle right, the time at which the tracking program confirmed that she'd been there. The final column was the difference, in hours between the second and third columns. The figures in this one were getting bigger and bigger as they went down the page: she was getting away.

Graham punched the tabletop. Damn. The problem was that while his program had to search quite a few possible paths every second, she knew where she was going and went there. Logically, she was getting further and further ahead.

Well, she has to stop eventually, he thought, and tried to concentrate on something else for a while, which, of course, was impossible.

He needed air. He'd been on call either inspecting the ruins or trying to track the viruses or attempting to find Jarrien for days, occasionally napping on one of the sofas in the lobby, much to the consternation of some of the Town Hall's guests, who seemed to be going on with their lives as if nothing was wrong in the world. A walk would do wonders for his head.

In the end, he simply told Odessa he was going out for a few minutes and walked out the door. Assaulted by sunlight, he blinked a couple of times and checked his watch. Mid-morning. When had that happened?

***

The speed with which they got Emily seated in front of a monitor surprised her, especially since what that monitor was showing indicated that it would still be some time before the robot she was supposed to be piloting could go anywhere. The scene showed at least two other robots from the New York maintenance division crawling all over her own device, their glossy enameled carapaces making them resemble giant chitin-covered spiders.

Kate, looking over her shoulder, explained quickly. "We should be ready in about half an hour, but I wanted to let you look at the controls before we started—they're a little different from the ones we had back in Denver. We have some advantages and some disadvantages versus our robot back home."

Emily nodded. Just by looking at the insectoid robots, she could see that they were much more advanced than the two-legged walkers that did maintenance in Denver. It was obvious that these scurrying, low-mounted frames would be able to cover ground more efficiently and she wouldn't have to worry about tipping over, even if she encountered enormous mounds or craters. She could understand why that particular design had been chosen, but still, the scurrying on the screen gave her the creeps. Living things weren't supposed to move like that.

And then she laughed at herself. Of course they were. And they did. Only no insects other than the occasional ladybug or butterfly had been programmed into their cyberworld.

"The main advantage we have is that since we won't be leaving the Manhattan mainframe's area of influence, we weren't forced to disconnect the robot's main computer, meaning that a lot of the stuff we had to do manually in Denver will be automatic here. This should be especially useful for fine motor control and spectral analysis. We won't have to rely on visual input from the monitors so much."

Emily nodded. "I'm guessing that's what those green buttons are for," she said, pointing at a row of obviously hand-fitted controls embedded in a black panel.

"Exactly. The buttons are automated functions that include assembly and disassembly—you select the structure and the robot takes it apart, analyzes it for failure according to blueprints on the Mindnet, and then the second button orders it to put it back together. Any physical structure built in New York is within its capacity. The other buttons allow you to weld, take core samples, mark with radioactive ink, and cut through metal walls."

"Handy if we run into something damaged on the surface. We can do maintenance as we search for our intruders."

"Exactly," Kate said, ignoring the sarcasm. They were all tired. "Here's the joystick. This control moves the robot's body, forward, backward or to the sides—the thing walks just like a crab. The secondary lever allows you to move the camera in three dimensions. That button allows you to climb structures like poles or columns. The button on the right flattens the robot against the ground, turning it basically into a three-inch-tall metal pancake. We haven't figured out any uses for this. We thought it might be a method for squeezing into low spaces, but we haven't been able to get the robot to move in this mode."

"Evasion," Emily replied. "Just like in Wolfhunt. Sometimes you come under attack and have to flatten yourself against a wall or onto the floor. The pancake function is a defensive thing."

"But defense against whom? What kind of enemy would attack a three-foot-long metal spider? There are no enemies out there!"

"There are no enemies out there now," Emily corrected.

"Remember that these things were designed before the whole world was integrated into the Mindnet. Maybe they were afraid of protesters or saboteurs or something. There have been radicals in human affairs forever."

Kate didn't look convinced, but said nothing, and was immediately called over to inspect part of the retrofitting procedure. "Just about fifteen more minutes," she said, and walked to where Prakash was in a heated argument with one of the local techs.

Emily sat, looking at the monitor, watching the grotesque insectoids do pre-programmed things to her own insectoid. There was something bothering her, something that had been making her uneasy since Graham had teleported her here. She couldn't quite put a finger on it, but the whole process had seemed somehow wrong, as if the act of shooting through the program without the structure imposed by the appearance of physical transport somehow broke one barrier too many. That the very fabric of their society was threatened by it.

She got hold of herself quickly enough, but the feeling remained, buried but present. There were still five minutes before Kate had promised to have the robot up and running. Emily decided that she would rather watch what was going on than wait any longer.

She was just in time to catch the end of the three-way argument between Kate, Prakash, and the tech, after which the tech went off to program some more parameters for the robot. Emily asked what it had been about.

"They were trying to convince us to keep the maneuvering under robotic control, just program coordinates and let the robot do the walking, but we specifically want you driving the robot. We'd rather have a human aboard, in case anything unpredictable comes up. And you're the best human we've got."

Emily smiled her thanks.

"And besides, I didn't want that pretentious ass to think he was running the show," Kate smiled back. "Come on, we're nearly ready. The programming to give you manual control has already been imbedded. All they've got to do now is to activate it. And you've got a robot to drive."

Emily walked back to her assigned position, noted with satisfaction that her chair was much more comfortable than the one they'd given her in Denver—Graham never thought of that kind of thing—and sat down.

The screen was clear of scuttling spiders.

Her first action, before attempting to move the robot physically, was to test the sensibility of the camera mount. About what she'd expected: well thought out and sensitive without being excessively so. The range of movement was phenomenal, however. Nearly a full sphere, limited only at the bottom by the mounting pin.

She quickly realized, also that, due to the configuration of the cameras and nearly circular disposition of the legs, there wasn't a real 'forward' direction, just the direction in which the camera was pointed. She hoped the designers had taken this into consideration when programming the reaction to the joystick. She tested it by rotating the camera ninety degrees and pushing the joystick slightly upwards, the direction marked forward. The robot responded by taking a pair of very slow steps in the direction the camera was pointing.

Prakash, noticing the maneuver, smiled over at her. "Yeah, we caught that one," he said.

Emily nodded back and began to experiment with the range of movements offered. Once she was satisfied that there were no unpleasant surprises hiding in the linkage, she tried something slightly more ambitious. There was a pair of small metal boxes to one side. She walked the robot over to them and tried to make it climb them. The robot, on meeting the resistance, initially stopped, and only climbed over on insistent use of the joystick.

Emily called Kate over. "We need to fix that," she told the tech. "I can't have it stop each time it meets an obstacle I need to climb."

Kate nodded and walked to where the local tech was stationed. Another, smaller argument ensued, the tech saying something about built-in safety features and Kate coaxing a smile from Emily with her response, which was basically that she didn't give a flying fuck about built-in safety features.

Ten minutes later, the robot was climbing all small obstacles without hesitation, and even, with application of the correct button, up a column that stood, somewhat strangely not supporting anything, in the center of the maintenance room.

"Time to go outside," Emily announced.

The techs, except for Kate and Prakash, who grinned at each other, looked a bit scandalized at this, probably feeling that something as daunting as the real world surely needed more than just ten minutes of testing and one small overhaul. Emily could certainly understand the way they felt. The first time they'd asked her to drive the Denver robot outside, she'd felt more than a little trepidation. There was something gut-wrenching about facing the fact that your whole existence took place within the confines of a computer mainframe, which itself was part of a much larger world.

Nevertheless, she directed the robot towards the long dimly illuminated tunnel to their left, first walking sideways, and then turning the camera to turn that sideways into forward. The tunnel, according to their schematics was several hundred yards long, with two small curves along the way.

A few minutes later, they'd navigated the second curve and were suddenly confronted by the sight of a small point of brightness well ahead in the tunnel. Emily, feeling the tension in the control room, gave the robot its reins, which resulted in a spurt of unexpected acceleration, getting 'ahhs' from the crowd and causing the brightness ahead to grow at a much faster rate.

She took the robot to the edge and stopped it there, teetering right on the border between the concrete tunnel and what lay beyond. While she waited for the robot's camera to adjust to the daytime brightness, she reflected that she'd been showing off, but she needed the tech team to trust her skill.

Anyhow, it quickly became apparent that there was no real danger. The outside of the maintenance bay was similar to the inside. More concrete, as far as she could see, and more metal. Manhattan was different from Denver. The vegetation that had overgrown the city was a lot less extreme—grasses mainly, as opposed to the bushes present in Denver. Nevertheless, the tech's grips on the back of her chair showed a collection of white knuckles.

She didn't let them catch their breath. She immediately pushed the joystick forward, ordering the robot into an easy eight-legged lope that looked a little like the running motion of a cantering horse. An arrow on her monitor pointed the way to the external data port that Kate had identified as the entry for the virus. The going, after the tortured mounds of rubble in Denver, was much easier. The robot pushed through the two-foot tall grass without major difficulties, and the buildings seemed to be a lot more solid than Denver's had been. A lot taller, too, which struck her as a bit of an absurdity. Shouldn't taller buildings collapse more often than their shorter brethren?

Anyway, progress was acceptable, if not fast, and the map screen showed that they were approaching the access port. It was near an area the map said corresponded with the actual physical location of Central Park. Emily smiled, comparing the geography of the old physical New York she could see on the map with the cyberworld city. Trust New Yorkers to leave everything exactly where it was, despite the opportunity of changing anything they'd wanted to.

Five minutes later, they were standing at the entrance to the shallow tunnel that housed the data port.

"Well, it seems you were right about this," one of the local techs conceded grudgingly.

It didn't take a genius to realize it, either. The grass all around the entry had been trampled and flattened, as if it had been walked all over by a number of people in the past couple of days. In actual fact, Emily thought, it was more likely that a single large robot had caused the damage.

A black cable snaked out of the mouth of the tunnel around a corner and, it seemed, into the park.

"Should I follow the cable?" Emily asked.

"Probably," Kate replied. "But let's make sure that it's connected to the port, first. I'd hate to follow a false alarm."

It took thirty seconds to confirm that the cable was, in fact, connected to the external data port, a small panel consisting of a couple of cable sockets and a single dim light. The cable inserted into it ended in a plug that looked like it had been built from scrap metal and copious amounts of adhesive insulation.

"Okay. Now follow the cable."

"How do we know it's working? Shouldn't we check the temperature?"

"It's a data cable, not a power cable. Won't be much warmer than the surrounding wall."

Emily maneuvered the robot so that it straddled the cable and set off. It was not a difficult trail to follow, and she could have done so even without the cable itself, since the cable was roughly placed in the center of the corridor of trampled grass.

About three hundred yards later, they came to the end

of the cable, but not to the end of the trampled grass. The corridor they'd been following expanded to an area hundreds of yards across, clearing in the heather unlike any they'd seen before.

And, sitting in the center of the clearing was what could only be a spacecraft.

"What the fuck?" Emily blurted.

"That looks like one of the spaceships in my daughter's coloring books," the New York tech pointed out. Heads nodded at every console; space flight was not something their world was interested in, or even capable of, but they'd all read books, played video games, and watched the TV shows. This one was unmistakable.

"But who…" Emily began before drifting off.

"The question might not be 'but who?' It might be 'but what?'" the tech replied.

Silence followed that proclamation as they pondered the possible consequences of that statement.

They were all very relieved when an unmistakably human figure walked into view from around the corner of the ship. Unfortunately, it lasted a short time, as the figure immediately spotted their robot and, after a moment's hesitation, ran straight towards it.

Emily barely managed to take cover in the tall grass to evade the charge.

Chapter 11

"There are people there. Outside! People!" Kate repeated, for the millionth time. "But that's impossible. Who are they?"

"I bet it's that Prophet guy," Prakash replied. "He's been urging us to go out for months. He probably got some volunteers and they built that ship. Now they'll try something insane like going to Mars to start their ideal society."

"It isn't the Prophet," Emily said. She'd been silent, seated on a sofa in the background, since they'd safely hidden the robot an hour before, up a tree where it was nearly invisible behind the foliage, but could keep watch on the goings-on in the clearing. Her sudden participation startled the others into silence. "I was watching him on TV this morning, and he's changed his mind. Now, he doesn't want anyone to go outside at all."

"Of course not! That way nobody will find out what he's doing."

"No," Emily said. "You didn't see his eyes. I think he was telling the truth."

"Whatever," Prakash said, obviously unconvinced. "Anyway, there's someone out there, and they've built themselves a spaceship of some sort."

"We don't know that it's a spaceship," Kate pointed out. "Might just be a shelter of some kind."

"On landing stilts?"

"Maybe they need them for some reason. What do you know about living in the real world? Your body is cocooned somewhere in a nice warm birthing chamber, just like mine."

Emily felt a chill as she remembered the birthing chambers. How long would the life-support for the Denver I chambers hold? After seeing the crater, she felt that she shouldn't even be alive anymore.

"Damn it," she said, vehemently. "Stop arguing about it and try to see if it has a thruster or propulsion device. Could it be someone that the sweeps missed? People who never got uploaded? Anyway, they're not looking for us anymore." It was true—after the first few minutes, the people, whoever they were, had gone back inside the structure.

Emily knew she shouldn't be working her feelings out on the team, but she had to vent at someone. Her sense that something was terribly wrong had only gotten worse with the discovery that there were persons unknown standing outside on the surface. Not part of a simulation, but real, physical people.

The problem wasn't that they were out there. All the techs knew they were out there, too, and were dealing with it without any issues. Everyone else pointed smugly at them and dismissed them as some kind of weird, unnatural curiosity.

And, though that had been Emily's first reaction as well, she knew that it was artificial. The more she thought about it, the more the world she'd lived in all her life seemed insubstantial. First Graham cut through the fabric of reality as she knew it with his little teleporting trick, and now this. People on the surface using a cable to send tremendous monsters into her world—creating new and terrible life just by tweaking a couple of parameters.

All she really felt was that the world they were observing in the monitor like some interesting yet ultimately irrelevant specimen was much more real than the one she knew.

And they were all so fascinated with their new project that no one was thinking about the logical next step.

"We need to talk to them," she said.

Silence ensued.

"Talk to them?"

"Of course, at least try to find out who they are, how they got out, and what they're going to do now. They might be dangerous."

"Shouldn't we alert the authorities?"

"What are the authorities going to do? Threaten to restrain their movements within the simulation? Those people out there are real, flesh and blood humans. The authorities have no way to control them."

In the end, Emily was outvoted, and the mayor of New York was brought up to speed on the latest developments before they did anything else. The only concession she managed to get was that, while the government deliberated, the tech crew would retrofit the robot with audio gear.

She drove the thing back to the maintenance bay and began the impatient wait for the conversation to come, one that she felt would probably be the most important she'd have in her life.

***

Rome Permek had been the only one to see it. A giant black metallic spider, obviously artificial, had ambled into the clearing, and bolted when he'd tried to run after it. Fortunately, the tracks it left were distinctive enough that they couldn't be mistaken for anything brought here on the ship. Distinctive enough to convince Captain Nartiya that there was no need to move, that whoever was left on the surface running the simulation—and what a magnificent simulation it was, the whole world being modeled in a globe-spanning series of linked computers—they'd been observing the past couple of weeks would soon be in touch with them.

Their long trip would soon be over, and they'd finally get to live the Tau Ceti dream of making contact with the people of Earth.

****

Graham knew that he could get into serious trouble for what he was doing, but only if someone from Joe Fan's team found out about it—and it would have to be one of the two or three more knowledgeable members at that, otherwise they wouldn't have the faintest idea what was going on. He didn't care.

The last week had made Graham reexamine his whole attitude towards life. He'd always been relatively content except for one thing: the vague feeling of guilt caused by his consciousness of the fact that his existence didn't conform to the expected norm. Unlike his friends, he didn't go to work every day, secure in the knowledge that, if worse came to worst, he could just slap together some code and continue to live the life of luxury he'd been enjoying.

That one could never starve in the cyberworld ironically made things harder instead of easier. The prevailing wisdom seemed to be that, in those circumstances, not working was somehow immoral. And despite his efforts to ignore them and enjoy life, he realized it was, somehow, affecting him.

But now... Now, the guilt was gone. The sudden complete upheaval represented by servers going down, big ugly monsters coming into the Mindnet through external data ports and, most of all, a hacker who could teleport faster than his tracking programs could follow her made him feel a freedom he'd never experienced before: the freedom of knowing that, no matter how he lived his life, it would not affect the world in any truly noticeable way.

So, he programmed furiously on the source code, which

was completely illegal, of course, but who would question him? He was the leader of the programmers who were going to fix the world. There was a reason the government had given him access. The first thing he did was write himself an invisible air-keyboard, which would allow him to type commands directly into the simulation without the need of being physically seated at a console.

Having finished the code, he tried it out. He typed the command to teleport him home in the empty air in front of his chest, like he'd seen Jarrien do. He was immediately whisked, without drama, to his tiny Denver apartment.

The next thing he did, using this newfound talent, was to create a screen in the air in which he could watch the progress of his hunter-seeker program. The column showing how long ago Jarrien had been to each spot was still growing. No matter, she had to stop sometime—a human couldn't live in a constant state of teleport, no matter how unbalanced she might be.

In the meantime, there had to be another way of tracking down a woman who was bouncing from one mainframe to the next. She had to leave a scar in the system, something he could identify and cut off without having to follow her jump by jump.

He waggled his fingers and began to type in the air.

***

"All right," Kate said. "We've supposedly got audio—both transmission and reception. Now let's test it. Here." She handed Emily a mic cobbled together from the remains of a comm unit.

Emily wondered whether her role as driver really meant that she was the one who should be tasked with testing all the systems, but was feeling much too impatient to truly argue the point. The mayor had taken nearly a day to decide to authorize the decision to talk to the people outside—it was already past noon. And, even then, only under official supervision, which is why there was a grey-suited, nervous-looking individual standing off to one side, not really understanding any of what was happening, but officially in charge of the whole thing. "What should I say?"

"Just say anything. Numbers, whatever."

Feeling truly self-conscious, Emily spoke into the mic quickly counting to twenty.

From a console off to one side, Prakash, who was wearing two makeshift headphones, also built from cannibalized comm units, looked over and gave them a thumbs-up. "Loud and clear, both projection and reception."

"Good," Kate replied. "Now all we have to do is hook the reception circuit to the speakers on this console, and we're good to go. Ten minutes, tops."

Emily fidgeted while they worked. She admired the way Kate had become the de facto leader of the tech team. A combination of bullying the New York team and sweet-talking Prakash had effectively made her word law on all development and technical issues. And yet, Emily wished she could order the woman to speed up the process. She wanted them to hurry, to allow her to drive the black spider to those people, and get them back into the Mindnet where they belonged. That would be one less loose end, and they could get back to the central problem of how to rebuild Denver I, so she could stop worrying about the health of her body.

And yet she knew it wouldn't, couldn't, be quite that simple. The people they were tracking had committed serious crimes. They'd released viruses into the system, not only wreaking incomparable havoc, but also causing enormous damage to the Mindnet's basic simulation programming at some points. Not to mention the even more disturbing fact that some of the people the viruses had disintegrated still hadn't regenned. That was the most unusual part of the whole thing. Everyone found it hard to believe because one of the lowest-level, basic security functions of the Mindnet was that when a physical body in the simulation was disintegrated through system error, it immediately reset to saved parameters, and the person had a nice anecdote to tell. The reports of non-regenerated disintegrations were being checked and rechecked by Joe Fan's team in Denver, but Emily's gut told her they were true.

So, how to convince these people that what awaited them if they surrendered was anything other than immediate incarceration? They weren't coming. As simple as that.

But the authorities had to try. There was no choice—how else could they return the world to normal? She could recall the days when she used to hate her predictable, easy life. When she would latch on to a guy like Graham just because he seemed to be a brilliant jewel in the muck of a mediocre society. How she longed for certainty now.

Emily jumped when Kate touched her arm. Had she dozed off? Or was she simply so absorbed in her musings that she hadn't noticed the other woman's approach? Either way, it meant that she had to try to get some decent sleep— which she hadn't been able to do since this mess started. Not so much because she was on constant call, but because something in her makeup didn't allow deep sleep when the world was in such a mess.

"Up and at 'em," Kate said, but gently. She could tell that Emily was a bit ragged. "Are you okay?"

"Just tired," Emily replied. And then she smiled. "But I was absolutely exhausted in the final rounds of the Wolfhunt tournament, and I won that one. I can do a little thing like talking to a few unidentified criminals who own a spaceship in my sleep."

Kate returned the smile. "I know what you mean. When this is over, I think I'll sleep for a week. But now, we have work to do."

Will this ever be over? Emily asked herself. But she kept smiling and faced her console, all business once again.

Having done it once already, and taking into consideration that the New York spider robots were much more suited to high speed than the Denver humanoid model, she guided the robot out of the hangar bay at a breakneck pace. She wanted this done now.

She quickly located the beaten path that led towards the spaceship—or whatever it was—in the park and shot down the path. Only when they were about two hundred yards from their objective did she veer off into the relative concealment offered by the tall grass. The plan was to try to remain unseen until they were almost on top of the people outside and keep the element of surprise on their side.

The robot moved slowly through the grass, trying to disturb it as little as possible. Soon, they were about ten yards from the edge, and Emily ordered the spider to stop. "All right, what do we say to these guys?" she asked the grey-suited fellow from the mayor's office. "Do you have a script prepared or what?"

The guy looked embarrassed. "Er... Not really. The whole thing was put together so quickly that no thought was given to what you should say. I think the mayor was more worried about you guys not making any promises he wouldn't keep, so please don't promise anything without my okay. The rest is up to you, I guess. Maybe find out who they are first."

"All right," Emily replied. She'd already dismissed the man. Typical bureaucracy—waste a day for no reason whatsoever. The robot crept forward and stopped about a foot from the edge of the grass. The camera could already make out the outline of the supposed ship through the tall blades.

"Now, all we have to do is wait for someone to come by and ambush them." She told the crew. A pin dropping in the control room would not just have been heard, it would have caused the entire team to jump clear out of their skins.

***

Rome loved the summer here. Yes, the Earth was a wild, overgrown wilderness, and the ruined city beyond the Park was about as depressing a vision as it was possible to get. And yet, the summer, the breeze, the sweet air were a bit different from what he was accustomed to on Tau Ceti II. The fragrance carried in on the slight summer wind seemed somehow… right. As if he was meant to be here, in much the way that he wasn't meant to be on the terraformed Tau Ceti worlds.

The variety of plants and animals he'd seen was simply amazing. There were species that had never been introduced into the colonies—he knew the name of every tree and flower and bird on Tau II, but here, he could spot ten species he couldn't identify without doing more than moving his head.

And the temperature, a bit hot and muggy, was a few degrees warmer than the best his home had to offer. It was possible to bask in the sun here, feeling the caress of it on his exposed skin.

He'd finished his morning scan of the simulation—his avatar in the system reported that everything was basically the same as yesterday. Although the news reported that some government groups were attempting to find a solution to the damage in the network, the rest of society had gone back to their daily lives. It was obvious that the simulation had an extraordinarily well-damped feedback control logic. Most systems faced with such extensive damage would have grown unstable and torn themselves apart.

Now he attempted to relax on a towel on the flattened grass in the park. He knew that the city around him was legendary but was completely disinterested in exploring the ruins—he much preferred to lay in the sun.

But, try as he might, he couldn't enjoy it completely. The robot that had appeared yesterday was a sign that something, somewhere on this planet other than the simulations was working well enough to find them, and to avoid capture afterwards. That could mean either a sophisticated automated system or humans. And they would be back, he was certain of it.

As he pretended to relax, he scanned the grass for any sign of activity, and therefore was the first to see the robot emerge from the foliage. He pretended not to have noticed, watching what it did with his eyes half-closed. Only when it became clear that the enormous spider was walking straight towards him with its unnatural clicking gait did he get up and prepare to defend himself or rush the thing.

The spider stopped dead in its tracks.

"Wait!" an unmistakably human voice said.

Rome froze and looked around. There was no one in sight. Could the sound have come from…

"Over here."

There was no doubt this time. The robot was speaking to him in the voice of a young woman. It was slightly scratchy and filled with static, but he thought he could make out the anxiety it contained. What did one say to a giant metallic spider?

The problem was solved for him. "Greetings," the spider went on. "We are representatives of the government and would like to know who you are." The spider's Hanglish was heavily accented, but understandable.

"Er, hello," he replied, speaking slowly. "I'm Rome Permek."

There was a pause before the spider responded. "We have no record of anyone with your name on our database—could you tell us your unique ID number?"

He scratched his head. This certainly wasn't the kind of conversation he expected to have as the first man to contact Earth-dwellers in five hundred years. He unobtrusively put a hand in his pocket and hit his comm's ping button five times. He hoped the message got through, and that Stell, his default emergency contact, would understand that Rome needed him here pronto.

"I don't really know what you're talking about," he replied. "My name is Rome Permek. I'm technically a civilian, but hold the temporary rank of Technical Ensign on the HSV *Unity*."

"Yes, of course," the spider replied, a bit testily, it seemed. "But we mean in the real world. Couldn't you at least tell us which mainframe your birthing chamber is administered by? We need to know who you people are to offer you terms. And we can't do that until we know how much damage you've caused."

Rome was even more confused than before but was saved from having to reply by Stell's arrival, panting and breathless.

The spider, startled by the new arrival, skittered back a couple of meters, stopping only when Stell halted beside Rome.

"What is that?"

"That's the robot I told you about earlier, Stell. You're eventually going to have to believe me when I tell you stuff."

"And what's it doing here?"

"We're having a little chat." Rome, having relaxed once he'd ascertained that the robot was not going to harm him at all, wanted to rub his absolute coolness in. "I need a favor. Can you get the captain?"

Stell nodded, still staring at the spider, and hurried off towards the ship. The spider returned to where it had been standing.

"I've asked the captain to come. She'll be here in a couple of minutes."

"The captain. Is that the leader of your group? Can you tell us her name?"

"Of course. We've been transmitting to you for nearly a month. Her name is Ashur Nartiya."

Another pause. "We have no record of any Nartiyas in the base. Where is she from?"

"Tau Ceti, like the rest of us." Rome shrugged. Customs had evidently changed, making Earth-dwellers very unusual. If an Earth ship had landed on Tau, the whole planet would have come out to greet them in force. This spider sounded like a tax inspector.

He giggled at the thought of them, the first diplomatic mission to this planet in half a millennium, being grilled by customs.

The spider evidently misinterpreted the laugh. "This is a serious matter. We need to know who you are and where you're from."

"I already told you. I'm Rome Permek from Tau Ceti II. Maybe the captain will be able to give you more information. There she is now."

A couple of minutes of silence ensued as the captain made her dignified way to where Rome waited with the robot. Stell hung a couple of steps behind her, still obviously nervous. Nartiya nodded pleasantly, impassively, towards the black metallic spider, and said, "Greetings."

"Greetings," the robot replied.

Rome, an arm's length away, was the only one who saw her jump, very, very slightly. Her self-control was amazing.

"I am Captain Ashur Nartiya. I am in command of the Human Star Voyager *Unity*. I would like to extend our respects and that of the Government of Tau Ceti II to the people and governments of Earth. We have crossed the great gulf between stars to reestablish communication, and, after five hundred years, it is a great honor."

The silence that ensued was the longest yet. The spider stood still, looking like the black-enameled fantasy of some deranged sculpture.

Rome expected that whoever was in command of the spider was uploading the welcome speech, the response protocol required to a pronouncement of this kind from a ranking naval officer.

But the robot surprised them.

"What?" it said.

*⁎⁎

You could have cut the silence in the control room with a knife. It was heavy, oppressive. No one wanted to be the first to speak, and anyway, what could anyone say that wouldn't sound inane or mundane beside the story they'd just heard? Billions of humans scattered across nearly a dozen planets light years from Earth. Could they be telling the truth?

Prakash finally spoke. "Bullshit," he said. "They just made up some names and a story to avoid being prosecuted for screwing up a good chunk of the Mindnet."

Emily spoke in a much softer voice, but she knew her voice carried the weight of conviction. "No. They're telling the truth. The whole thing is true." She didn't know why she was so sure. A few weeks ago, before the wall came up and cut the world off from the server that was supposedly keeping her body alive, she would have dismissed such an idea out of hand. The world was a tidy, ordered place, and though she'd often told herself that it chafed and that she was bored to tears by the structure, she'd known such things were impossible—and it was a comfortable feeling.

Now she knew that it was not only possible, it was real.

The only intelligent thing they'd managed in the whole bungled interview was to tell the purported star travelers / criminal masterminds that they would consult with a higher authority and meet them again at noon the following day.

"But it's ridiculous!" Prakash insisted. "Think about it. They claim that the last contact between the colonies and Earth occurred five hundred years ago. That's before the world was fully cyber-loaded. We have all the history books from that period scanned into the libraries, and nothing indicates that there are big gaps in the knowledge. I mean, we remember the Virus Wars, the Indian Famine, the Crimean War, the Renaissance. How could we have forgotten something quite as major as the colonization of the planets? Isn't it a bit illogical?"

"Who says we forgot? Maybe it was deliberately deleted."

"No one has ever deleted files. That's not the way the world works."

Emily smiled sadly. "Yeah, that's what I thought, too."

Prakash was about to retort, but caught himself. He blinked a couple of times. "Do you really think that…"

"I don't know what to think anymore. Would you have believed the possibility of people outside? Of servers disappearing completely? Of teleporting from one place to another? Who knows what else is hidden in the programming, if we just look hard enough."

Kate, standing beside Prakash, nodded. So did most of the New York techs. They'd felt it, too.

Emily turned to the government man, who stood pale and silent to one side. "We need to get hold of the mayor right now."

The man hesitated a second before betraying his boss. "Do you really think he has the authority for something like this?"

Emily snorted. "It's his city. If he wants to call the global council together, that's his call, not mine. Pass me your comm."

Chapter 12

Graham watched Emily's conversation with the alleged space travelers through a window in the air. His mind boggled at the thought that the power of the whole simulated world, right there at his fingertips, had never been fully exploited by anyone before. A slight sense of awe at what Jarrien dared to do with her skills was replaced by a slight feeling of disappointment that she would be so restrained. They could do anything. The voyeuristic possibilities alone were unimaginable.

But right now, he was intrigued by the possibility that the people from the starship might be telling the truth.

Interesting, he thought as he drilled into the most deeply buried of the government's classified files, blowing by the security—it wasn't so much that he was overpowering the safeguards, more like ignoring them. They were built to protect against hackers coming through the system, not highly talented people willing to think outside the box. Entering from the side, as it were, through the very fabric of the simulated reality, he soon had the information he needed.

So it's true, he mused.

He typed a couple of commands in the air in front of him and blipped over to the control room. It might be educational to watch Emily's meeting with the mayor in person.

***

It was so like Graham to appear just when everything had to be explained to the mayor, Emily thought. As the public face of the repair efforts, he would probably get all the credit after having done nothing whatsoever. And he looked different, somehow. Pale, maybe, or thin. She couldn't quite put a finger on what it was exactly, but there was something. It was probably caused by spending too much time staring at a computer screen, but it still made her uneasy.

The mayor, as usual, was unavailable. He'd called in to say he would be there in ten minutes, but that had been half an hour ago. Where was he? When Emily had explained the situation to him, he'd sounded all concerned—but then, that was his job. He was probably out kissing babies as they waited.

Between Graham, who pretended to not know or not care about what had been happening over the past few hours, and the idiot politicians, she was ready to explode.

The door to the control room opened, and the mayor, a fat man in a blue suit, walked in, followed by a pair of functionaries that she uncharitably dismissed as that day's selected sycophants.

"Finally," she said. "I did mention that this was important, right?"

The mayor held out his hands apologetically. "I'm sorry about the delay. I had Caroline," he pointed at sycophant number one, a pretty young woman with shoulder-length black hair, "look up the possibility of the space people telling the truth. We've got all the classified information on the subject printed into this folder."

"Oh," Emily replied, staring at the floor.

"Don't worry about it." The mayor smiled the charming smile that had gotten him elected. "We're all a little on edge lately. You shouldn't assume that just because we're trying to get the public to think about other things means that we've forgotten the real problems; it only means that we'd prefer not to start a panic. We have enough to worry about as it is."

Graham smiled knowingly at her. Only the mayor's presence kept her from hitting him.

The mayor went on, "Caroline?"

Caroline handed each of them a printout and logged in to the system, commandeering the main screen for the presentation. After an impressive number of security and password prompts, an image appeared on the screen. They were all surprised to see that it was a starchart.

"Before passing to the cyberworld, humanity had expanded all the way through the solar system and had sent probes to the Tau Ceti system. It seems that the second planet in the system was deemed suitable for human life—not perfect, since it was a lot colder than Earth, but good enough, with an oxygen atmosphere and liquid water. Much better than any of the planets that were being terraformed in the solar system, and worlds beyond the habitats."

"Habitats?" Emily inquired.

"The habitats were essentially enormous cities built inside hollowed-out asteroids. They were nearly self-sufficient and could last for centuries without being replenished from any of the planets. This, it seems, became relevant because the plan, when Tau Ceti II was discovered, immediately became to strap enormous engines onto one of the habitats and send it off into space on a two-hundred-year flight. This happened just before we ended the cyberworld entry phase and contact with the outside was severed."

∗

Later, Graham smiled at what the mayor had said. That hadn't been quite how it had happened. The records had been intentionally fudged—even the timescale on quite a few other functions had been modified to fit the official story—but, bureaucrats being bureaucrats, they had saved an even more deeply classified version of events in a seemingly unrelated file. A file which Graham had accessed earlier that day.

He smiled and said nothing, however. Let the self-limited members of the team find out the hard way. The offworlders would tell a different story, and the timelines wouldn't fit, but that wasn't his problem. His problem was how to forestall the action that would be taken against him once the deeply buried files that told of the nearly four hundred years that had been expunged from the official histories came to light once again.

Most people at this meeting wouldn't believe him, wouldn't want to know just how much freedom had been allowed in the early days of the simulation, until they read it for themselves. In the course of the coming days, it was clear that they would. A whole bunch of ancient history would come to light, and the old disagreements would be revived.

The one good thing about having seen it first was that he'd have his own arguments ready when the time came.

***

Emily sweated a little at the controls. She told herself that it was just the pressure of having to perform in front of so many people, but the truth was that she was a bit angry about the way she'd been relegated to the role of deluxe chauffer. Everyone who'd been absent while she was struggling to keep the team together as they searched for the Outsiders over the past couple of days had suddenly seemed to reappear.

The mayor was here, of course—he'd been in touch with a couple of the politicians on the worldwide steering committee and knew what was expected of him. But Odessa, who'd been jumping in and out of the picture since the beginning, was in again. It seemed that whenever powerful individuals were present, so was Ms. Varzi. But it was also evident that she strongly preferred to leave the drudgework to the little people.

Most irritating of all, however, was Graham. He'd been gone while they searched, and when confronted with the question of where he'd been, he just shrugged and said, "Coordinating," with that infuriating grin of his. And then he just took charge.

The worst part of it was he didn't even do it on purpose. He just walked into the room and everyone deferred to him, even Odessa and the mayor, who'd been getting on everyone's nerves with their orders and imperious tones. Even the mayor's numerous aides, who'd acted as if Emily were just another lowly tech.

One look around was all it had taken to understand that only frustration lay in trying to take back her role as leader. She'd sighed and taken her seat at the robot's controls.

Now, they'd reached the agreed rendezvous point in front of the spaceship, and they'd been deliberately early so that the mayor and the rest of the entourage could see the ship firsthand. They'd all seen video, of course, and the monitor quality was no better than that, but they still expressed amazement when presented with live feed. Emily fought back the nearly irresistible urge to make snide comments.

She contented herself with giving status reports every once in a while. "They should be arriving in about ten minutes."

No one replied, they just stood, looking at the monitor as if that would make the offworld delegation arrive any quicker, and shuffled their feet. At exactly one minute before noon, the large access ramp to the ship opened, and the woman who'd introduced herself as the ship's captain appeared, flanked by the two men who'd been present the day before. As they approached the robot, other people could be seen emerging.

The newcomers maintained a respectful distance. Emily thought they were probably just curious. This was, after all, a momentous occasion.

"That's Nartiya," an aide whispered needlessly. Needlessly because the mayor was armed with printed video captures, and needlessly because, since the microphones were still off, there was no need to whisper.

Emily held up a hand for silence and, when she got it, switched on the mic, which she handed to the mayor. He nodded thanks.

"Hello Captain Nartiya. I am Mayor Steven García. I would like to be the very first to bid you a warm welcome both to Earth and to the city of New York. It's an honor to be able to greet interstellar travelers on such a momentous occasion."

This was followed by a predictable amount of obviously rehearsed diplomat-speak, which Emily tuned out after a while. It seemed that everyone was thrilled to be a part of this, and they repeated it until there could be no further doubt. And then they repeated it again, just to be on the safe side.

It took nearly half an hour for anything of interest to occur, and that occurrence was also dictated by protocol. Specifically, invitations were exchanged for each party to visit the other's environment.

In the end, having been established that a technical meeting would take place to coordinate the offworlder's visit to the Earth cyberworld, Emily found herself driving the robot up the ramp into the ship as everyone crowded, by order of precedence, closer to the monitor, hoping for a glimpse of the exotic, star-spanning tech that the Outsiders obviously had to have.

Over the next hour, she guided the robot along corridors that could easily have been present in any luxury liner on Earth. Everything Nartiya pointed out was humdrum to the point of being boring—to Emily's eye, most of the furnishings looked perfectly standard, and the controls in the bridge seemed tremendously outdated, although she had to admit that there were an awful lot of them.

Rapt had long been replaced by bored on the onlooker's faces when the fact that they weren't dealing with cyber-simulated humans was suddenly and unexpectedly thrust back upon them. Nartiya had entered a large chamber filled with beds, machinery, and some sliding plastic curtains.

"While the rest of the ship," the captain said, "is military-grade—meaning utilitarian, but not very glamorous—this is one area we are really proud of. No expense was spared, and it's the one area of the ship that is truly state of the art."

The control room around Emily was silent as everyone stared at the place. The whole room was painted white, and the machines, many of them mounted with robotic arms, had a slightly sinister air about them.

"Er…" the mayor began. He looked around the room and, receiving only shrugs, continued. "What exactly is this place?"

Nartiya looked surprised. "It's the infirmary, of course."

"What's an infirmary?"

***

The next day, Emily found herself alone with the technicians again. The mayor, realizing that despite the novelty and implications the Outsiders posed no immediate threat, had decided to give priority to other issues and had invited them to visit him in the simulation as soon as they had the technical side worked out. Of course, all the high-profile members of the team seemed to have vanished now that there was actual work to be done. They probably didn't expect to be needed for another few days, at least.

Emily smirked. What the fat cats weren't taking into

account was that the process of integrating systems so that people from the ship could enter and interact with the simulated dwelling of the Earth-humans was well advanced. The 'virus monsters' they'd been chasing had been produced by the first ham-handed attempts by the crew of the *Unity* to assess what was going on inside the huge simulation they'd discovered on what they thought was an otherwise empty planet.

The offworlders had, of course, improved their programming, and their current 'body', controlled by one of the crew, was nearly indistinguishable from any of the regular inhabitants of the cyberworld. Only the fact that Graham was unbelievably insightful—Emily admitted it freely, even though it caused her to gnash her teeth—and that Kate and Prakash were very good at what they did had made detection possible.

All Emily had to do now was wait for the guy's arrival—they'd decided not to teach him how to teleport just yet—and show him around. They'd agreed that he would meet her in the control center at the mayor's office.

Emily and the techs had employed the downtime while they waited in speculating about how the visitor would look. Since he could program his appearance to be whatever he chose, they'd agreed that he would probably appear to them as an imposing figure—probably over six feet—in order to have the physical advantage in any negotiations. They'd also concluded that he would appear handsome, probably extremely handsome, for no reason other than that humans are vain.

A knock on the door heralded his arrival, and Emily nodded to Prakash, who was nearest, to open it. Beyond was revealed a slightly nervous-looking young man whose aspect caught them completely by surprise, and they exchanged sheepish, slightly guilty looks.

He had sparse dark hair, was about average height, and was a bit on the thin side. All in all, he wasn't bad-looking, but he certainly wasn't what one would have created for oneself if given free rein in an avatar.

Emily recognized him immediately. "Hey, I know you! You're the guy who saw us the first time we approached the ship!"

He just nodded, looking around the control room nervously.

"I'm Emily Plair," she said, holding out a hand.

"Rome Permek." He hesitated a moment before shaking and then smiled sheepishly. "Sorry about that. We no longer have the custom of shaking hands. They briefed me before coming, but I forgot for a moment."

"Don't worry about it," Emily said, remembering her nearly physical reaction to the infirmary. "I have a feeling that we're all going to have to get used to some things we find strange before we can really get down to business. Here, let me introduce you to Kate and Prakash. They're the ones who'll actually be able to help get our communications up and running, since they know the system—I'm just the chauffer."

"Pleased to meet you," Rome said, this time shaking hands with no hesitation. He turned back to Emily. "I was told you were the person of reference."

She laughed—a short sound that was nearly a snort. "That's Earth for you. I seem to have been chosen to lead a team assigned to solve a problem whose technical points I don't understand in the least. But trust me, the techs know exactly what they're doing, so why don't I just get out of the way?"

Emily faded into the background as the three programmers got down to business. She could follow the less technical aspects of the conversation without too much trouble and understood that main problem would be how to make the ship's system understand the cyberworld without having to program specific avatars. The word 'interface' seemed to come up a lot after that, and then they lost her. She wandered out to see about getting something better than the coffee they'd been making in the office.

***

By the time Emily returned to the control room, the three techs had seemingly finished their unintelligible babbling about connectors. She found Prakash and Kate listening raptly as Rome told them about life on Tau Ceti II.

"All done?" she asked.

"Not really," the offworlder replied. "I still have a couple of days' work to do on the ship before we can send more people through—remember we don't use brainjacks like you do, so the avatars need to be scanned and made to move naturally through complicated damping programs. But, your techs have just showed me the way your simulation does this, so I can just create basic parameters and let the cyberworld take care of the rest."

"So you can program a lot of different people simply and without fuss?"

"Exactly. The avatar you're looking at now," said Rome, posing for her, "is a tremendously complex thing that took me more than a month to get up and running. The first probes I created were much too unsophisticated." He grinned. "The techs told me you thought they were monsters or viruses. Sorry about that."

"No need to apologize to me. But if you happen to meet a guy called Graham, I would get on my knees and beg his forgiveness. He's been tied in knots over the whole thing. But don't worry about it, it serves him right." She paused. "Want to look around?"

"Sure. I've seen quite a bit of your world already, but it'll be a change to be able to ask questions. And, trust me, I've been at a loss about a great many things ever since we got here."

They went out the door and into one of the wood-paneled corridors of the mayor's office.

"So why didn't you just contact someone in authority and introduce yourself? All you had to do was to prove you'd come in from an external jack for the government to take you seriously."

"Frankly, it didn't occur to us. We thought that your cyberworld was just a big, complicated simulation. When you found us, we were trying to figure out what it was all about and why it had even been built. That's why, after the first couple of entry attempts, we programmed the avatar to fade into the background as much as possible. I'm not really sure how you managed to find us."

"As a matter of fact, I have no idea what they did. One of the techs did the actual work, but Graham came up with the concept. Anyway, you've got me now. This is your chance to get those answers—or at least the non-technical ones."

"Well, the main question I have is general, but I'm not really sure if you'll appreciate my asking," Rome said. They'd made their way out of the building and were enjoying the early afternoon sun.

"Go. I won't be offended. We do, after all, come from different worlds, and I guess I can take that into account. But just this once." She smiled.

"The thing I can't understand is why you keep everything so normal. Actually, I don't see how either, but let's start with why."

"Normal? What do you mean?"

"Well, I just think that, since the people I see are just avatars anyway, there seems to be some scope for improvement."

"You mean like making yourself thinner or prettier, or whatever? That's illegal. And besides, our physical aspect is fixed by the scanner in the birth machine, and all growth is extrapolated from there, as well as our feeding habits and stuff."

"I was thinking more on the lines of getting superpowers and stuff. In a world like this one, you would expect everyone to fly, to teleport from here to there, and to look like giant dragons, or clouds of blue mist. But everyone seems normal. You could be on Tau Ceti, living a normal, corporeal life. It just seems that you aren't achieving your full potential."

Emily felt a wave of nearly physical discomfort at what he was suggesting. And then the feeling that he sounded like a slightly more mature and responsible version of Graham. "There was a time when people used to do that, and did, hundreds of years ago. But it made them unstable—it seems the human brain needs certain boundaries, certain limits, or it just gets unhinged. We fought some major wars, in which gigantic one-person armies fought amongst themselves and blocked thousands of people out of the cyberworld. Do you have any idea what that's like? Waking in a dark birthing chamber, in a completely atrophied body, unable to move because you risk pulling the lines out of your brain? Unable to scream because your throat doesn't know how to talk? That's what happened when we could do whatever we wanted. The only improvements allowed are the pain damping, the fact that we aren't killed until our bodies die of old age, and that we don't have to go to the bathroom."

"So people just don't do it anymore?"

"They can't. It's not just illegal, it's impossible. They programmed safeguards into it."

"No, they didn't. I've seen your code, and there's absolutely no reason why you couldn't program yourself a pair of wings right now. Hell, I could do it for you from the ship."

Emily thought of Graham and his teleport. He'd claimed that they could only do it through a special permit program controlled from the mayor's office. But if, as Rome said, it was possible for anyone to access the code, then Graham knew it. For some reason, that thought made the already shaky foundations of her world give a little more. More and more, she was becoming convinced that there would be no going back to how things were before. Ever.

She walked silently for a couple of minutes, and he waited patiently. Finally, he spoke. "What's wrong?"

"It's just that nothing seems to be working anymore. First, the black areas, and now this. Can you believe that we actually lost a mainframe?"

"A mainframe?"

"Yes, a big computer like the one that controls Manhattan, only this one had half of Denver. Each machine is situated in the geographical area that corresponds to it. Just before you started trying to get in, one of these went offline, and when we went out to have a look, we only found a big hole, as if it had been hit by a meteor."

"Oh…" Rome said. Now it was his turn to be lost in silence. "I think that might have been us."

"You?" The shock and horror were clear in Emily's voice.

"We were trying to get the planet to respond, so we plugged in to a couple of the high-energy nodes. We were looking for a way to talk to the simulation, and we used a bit too much power trying to call attention to ourselves. Two of the nodes seem to have been damaged, and one exploded."

The few remaining solid pieces of her world slipped. She could feel them as they went. "But…" she began, and paused to compose herself. "You might have killed millions! You probably killed me!"

"We didn't kill you. You're right here!" he protested. "And in our defense, the reactor in the one that exploded was completely unstable. It should have been replaced ages ago."

She broke down, tears streaming down her face. Rome watched her for a few moments before ordering his avatar to put its arms around her.

Chapter 13

Rome watched as Emily drank her coffee.

She'd finally managed to calm down. Her body, she'd explained, was in a birthing chamber that, as far as anyone had been able to decipher from the technical documentation they'd found, should be under the control of the Denver I mainframe. With the ship's destruction of the computer, the life support on her birthing chamber should have gone down—and she should have been dead.

"That obviously didn't happen," he pointed out.

"No. But I'm living in constant fear that my reprieve is just temporary, and that I'll die at any moment. The way I imagine it is that my body will die and my avatar will just stand there, and nobody will know I'm dead until they notice I'm not moving and trace the program back to the source." She smiled, and Rome relaxed a little. "I just hope they don't decide not to erase me and leave me standing there as an ornament. Or a nude statue."

He chuckled. "Or worse yet, that the simulation keeps you on autopilot and nobody ever realizes what happened." It was immediately apparent that it was precisely the wrong thing to say. Her eyes widened for an instant before brimming full of tears again. He went on hurriedly. "Don't worry, that can't happen. The programming wouldn't allow something like that."

She smiled wanly, as if knowing that he was trying to comfort her. And he was. He wasn't all that sure the programming wouldn't allow an uninhabited body to go on exactly as it was—as a matter of fact, that's precisely what he'd thought in the first place. Until the robot had appeared and said, "Hi, we're Earth people and we're alive," they'd all assumed that the simulation was just a program running without living input.

"Look," he went on, "I know I'm the worst person possible to try to comfort you, since I could never know what living this way would feel like, and also because I'm part of the crew that caused this to happen in the first place, but I can say that, technically speaking, if the destruction of the mainframe was a physical threat to you, you'd have felt something already."

"That's what the techs always say," she replied. And then she decided to be honest with him. Maybe, just maybe, a person who hadn't spent his entire life living in a simulated environment might be able to understand what she felt. "It isn't even me that I'm worried about. Well, at least not directly," she said.

"Huh? What is it, then?"

"I'm thinking of the millions of people who were inside the Denver I area when it went down. I can just imagine them trapped in their birthing chambers, unable to move their atrophied limbs, just sitting in the darkness, in the silence, gradually coming to feel levels of pain well beyond what the simulation allowed, and wondering if they were dead. My parents were there!" Emily broke down and cried.

Not knowing what else to do, he took her hand.

"And every day, I wake up knowing that the only thing between me and the same fate is a mainframe. A mainframe that can explode or get hit by a meteor, or, even though everyone says it's impossible, just break. I just feel like nothing is real." There, she'd said it. Now he'd laugh, and she could get mad and forget about her anxiety for a while.

He didn't laugh. Or, rather, he did, but for unexpected

reasons.

"Finally!" he exclaimed. "That's the first time I've heard anyone here say anything sane about the way you people are living. I would go insane if you told me my body was immobilized and my mind was trapped in this nightmare of a simulation. I was worried that everyone on Earth had gone completely off their rockers."

She just looked at him, unable to reply. Here she was, telling him her deepest, darkest secret, the one thing she knew would get her only shocked, uncomprehending stares from her best friends, and he acted as though it was the most natural, normal thing in the world. "You don't understand," she told him. "What I'm feeling isn't normal. The cyberworld is the best thing that ever happened to us. This is the first time that humanity is truly free. We're free from pain—well, unbearable pain anyway, lesser pain was kept since it is a fundamental learning tool. We're free from starvation and poverty. Everyone knows that they have to work to get really good stuff, but nobody has to work at something they hate just to keep body and soul together. We are free to be as great or as inconsequential as our talent and our drive permits."

He said nothing, but it was still obvious that he wasn't quite grasping her point.

"Don't you see? The world obviously isn't the problem—it's kept us safe and happy for centuries. My insecurity must mean that I'm the one that's losing it, and that makes it worse. We can deal with any kind of physical illness—as a matter of fact, we don't even feel anything that might be affecting our physical bodies—but if I go insane, there's nothing anyone can do about it. And I'm definitely getting paranoid."

This time, Rome did laugh at her. "Insane?" he asked. "For being worried about being trapped inside a huge program that you've already seen can break at any moment? I think you'd be insane if you weren't!"

"Trapped? We're not trapped! All of us are here because we want to be. We understand true freedom in a way that slaves of flesh and blood never will."

"Can you leave?"

"What?"

"Can you leave the simulation? Can you order the program to let you take control of your body and just walk around in the real world?"

She paused. "I really don't know. I never thought about it, and I don't know anyone who has. Why would anyone want to leave?"

He seemed about to retort hotly, but then stopped to think. "I'm not really sure," he said at last. "But what I do know is that I'd never voluntarily allow myself to be locked in a computer program."

"Why not?"

"Because life would seem meaningless. As soon as the next generation arrived, everything I'd ever done could be wiped from the memory drives. Hell, I wouldn't even leave a body to feed a new generation of worms. It just seems that nothing would be real."

Ouch. That one hit a little too close to home. "Of course things are real. A beautiful building is no less remembered because it's inside our world! A novel can still be great, even if it can only be uploaded through the Mindnet. After all, this isn't just a temporary uploading of Earth's people. We live here, and will do so forever. Things that happen on the outside are what isn't real."

He nodded, not looking convinced.

She wasn't surprised. If it had sounded as hollow to him as it had to her, he wouldn't be buying it.

***

The meeting room held an air of unmistakable tension. Word had quickly gotten around that the destruction of the mainframes had been the offworlder's doing, and the meeting, which had originally been planned as a cheerful welcoming soiree had, in reality, been tensely formal. Nothing had been said about the matter yet, but it was clear that both sides understood exactly what the silence signified.

The delegation from Tau Ceti stood to one side, unattended, two of its member's avatars—Captain Nartiya and her aide—having been specifically created for the occasion. Rome wore the same avatar he'd shown for his meeting with Emily, Graham noted—he hadn't been present, but he'd been watching.

Soon, ushers led the visitors to a long, white-clothed table that had been set up in the center of Town Hall's main conference room. The three people from the ship seated themselves on one side of the table. Their seats had been placed in the center of the expanse, right across from the mayor's seat. The Earth delegation sat facing them, its more important members in the middle, and lesser aides and hangers-on who'd only been invited because they were the mayor's friends and allies seated farther away. Many of them would have to strain to hear what was being said, despite the table's shape: they'd chosen an oval table so that the New York delegates could not only see the people facing them, but also each other.

Graham was seated directly to the mayor's right, which earned him a dirty look from Emily, who was considerably farther away. He took his seat last, watching the rest of the dignitaries—those without specifically assigned places—jockey for position. He noted with interest that the only people not from New York were the technical consultants from Denver. There was not one single government official from any other city. Not even Denver or

Stuttgart. Well, maybe Stuttgart's politicians had been wiped in the mishap, but it was still strange.

There was no world government, of course, and even national governments had been consigned to the scrap heap of history after the mainframe agreement at the Place de Concord established that each local mainframe would govern itself and that each government would uphold the agreement. And, despite dire predictions, it had worked flawlessly ever since. Not one single mainframe had ever successfully rebelled against the system, and only one had ever tried it: the individualistic terrorists of Copenhagen, nearly four hundred years before.

So all the other mainframe governments regarded the fact that there was a human starship sitting in Central Park as a local issue with no real importance anywhere else. The prevailing attitude seemed to be "it isn't as though the Mindnet went down or there's a new worldcast channel, so why get all worked up about it?" Graham thought it was like a report of a hurricane flooding a mainframe bay. It was the mainframe government's responsibility to deal with local weather. Or local animal infestations. Or anything else that went on on the outside in their area of responsibility.

But it still surprised him. This meeting was likely to be the most important event in human affairs on Earth, and, possibly in the galaxy, in the last half millennium, and it was being treated like a minor infrastructure malfunction.

With everyone seated, the mayor of New York opened the hostilities. "We are extremely concerned with the reports we've received that your ship was responsible for the destruction of at least three mainframes worldwide, causing, we suspect, the death of millions of people on Earth. Can you shed any light on these reports?"

Nartiya straightened in her chair. It was obvious that she was not as well-versed in the control systems of the avatar that had been created for her. The projection of Nartiya moved woodenly, haltingly, much less smoothly than the more practiced Rome, who presumably had access to the same technology. "Yes," she said. "We can shed light on it. As a matter of fact, we were responsible for it, and would like to apologize and offer any aid that might help the victims. It wasn't our intention to do any damage—in fact, we weren't aware that our actions could possibly affect the lives of anyone living."

A murmur went around the table. Most of the seated delegates had heard the rumors but had expected a political maneuvering and a drawn-out battle. No one expected a quick admittance of guilt and an offer of help. Even the mayor, who'd likely planned a response to any possible contingency, seemed at a loss for words.

"Unaware?" he said finally, incredulous. "How could you possibly be unaware of the consequences of what you were doing? You knew about the treaty—you even have a copy in your data banks! It even says that the treaty had been signed between the colony on Tau Ceti II and the cybernations of Earth. How could you possibly assume that destroying a mainframe would leave cybernations unaffected?"

"Well, the truth is we didn't have any data concerning the cybernations themselves or Earth's social structure. For some reason, that knowledge was never installed in the Tau Ceti data banks and went to the grave with the original delegates who signed the treaty. We had centuries to theorize about it and came up with two main theories: Earth was a kind of police state in which computers monitored and defined the lives of everyone living there, or humanity had developed technology that allowed them to interface with their machines—some of us even argued that a kind of post-humanity had been achieved by mixing humans and machines to create a new kind of organism. But all our theories led us to expect that there would be some kind of life on the surface, some activity, some physical human or post-human presence we could interact with. We certainly weren't expecting this." Nartiya gestured jerkily towards everything around her.

"Is this the way you react to everything you don't understand? By trying to overpower it without thought to the consequences?" the mayor retorted. "No wonder Earth felt compelled to force you into a treaty through which you agreed to have no contact with us for five hundred years. Sadly, it doesn't seem to have done any good."

Nartiya made to reply, but Graham wasn't listening. Something she'd said bothered him. There was no reason for the records of the treaty to be incomplete in this way, unless it had been done intentionally. He wondered why it had been done. What were those long-ago delegates trying to hide? Why had they hidden the nature of the original conversations? It was obvious that they had, at least to some extent, since the original talks had taken place with the same cyberwold Earth that existed today, which meant that either avatars were employed, or the meetings took place on neutral ground—electronic neutral ground.

Discreetly, Graham typed a pair of commands into the air in front of him and immediately felt his awareness split in two. Though part of him was still seated in the conference room, listening to the Tau delegates trying to explain what had happened to the unsympathetic Manhattan dignitaries, an equally important part of him was suddenly standing in his own quarters.

***

He'd experimented with duplication before, but this was the first time he would be able to test the newfound skill in real-world conditions. He studied his duplicated avatar in the mirror. *Perfect*, he thought.

He moved the double to the console and began to type. No matter how effective the air keyboard was, he still preferred to do his programming seated at a console. He supposed it was a lifetime's habit that made it so. Anyway, he soon hoped to be able to dispense with typing altogether. The direct neural interface program he was working on would enable him to twist the simulation into unintended knots with a mere thought.

In the meantime, his highly illegal duplicate had a job to do.

***

"No," Nartiya replied, ignoring the sarcasm, "of course we don't use overwhelming force on everything we don't understand. And we didn't do that with your mainframe straight away, either. First, we tried to communicate with you from orbit, then from the surface, on every wavelength ever used for communication. We finally concluded that either humanity was gone from the planet or deliberately hiding. We needed to send a message you couldn't ignore, which is why we tried to get into the mainframes. We chose widely separated ones so that the damage to any one sector would be minimized. Since the big computers seemed to be the only functioning technology on the planet, even the only signs of intelligent life, we saw it as a last chance maneuver. If that failed to elicit a response, we would fuel up and return to Tau Ceti. By the time you showed up, we'd essentially given up hope of finding you here. We were going to return in a week or so."

"But that's ridiculous! You had managed to infiltrate one of your technical people into our cyberworld—and did quite a bit more damage while you were at it. You knew we were here."

"To tell you the truth," Rome interjected, "we had no idea you were here. The simulation is so complex that we thought that the humans inside were just more programs that we hadn't had time to unravel yet. Nothing seemed to indicate that there was actual, conscious, intelligent life present."

Graham suddenly jerked. He still wasn't used to being in two places at once, or to controlling two bodies at the same time. So when his duplicate unearthed an extremely interesting tidbit from the data cores in the Washington mainframe, the body at the conference twitched in surprise. He hoped nobody had noticed.

Interesting, he thought, and erased the duplicate copy. He had what he'd created it for. He also made a mental note to see how he could increase his capacity to be at two different places at the same time.

***

While the rest of the delegates were staring across the table at each other, Emily was surreptitiously watching Graham, who'd been acting strangely for the last ten minutes. He seemed to be only half-aware of what was going on around him, talking to himself silently, and staring, in rapt concentration at something a foot in front of his eyes. Every once in a while, he would seem to break out of the trance, look around guiltily, and focus on the meeting around him for a few moments before zoning out again.

She wondered what the hell he was up to now.

"But," Nartiya went on, sounding slightly guilty despite the fact that her avatar showed no particular emotion, "you might be right about the motives for the non-interaction treaty signed between the spacefaring sections of humanity and the people of Earth."

"What do you mean?" the mayor said.

"As I mentioned, our records are incomplete. We have no filed explanation as to why the treaty needed to be signed, just a pile of documents exhorting us to respect this treaty because Earth was our homeworld, and the people of the planet had long supported space exploration and had never left an unviable colony to fend for itself or starve. And, in return, the least we could do was to uphold our side of the bargain." She paused, trying to judge what effect her words were having. "As you can imagine, this lack of information has led to quite a bit of speculation among us. Why would Earth request this treaty? Was it military in nature? Or was it a case of simply wanting to be left alone? One of the theories that has been bandied about for the past couple of centuries is that Earth was experimenting with a radically new type of social system and you wanted to be certain that no outside forces interfered with its development while it was in stabilization phase."

Emily caught Graham grinning at this, then looking furtively around to see if the offworld delegates had noticed. Seeing their attention focused on the mayor, he relaxed. *Typical Graham,* she thought. Even during what was probably the most important meeting he would ever attend in his life, he was goofing off. What a jerk.

Nartiya was still explaining. "Of course, most scholars believed that this was just a dumb crackpot idea that someone had pulled out of a hat, and it was never really looked into by anyone with any credentials. But, they seem to have been right after all."

The mayor nodded. "The cyberworld," he said.

"Exactly. This whole experiment must have been extremely unstable when it started. Essentially, the government of the planet forced everyone to live inside the simulated world, and they must have enforced it pretty stringently since there's no sign of human life anywhere on the surface. If we tried to do something like that on Tau Ceti, we'd have an armed insurrection on our hands."

"So you think Earth asked for those five hundred years in order to keep spacefaring humans from siding with the resistance? Because the resistance would seem like the just cause to the outside-dwelling starfarers?"

"Maybe. But I think it was probably more along the lines of allowing the society to stabilize with no outside influences whatsoever. After all, if you just wanted to keep us from helping the insurrection, all you had to do was ban our ships from coming farther into the solar system than the asteroid belt. There was no need to ban all transmissions."

"You're probably right," the mayor said.

But Emily was watching Graham, who was grinning as though the conversation between Nartiya and the mayor was the funniest thing he'd ever heard.

***

Back aboard the *Unity*, Rome was thinking about the meeting. Of the huge number of things that felt completely wrong about the talks, and, to be honest about the social structure of Earth in general, there were two that bothered him particularly.

"But what was in it for us?" he asked Stell.

"As usual, you are making absolutely no sense. What was in it for us in what?"

"The treaty. So Earth gets left alone, but what did we get out of it? By that time, our combined military was much larger than that of Earth, since Earth had disbanded their fleet so they couldn't say 'you leave us alone or you'll pay the price', but it wasn't in the colonies' best interest to leave Earth alone. It was still a great place to get certain raw materials much cheaper than mining for them. And especially since the Earth people weren't going to be using them themselves. Or, failing that, destabilizing the cyberworld and keeping Earth's population active on a more physical level would have given the colonies a huge market for our goods. The treaty doesn't make sense from our side."

"I hate you," Stell said. "You get to actually go to the meetings, but everything seems to indicate that you didn't listen to anything that was said there. Life is so unfair!" The meetings had been broadcast back to the ship, of course, and a small hyperspace carrier had been dispatched to get the news back to Tau Ceti.

"You mean you believe the stuff about how the colonies owed a debt to Earth and that respect made us honor their requests? I think that might hold for something small, but something as large as having no contact at all with the home of, at that time, three-quarters of humanity? It just seems too much."

"Well, there's no way to go back and ask them, is there? So tell me about this girl."

Rome sighed, but had no one to blame but himself. He'd been the one who told Stell about Emily, after all. So he started to get into the details, but distractedly. Most of his attention was focused on trying to figure out just why the Earthlings had, after a couple of snarky comments, just let the matter of the mainframe damage drop when the Tau delegation apologized for a second time. Was it possible that they really didn't care about what happened outside their own mainframe, or were they setting up some well-planned ambush to obtain concessions?

It seemed unnatural, somehow, to shrug off a loss of life on that scale as just something that could happen. Any aggression even remotely similar on Tau Ceti would have sparked off a war that could last for generations. He felt that there had to be something sinister behind the Earth delegation's acceptance. He just hoped it didn't get too ugly.

Chapter 14

Jarrien stopped where she was and watched her data set incredulously. Up until a few moments before, she'd been certain that, regardless of anything Graham might do to try to catch her, she would be able to stay one step ahead of him. After all, he was a busy man, and it took time to track down the telltale signs of a teleport in the simulation's history files. It hadn't been fun, but it was imperative that she manage to stay one step ahead of him.

He was much too deeply involved in the investigations into the anomalies of the past month and the meetings with the visitors from the stars for her to risk speaking to him. He would definitely grill her about the little excursion she and the Prophet had undertaken, and she was not going to share information about what they were doing out there with the leader of the forces opposing them.

But now, Jarrien stared at her data feed in disbelief. She'd programmed it to show her where Graham was at all times, and what he was doing. She'd arranged to get this information through untraceable preexisting security systems that the simulation program itself used to monitor each sector. Not only were the systems untraceable, they were also infallible, with plenty of redundant backups built in. There was no way her info could be wrong.

And yet, the feed was showing not one or two Grahams, but four of him. She flipped through the versions: one of them was sitting, a slightly bored and distracted look on his face, in what appeared to be a formal meeting, while all three of the others were shown in locations that were on her back trail. Two were on false paths she'd programmed in, but the last was less than two hours behind her. There was no way she could avoid all three for more than a day.

Graham had copied himself. The thought was staggering, even to Jarrien, who'd scratched out a living by skirting the law, by hacking into the source code in places where no one would notice. By living in fear of discovery and on the margins of society for years. And here was the top programmer on the government payroll casually cutting through all the taboos and forking himself three times. He wasn't even bothering to hide the identity of the copies: all three were identifying themselves as Graham Johnson.

Running was no longer an option. There was no way she would be able to avoid the guy. Even if the copies failed to run her down, he would simply do something even deeper and more unpleasant to the simulation until he had her. And the simulation had to survive. Her only choice was to talk to Graham and explain, plead with him to live his life by the rules that had kept society together for hundreds of years, and forget that he'd ever teleported or seen her do so.

She had a feeling he would be very hard to convince.

***

The prophet was on TV again, Emily noticed. She couldn't quite understand what kind of game the guy was playing. For years, he'd been the voice of the lunatic fringe, espousing a 'back to nature' message that essentially screamed out to everyone that the only way they would survive was to go back to their physical bodies and leave behind the safe, soft cocoon of the cyberworld. He'd explained to anyone who was willing to listen that humanity had come to ascendancy through the conquest of hardship and standing up to nature. And the risk of turning their back on these simple truths was facing the possibility of species' extinction.

And then, with the huge malfunctions and the arrival of the Outsiders, proof of what he'd been saying all along was handed to him on a platter, as was a worldwide media audience. So, what did he do?

He did a hundred-and-eighty-degree turn and began spewing things that were the opposite of everything he'd ever said before.

The reporter, of course, had been well briefed and was trying to find out the reason for this sudden change of heart.

"Well, the fact that humanity exists outside our cyberworld removes the need for us to bear the burden," he said.

But she wouldn't be swayed that easily. "We've always suspected that there were other branches of humanity out in the galaxy, and yet, your position was that it didn't matter. That the homeworld itself needed to fight to regain our biological origins. You went on record quite vehemently on this point."

"That's true. But now I see that I was merely frightened because I didn't really, deep down, believe that there was anyone else out there. But now that I know better, I have come to realize that what we have within the cyberworld is a unique, valuable society. A society, moreover, that will leave no trace outside the servers if we should return to our bodies. The loss of my earlier fears has opened my eyes to this stark reality."

"So you truly believe that we should stay here? Or will you still ask for the laws to be changed to give everyone a choice?"

The Prophet's eyes blazed. "I don't think a choice is a viable compromise. Now that we're certain that humanity not only exists but is thriving outside our simulation, I really believe that we must do everything in our grasp to keep our way of life intact. And giving people the choice to establish a parallel society on the planet's surface would be counterproductive. How long do you think they would take to realize that the machines running the simulation could be put to better use, or that the people locked in the birthing chambers could be used for cheap labor?"

"You've thought this through," she replied.

The Prophet smiled knowingly. "I had years to think through the possible negative consequences of what I espoused for so long, and these were just some of the issues I knew I would have to deal with if my followers were allowed to live on the surface."

"So, what would you say your position is now?"

"Strict hermeticism. We need to stop speaking with the offworlders and suspend all forays to the surface. I have indisputable intelligence that indicates that a robot exploring the surface was the way contact was made with the offworlders. Not an automated maintenance drone—I'm talking about a robot guided by humans who saw everything it saw and chose what to explore and where to go next. We need to stop doing this at once."

"And if your followers don't agree?"

"It's natural that some of them might be a bit confused by the change of direction, but anyone who was following me originally obviously has a clearer head than the population in general and will be able to see the logic in what I'm saying."

"And if they don't?"

"Then I'll have to fight them, too."

Something about the way he said it made Emily shudder. It wasn't a rational thing, of course—she knew that the likelihood of anyone putting together an expedition to return to their physical bodies was extremely small. Why would anyone want to suffer the discomfort of corporeal existence when all the rewards had been programmed in to the simulation, and all but the least uncomfortable costs had been removed? And yet, she couldn't shake the feeling, more like a certainty, that it would happen and that the Prophet's war would take place.

Turning off the set, she caught a glimpse of the time display on the wall. Damn. The next meeting with the Outsiders was due to begin in three minutes, and there was no way she could walk there in time. She would have to teleport.

She hated teleporting. It was unnatural. It was wrong. And, to make it much, much worse, it was seductive. Each time she did it, she felt a little less guilty, a little less revolted, a little less convinced that in accepting teleportation as a way of life, she was pulling on a thread that would, in the end, unravel everything she'd ever known: her structured, easy life, the social fabric of the simulation and, in the end, the simulation itself.

But there was no way around it this time. She grabbed her comm, typed a command into the air, and disappeared.

***

The room was exactly as before, except there were much fewer people in the Earth delegation. The novelty had worn off, so the only people still present were those who had to be there. The rest, convinced that no invasion was imminent and that the Outsiders manifested as slightly less well-animated versions of cyberworlders, had gone off to find more interesting things to do. The meetings, as far as the rest of the world was concerned, had gone back to being strictly a local affair.

Consequently, while the Outsider delegation held the same three slightly jerky avatars, the Earth side consisted of just the Mayor, Kate, Prakash, Emily herself and, surprisingly,

Graham.

Well, she thought, *at least the Prophet won't have to start his war. No one is ever going to mount an organized movement to live outside the cyberworld.*

She took her seat beside Graham and immediately realized something was wrong with him. He seemed somewhat distracted, but with everything that had been going on lately, that was only natural. And anyway, he'd already been acting strangely before. No, that wasn't it. It was more a sensation of his not being substantial, which she knew was absolutely ridiculous but still described what she felt. He was somehow... absent. She even went so far as to allow herself to brush against him, seemingly accidentally. Unsurprisingly, Graham was perfectly solid, and irrational relief flooded her.

The mayor set the proceedings in motion.

"We've discussed the previous meeting and have come to a decision," he told the offworld delegates.

Captain Nartiya's impassive avatar showed no emotion, but her hands fidgeted with something—presumably something on board their ship, something physical which hadn't been reproduced by the interface program. "We would like to reiterate our apologies and await your decision."

"We feel that our society has managed, in the last five hundred years, to attain a stability, peace, and balance that are unprecedented at any time before this." It was obvious that the mayor was simply reciting a set piece he'd either committed to memory or nearly so. "We believe that the reason our forefathers requested this treaty is that the only way to maintain our balance, our way of life, and our current state of happiness was to remove any interference from our affairs and seal ourselves off from the rest of humanity. We believe they were correct to act this way and would like to request another extension of the same treaty—five hundred more years of non-interference with our culture."

"What?" Rome blurted, with no respect for any protocol or turn.

Nartiya turned to look at him, and spoke. "We hope you'll reconsider. Every human colony in the galaxy has one dream: to be reunited with the people of our beloved homeworld."

And suddenly, Graham moved. Any sense of vagueness was gone, his attention was quite clearly focused here, and there was no doubt that he was complete and present. He burst out laughing.

"I can't believe you'd say something like that," he exclaimed. "Do you people even know why the original treaty was signed?"

"The records have been lost in time," Nartiya responded stiffly. "We suspect that the transcripts of the meetings were either never recorded or deliberately erased afterwards."

Graham laughed again. "Yeah, that would make sense. Better to keep one's hands clean."

Everyone was staring at Graham now, the cyberworlders in shocked disbelief, and the offworlders blankly—but Emily could easily imagine the incredulous faces aboard the *Unity*.

Nartiya recovered first. "I'm sorry, Mr. Johnson, I don't really understand what you're saying."

"I mean exactly what I'm saying—either you are pretending not to know what was said in the original meetings, or, more likely, the delegation that attended the meetings declined to give details, simply reporting the treaty itself and explaining nothing further. They must have been really powerful people to be able to do that, though."

"We've always thought that the records had been lost to a clerical error over the centuries—why would you think that it was done on purpose?"

Emily was asking herself the same thing, and, judging by their expressions, so were the rest of the members of the Earth delegation. The mayor, in particular, was staring at

Graham open-mouthed, a mixture of surprise and fury written on his features.

Graham, of course, was enjoying himself immensely. He leaned back in his seat and glanced impassively at each of the faces at the table, as if trying to imprint the moment on his memory. He leaned forward as if to speak but stayed silent for another moment. Then, when the mayor began to say something, Graham spoke in a loud voice. "Unlike the colonies, Earth has an intact record of the sessions in which the treaty was signed. We know exactly what happened, and why."

"What?" The mayor finally managed to get a word in edgewise. "Why haven't I been informed? And why didn't it come up when I accessed the files regarding the treaty?" he spluttered. And his eyes also said, why did you bring this up here without warning me, you bastard? What's your game?

Graham just smiled. "The answer to both those questions is pretty simple. Nobody told you because I'm the only one who knew—as a matter of fact, I found out only after the meeting began."

"How—" Emily began, but he continued in the same loud voice. It seemed that when he spoke, all competing voices became somehow muted.

"And the reason you couldn't get access to the files is that the files you would have needed are buried somewhat deeper in the government archives. They date from a time when there were still centralized governments running things, and they were paranoid about security. Even though the big governments are gone, some of their secrets are still password protected and deep-encrypted in some of the local mainframes, if one knows where to look—or better yet, if one knows *how* to look."

"So, tell us about it!" the mayor exclaimed. All semblance of a diplomatic meeting had dissolved. Graham had kicked the table and had effectively eliminated the possibility of the meeting continuing.

"I don't think so." He crossed his arms.

"What?"

"Well," Graham continued laconically, "for one thing, the information contained in these files would be a bit of a shock to all of you. And for another, I believe it's going to take you a few days to get it, which buys me some time to do a few things I've been wanting to do, without the distraction of all these diplomatic meetings."

"If you think we'll ever invite you again—" This time, Emily could distinctly hear it. The mayor's voice dropped to a barely audible whisper the instant Graham's mouth opened.

"I don't need your invitation, but these meetings are a bit of a waste of time, so I might not bother anyhow. Well, as I was saying before I was so nearly interrupted," he said, directing a mischievous look at the mayor, who had stopped talking mid-phrase, with a dumbfound expression, "there are things I want to do. Cheerio, then!"

He disappeared. And with him, another small portion of Emily's hopes for a return to a normal, solid-feeling existence.

***

Rome looked over the faces at the table. It was somehow liberating to meet the gazes and know that what he was seeing was actually there, that the people looked exactly the way he saw them, as opposed to being images created by a simulation. *How much did Earth people resemble their avatars?* he wondered. Did they really have no control over how they looked? They claimed to be constrained by the simulation's rules so that they would look fat if they overate or untidy if they neglected to comb their hair, but he'd looked into the compilers they used and had found no actual blocks in the program that would keep them from doing anything they wanted with their bodies. Even the claim that their overall physical appearance was extrapolated from the way their actual physical bodies looked at birth, deep underground, was difficult to accept.

And, even though he'd been spending a lot of time with the captain lately, this meeting was a bit more intimidating than he was used to. Every single department head on the ship was present, from the bored-looking biologist, who was more interested in the wild animals of the surface, to the bearded head of the historians, who was stepping all over himself to either prove Rome's findings false or take credit for them.

"So, what you're saying is that you have an actual recording of the meetings during which the treaty was created?" Dr. Kamm asked from behind his beard.

"Exactly."

"And the media survived for hundreds of years? How can you be sure that this isn't some kind of hoax by the Earthers?"

"I can't be one hundred percent certain, of course, but my professional opinion is that this is the real thing. The files we had to access to get the information we're about to see had only registered one view in the past three hundred years—and that was supposedly by Mr. Johnson during the meeting. And, to put it bluntly, I don't think that, with their current programming knowledge, the people on the government payroll could have altered the records. These were some deeply protected memory files, and unless they've been hiding their good programmers somewhere, they just don't have the skills to modify them. What's more, I had the feeling that they wouldn't have been able to dig the files up without my help and seemed just as surprised as I was at what the recordings show."

Ashur Nartiya intervened. "Maybe we should watch the recording before passing any judgment about it, don't you agree?"

Kamm frowned, but nodded.

Rome went on. "The recording is in two dimensions. The Earth-based system had a tri-D of the meeting, but transferring it to our systems would have been time-consuming, and I felt that the information was more important than the format in this case." He looked around the room, anxiously searching for a clue as to whether he'd been correct to do so. No one stirred, although he thought he detected the faintest of impatient nods from Captain Nartiya. He hit the play button on the remote.

The wall behind him immediately came alive, the molecules excited to show an image. This could be done with any wall in the room, but he'd chosen the far wall because it was the least likely to be obstructed by people sitting in front of it. Unfortunately, this immediately made him the obstruction, and he moved out of the way as quickly as dignity allowed.

The scene was a meeting room—a chamber which was, to Rome's eye, depressingly similar to the meeting chamber in Manhattan's City Hall. It saddened him to think that Earth's culture had stagnated to a point in which five hundred years had resulted in nearly no innovation in architectural design.

The biggest difference between the chamber in the image and that in present-day New York was that the large dark table had been round five hundred years before.

Seated around the table were three cyber-citizens, recognizable by the fact that their avatars were indistinguishable from real humans. The Earth delegation was composed of two silver-haired people – one male and one female, and a much younger woman with light brown skin and black curly hair. Seated in front of them, clumped together as if for warmth were three cartoonish simulated humans, presumably the delegation from the colonies. Lettering appeared on the screen, identifying each member of each delegation in turn. On the Earth side, the signs identified the younger woman as United Cybernations Coalition President O'Connell and the older pair as senators Yang and Angellini.

The Colonists were represented by Ambassador Timur from Tau Ceti and his aides, Wasyl and Minussain. It was impossible to tell anything about them, physically, other than that they animated identical mannequin-like avatars. As the recording began, Timur was speaking—evidently replying to something O'Connell had said.

"I'm afraid it's not the same to us. If you insist on this insane course of action, we need you to guarantee that it won't spread to the colonies. We simply aren't at a state in which we can afford to have our people living that way—our infrastructure just isn't ready," the ambassador said, the expression audible in his voice giving lie to the avatar's immobile features.

O'Connell looked back at him impassively. "It isn't our fault that the people in the colonies prefer the standard of living inside a cyberworld to the hardships of your half-terraformed planets. And we certainly aren't going to go back to the way things were just because you're afraid for your precious little colonies. We like it this way—comfortable living, no pain, and since everyone is in here, there's no resistance, no one saying that we should live in the real world. This is the real world."

"Not to us, it isn't," the ambassador said.

"Then that's your problem, isn't it? We've found a way to make everyone in the world comfortable and content, created a society in which those who want something more can strive to get it, and the rest can use their time as they wish. We have flourishing cultural life, more artists and poets per capita than any other era of human existence. Everyone is happy."

"The fact that we're even having this discussion means that

not everyone is happy about it."

"You mean the colonists? You've been gone for a hundred and fifty years. And all the malcontents left with your colony ships. Our final sweeps caught the ones that didn't, and we uploaded them," O'Connell said.

"The people you so lightly dismiss as malcontents are the ones who saw the internet age and the Mindnet that followed as a sign of stagnation. The ones who saw that humanity was looking ever more inwards and becoming self-referential. The ones that thought that there must be something wrong when individuals prefer to spend their time involved in online pseudo-sex than exploring the galaxy. Remember that this was just after the quarkdrive became stable and other star systems became a viable option."

Anger flashed across O'Connell's features, but she quickly brought it back under control. "You must be referring to the misguided individuals who, when the world was on the verge of solving the problems of hunger and social strife, insisted that the resources would be better spent exploring cold balls of rock with no relevance whatsoever to the same real life you're always so fond of throwing back in our faces. Well, all I can say is that it's a good thing Earth was a democracy in those days, and we were able to ensure that the good of the many prevailed over the ambition of the few."

"Ah, yes, the virtuous middle path that leads to stagnant mediocrity, how noble. Fortunately, those few were able to get private funding to get where they needed to go. Fortunately, the cream tends to rise to the top and has money available to it. Fortunately, humanity was able to achieve its rightful place among the stars despite the anchor of the masses."

"So if your way of life is so perfect, then why are we having this conversation?" O'Connell asked, a sarcastic twinkle in her eye.

"Like any disease, the stagnation of life inside the Mindnet will spread if unchecked. We've already had to take down a series of clandestine nodes on Tau Ceti, which is the most advanced of the colonies. As you said, it's seductive. Why do backbreaking, dangerous work on a cold planet when you can spend your time in a warm simulation?"

"What do you propose?"

"As you said, Earth is self-sufficient now. We want you to voluntarily isolate yourselves until our society is mature enough to make full-immersion networks less of a threat to our survival."

"How long do you propose?"

"Five hundred years?"

"What? That's ridiculous!"

"I don't think so," the ambassador replied. "Think how long Earth had to prepare for it, and you were still overcome in less than two centuries."

"We weren't overcome—we chose this voluntarily. You could choose a different path without resorting to this extreme. What if we refuse?"

"Then we will blockade the planet. Anything trying to leave the surface will be destroyed. We will jam all outgoing transmissions."

"Hah! There's no way you can do that! Your navy is a puny, ineffective force."

"Our navy was a puny, ineffective force seventy-five years ago, when the last of you hid in the cybersimulation. You will find that things have changed, and the combined space fleets of the colonies are more than enough to reduce Earth's defenses to glowing piles of slag. Please don't force us to do this. We just want the chance to set our own course."

O'Connell glared at him, and the recording ended, leaving the meeting room in darkness.

A stunned group of shipboard directors waited silently

as Rome turned the lights back on. Pandemonium broke out immediately.

"Bullshit!" Kamm exclaimed. "Everyone knows that Earth has been left alone because they requested it. Where did this come from?"

"Everyone knows what became popular knowledge. Perhaps it was just the most comfortable explanation that fit the facts. How can you be so certain that what they taught you is true?" Rome replied.

"I would be much more willing to believe that the Earthers faked this to mislead us."

"My professional opinion, as an expert in the matter, is that this recording is real."

Nartiya broke in. "And I agree with Mr. Permek. This was as new to the Earthers as it was to us. They thought the same thing you did, Dr. Kamm. They thought they'd been isolated because they'd requested it." She smiled. "Now they're doubly pissed at us—they think we're complete morons because first we locked them on their planet, and then, having forgotten about it, we destroyed a good chunk of their infrastructure when we came back. Have to say they have a point."

Kamm didn't look convinced, but decided to hold his peace.

"What I don't understand is how they survived in the first place. I mean, how do you make babies in a simulated world?" said a voice from the back of the room.

All eyes turned to the biologist, who, having obviously missed the historical significance of the recording, had let her mind wander on a completely different path.

"Think about it a minute. Rome, you've spent a bit of time there—do you know?"

Rome blushed. He'd been thinking about how to get his brain plugged into the simulation to experience the sexual side of things—and Emily was beginning to figure quite prominently in his fantasies—but he hadn't given a thought to the biological side. "I have no idea," he replied.

Chapter 15

The computer took quite a while to pull up the file. No one had accessed this particular group of history archives since the ship had left Tau Ceti, and they had been sent into a secondary memory buffer. Finally, the screen lit up with the interactive menu of the Encyclopedia Colonialis's special edition, which consisted of quite a few terabytes of information and images referred specifically to the Second Dark Ages, a period that spanned approximately from eight hundred to six hundred years before—or from about 2050 to about 2250 in the old Roman calendar.

Stell rubbed his eyes. He'd been roped into looking for information that Rome felt they couldn't do without for nearly four hours. And he still wasn't at all convinced that this collection of ancient historical knowledge was going to be of any use. But Rome had been adamant, and Stell had grudgingly acceded among dire oaths of retribution and claiming a steep price for the services rendered, which he knew he'd never make good on.

And what for? So that Rome could get into that cybergirl's pants, probably. Who knew what that incurable pervert was doing, locked in the lab with all that computer equipment. He claimed he was running tests, but Stell was half-inclined to believe that the tests were mainly aimed at modifying this Emily's libido programming in the simulation. He smiled to himself and kept searching the databases for anything remotely related to the root causes of the colonization. It was interesting enough in a dry kind of way; he'd never known that humanity had once been so deeply divided about space exploration.

It was something that all Tau Cetians took for granted—stars were there to be colonized, and not a single year passed without a ship bearing tens of thousands heading off into some unexplored sector.

But then, humanity had never been so tightly packed onto one planet since those days. So Stell read on, absorbed in the subject despite himself and learning about such atrocities as overcrowding, hunger, and the greenhouse effect.

***

Despite Stell's misgivings, Rome actually had been running tests—tests that had nothing to do with Emily—and he was now sitting at his desk looking over a couple of hard copies of the results, trying to understand what they meant.

The numbers themselves were easy enough to interpret: there was some kind of damping factor present in the structure of the simulation. It was the kind of thing one built into any program that could go way out of control if it went into a positive feedback loop. The dampers built into the simulation were essentially of this kind—they were programs that functioned in such a way as to keep the parameters of the entire cyberworld within strictly-defined control limits.

This was easy enough to understand: one wouldn't want to have the climate go completely out of whack, which was always a threat with any chaotic system such as a climate pattern. What surprised Rome was that the same kind of damper seemed to be applied to each individual person within the simulation. Although he wasn't certain, it seemed to mean that their emotions would only be allowed to run within a strict set of parameters.

Which would have been fine had the people been simulated as well. But, as far as Rome was able to determine, the personality functions were supposed to come from a different source—he assumed that it was the famous birthing chambers where their bodies were supposed to live by way of an interface between brain and mainframe.

So why the dampers? To keep everyone happy? To prevent insanity? He didn't know and hadn't yet penetrated the system deeply enough to ascertain what the precise damper settings were. Just another thing he'd have to ask Emily about when he met her.

Emily! He'd completely forgotten that he'd agreed to meet her nearly a quarter of an hour before! He looked down at himself—he hadn't bathed in two days, his shorts smelled distinctly funky, and there was no way he could get there before she left.

Then he smiled and, thinking that old habits really did die hard, keyed a couple of commands into the ship's computer.

He was immediately transported to the cyberworld through his programmer's optic shunt. He was still sitting at his desk, of course, but at least it looked like a coffee shop in Manhattan. He noted with satisfaction that Emily was seated at a round table by the window and that his tweaks were slowly but surely improving the resolution every time he returned. Now, if only he could design a full five-senses interface.

Emily looked up from her book and smiled. "You're late."

He shrugged. "I was taking a shower, and the time just got away from me. I wanted to look my best for our meeting."

This, at least, got him a laugh. She was smart, and he liked that. "Meeting? I didn't know it was going to be so formal. I would have prepared a presentation. And here I was just hoping that we could have a cup of coffee and get to know each other a little better—I wasn't really at my best last time."

"Of course. That's what I meant." It sounded so lame. But he pushed on regardless. "Tell me a little more about yourself. How long have you worked for the government? When's your public service time due to end?"

She laughed again. "We don't have public service time here on Earth. Our public servants are paid salaries and free to leave government employ whenever they feel is most convenient for them."

This surprised him. If what Emily was telling him was true—and he had no reason to believe otherwise—then the government had no way to insure a steady supply of talent. On Tau Ceti, everyone complained about their service time, but everyone also agreed that the law insured that the government would have access to every level of the available talent pool. It insured that lucrative private venture wouldn't deprive the colonies of the leadership they needed. "So, you choose to work for the government?"

She laughed again. She was obviously in a good mood, for some reason. "I don't work for the government."

"Then what—"

"Am I doing here? That's a good question. I got roped in at the beginning because Graham knew me. I don't know anything about computers, and I certainly never imagined working for the government. I work as an account director for a major media company."

"Oh, so you were brought in for your managerial skills? To help coordinate?"

She paused, as if embarrassed. "Well, that is what I'm doing now, anyway. But I was originally brought on board to drive the robot."

"What?"

"It's a long story. Just let it be for now. You sure seem to have a lot of questions today."

Rome, immediately remembering the one question he was

supposed to ask, felt himself blush furiously. For the first time, he was thankful for the fact that his real body wouldn't be reflected by the expression of his avatar.

She kept going with a smile. "So now it's my turn to ask questions. Tell me about yourself. What do you do on the ship? I assume it's some boring thing with computers, but tell me anyway. What's life like on the surface of your planet?" Rome could have sworn that her smile turned coquettish, would have been certain of it had she been a flesh and blood woman instead of a simulated avatar. "Is there a Mrs. Permek?"

"Er—" he began, and felt himself chickening out even before he spoke. "I'll try to take that in order. The surface of Tau Ceti is pretty cold. We're used to it, but it isn't always comfortable. It's a question of too much heat reflecting back through the atmosphere. We're working on it, but it will take us at least another couple of centuries before the planet is terraformed to the point where we have an Earth-like climate."

"That wasn't my first question," she said. She seemed to be enjoying herself immensely, at his expense. "I asked what you do for a living."

"What do you think? I'm a computer engineer, of course!"

"Oh. I thought you were like the captain or something." There was a twinkle in her eye, which Rome decided to ignore.

"You've met Captain Nartiya, and you've probably even seen enough of her to be quite aware that there's room for only one captain on the *Unity*."

She laughed. "All right, not captain, then. But I had assumed you were part of the diplomatic team—you've been in every meeting. I assume others have been left out."

"Of course they have. There are over two hundred people on the ship. But the real reason I was invited along is that I was the first one to find you."

"Do you mean you knew we were here before we found you with the robot?"

"Not really, we thought it was just a big simulation. Come on, we've already explained this!"

The twinkle in Emily's eyes had spread to the corners of her mouth. She was obviously trying to suppress a smile, so he gave her his best baleful look, which he remembered too late the avatar wouldn't be able to transmit. She burst out laughing.

"You shouldn't tease me about that. We feel terrible about breaking three of your cities. And, besides, we don't really understand you people at all. How can you allow yourselves to be caged inside this simulation?"

Although it looked to Rome as if Emily was about to launch into her defense mode, she caught herself in time and shrugged. "You have to remember that we were born in here. None of us have ever known anything else."

"But you can leave any time you want!"

This time, she thought about it a long while before she answered. "That's true. But you have to remember that we've never lived a corporeal existence before. Sure, we can feel what happens to our bodies, and we know what it's like for a gentle breeze to caress our arms," she said. "But, deep down inside, I think most of us wonder if what we're feeling is actually what our real bodies would feel if we could inhabit them."

"You could find out easily enough."

"It isn't easy—the technical knowledge probably exists, but I have no idea where to find it, and other laymen are probably in the same situation. And there's the pain to consider."

"Pain?"

"None of us has ever truly felt real pain. Pain gets damped by the system, although when we are very young, we're allowed a bit more—to help us learn what not to do, I guess. Whoever designed the system wanted us to learn, but not suffer. We don't know what it might be like to live with constant pain. That's the real reason we never seriously consider pulling our bodies out and going for a quick walk over the surface. We think it will hurt."

Rome thought about the unused bodies in the birthing chambers. If they tried taking a body that had been immobile for decades out for a 'quick walk', he knew damn well that it would hurt. But he decided not to tell her. "Life doesn't hurt," he said, trying to give his voice the tenderness that his expression was incapable of conveying. "Just sometimes, and the comparison makes healthy normality seem all the better. What about disease, surely you feel pain then?"

"We don't get sick. Ever. Our bodies are ensconced inside the birthing chambers with machines watching over every parameter. No microbes could ever get in, and genetic defects are corrected surgically whenever a need arises."

"What about cancer? That's unpredictable."

She shrugged. "I don't know much about cancer. I know it used to be a big thing, back before the cyberworld. I suppose the system cures it when it finds it."

"I guess, if it finds it early enough, it might be possible to deal with most cases, but all of them? There have to be some cancer deaths, no matter what kind of technology is keeping you alive." And besides, he thought, your tech is already five hundred years old. If we can't cure cancer, you certainly shouldn't be able to.

"So you just trust the birthing chambers to do their jobs? What it there's a malfunction?"

"They don't break—they teach us about them in school. Multiple redundancies keep them up."

Rome nodded, but everything she said brought up more questions. Complex machines that never break? Pain-inhibiting systems that keep everything pleasant, and yet no one abuses them? Not to mention the feedback dampers he'd found earlier. What about that? But there was one question that forced itself to the forefront. And though the other questions were more interesting to him personally, he needed to get this one out of the way or he'd never rest.

"And how do you…" he began, but let the question drop in midsentence. It felt even more awkward than he'd imagined. Maybe he should ask someone else. That Prakash guy looked to be someone who would only find technical interest in the question.

"How do we what?"

"Well, the biology people on the ship were wondering how… how you make babies."

She laughed. "I wish I could see your face. I do believe you're blushing," she said. And then her grin became mischievous. "Would you like me to show you? How well have you got that avatar hooked up?"

He was speechless, and she laughed even more, tears forming in the corners of her eyes.

"Men," she exclaimed. "I see you're the same, no matter what part of the galaxy you come from."

He found himself thankful, once more, that the avatar couldn't show his features. She would have laughed even harder at the crimson shade of his face. "Er, the avatar can't do much," he admitted.

"Pity," she said. But, by the way she said it, he suspected that she'd known it all along. "I'll just have to tell you, then." She paused until he was about to open his mouth and ask her to continue. "Babies… Well, they're made the same way as always."

"But…"

She laughed again. It would have been irritating if she hadn't had such a nice laugh. "I know, two simulated humans would never procreate. The actual biological side takes place in the mother's birthing chamber, through artificial insemination. But in order for the insemination to happen, a man and a woman here in the cyberworld need to have sexual intercourse, just like on Tau Ceti II, I imagine."

Not quite like Tau Ceti, Rome thought. If it were, the asexuals would never have any children. But close enough.

"And the possibility of pregnancy is based on the natural cycle?"

"Of course not! We inform the central computer that we want to have children—both male and female consent is required. Only after consent is given can the insemination be performed."

Now he smiled, although she couldn't see it. "There must be some pain in childbirth, at least—or discomfort from the pregnancy?"

"Oh, we don't have to carry the baby around in the cyberworld! We let the flesh body do that. When the baby is born, it gets delivered to us at home."

"But you should be able to feel the pregnancy! After all, even if most of your sensations are fed to you through the simulation, your body would definitely let your brain know what it's feeling!"

"It doesn't. And don't ask me why! I work in advertising!" She pouted. "And enough about me. I want you to tell me all about your life on Tau Ceti. Is it very green?"

"It's very cold."

"Don't give me that. You're not going to get out of it that easily. Tell me everything. What do the houses look like?"

Rome could feel unanswered questions burning in the back of his mind, but, now that he'd gotten the breeding question out of his system, he was beginning to relax and just enjoy being with Emily. He found himself wishing she were real.

***

"Maybe we should just disconnect them and see what happens," Stell said.

Rome shook his head. He hadn't been able to stop thinking about Emily for the past couple of days—he wasn't at all sure what he felt about her, but one thing was certain: he didn't want to do anything that might harm her. And he suspected that disconnecting the cyberworld would be enormously harmful, not just to her, but to everyone else on the planet as well. "We can't do that, Stell."

"Why not?"

"For one thing, they'd starve," Dr. Senni Unameya interjected. The head of biology had taken a much more active interest in the goings-on within the cyberworld once Rome had explained the procreation method. Far from the boredom she'd expressed at the meeting, and even from the idle curiosity about the planet's reproductive cycle, she'd become fascinated, almost obsessed with the way humans were living there. She'd explained that it was a unique opportunity to examine life support systems used in a way that they hadn't before. Rome found that, whenever he wasn't working, she seemed to materialize out of thin air and ask him about this or that aspect of the cyberworld, or to obtain technical details of some other.

Stell snorted, an unusually crass expression from the normally hyper-polite analyst. "How could they starve? They live on a perfectly temperate, already terraformed planet that in the past has had eight billion people living on it. What are they now? Two billion at most?"

"A little less. One point eight," Rome said—his analysis of the simulation had managed to count the personality feeds, once he understood what was going on.

"Exactly. They should be fine. And we could all get to meet

them face-to-face instead of having to go into their macabre little simulation."

"It isn't quite that simple," Senni replied. She began to count on her fingers. "In the first place, when the planet was supporting eight million people, or even one-point-eight, agriculture was well developed. There's no way the current population could just walk out of whatever kind of bunker they're stashed in and live off the land.

"Secondly, their bodies have been immobile for their entire lives. Won't be able to get out of their beds and walk around. They'll be completely atrophied. Many of them will never be able to walk at all, while the rest will require months of physical therapy to be able to do so.

"And finally, even if we just revive a few and get them mobile here on the *Unity*, the shock of not having the safety net would probably render most of them inoperable. I, for one, would hate to share our ship with a bunch of psychotic people who have no idea how to behave in a real society."

"Still," Stell insisted. "I think we should find a way to disconnect them, at least gradually. And most of the crew agrees with me. We think it's an abomination."

This was news to Rome, who, admittedly, had been a bit out of touch with the goings-on aboard the ship. What little time he didn't spend investigating the cyberworld was used to daydream about Emily and improve his sensorial avatar interface.

"I know," Senni said. "Some members of my team have mentioned it. I told them the same thing I'll tell you: the fact that you think we can just waltz in here and destroy these people's way of life is the reason you are crew and not officers."

Stell got up without a word and left.

Rome had to smile. "You certainly are direct, aren't you, doctor?"

She returned his smile. "I'm a biologist and a medical doctor. I believe in telling people the truth, even if they don't have the maturity to accept it." She paused. "And Captain Nartiya asked us to send the message that we won't tolerate any speculation about disconnecting the cyberworld. If the Earthers want to disconnect, they are more than capable of doing so without our intervention."

"I know. I never asked to disconnect them."

She smirked at him a bit evilly. "I can't imagine why."

"Does everyone on the ship think I'm in love with her?" Rome asked.

"Not everyone. Just anyone who's come into contact with you over the past couple of days."

Rome sighed.

Senni went on. "Do you think she feels the same way about you?"

Good question, Rome thought. It was something he'd been wanting to talk about with someone – anyone – for a few days. Stell, being a militant asexual, wouldn't understand it. Even so, he'd never imagined he'd be discussing it with one of the senior officers on the ship. "I'm not really sure. She keeps bombarding me with double entendres and innuendo, but I can't tell whether she's trying to get me to come closer or to scare me away."

Senni laughed. "Well, the fact that you managed to spot both possibilities shows that you're smarter than the average clueless guy. I can't really give you an answer. Sorry. I'd have to see how she looks at you, how she acts around you when she's not sending this mixed message."

They sat in silence for a few moments before the doctor spoke again. "I wasn't just asking out of morbid curiosity—I was actually asking out of professional interest."

Why does that not surprise me? Rome thought. He raised his eyebrows, indicating that she should continue.

"As I told your friend, we can't disconnect the entire planet—it would be genocide. But a single person might choose to disconnect, and we could accept that, don't you think? If we incidentally got a lot of information out of it, it would just be an added bonus."

"Are you suggesting that I ask her to disconnect and to come back to Tau Ceti with me?"

"No. I'm asking you to think about it."

She left him sitting there with his head spinning. But she'd achieved her stated goal: he was definitely thinking about it.

Chapter 16

"They called it the Second Dark Ages, Graham. That's what you're trying to bring back. The Second Dark Ages," Emily said forcefully. Once her surprise at his sudden appearance and her words of anger about the way he'd left the meeting had finally petered out enough to allow her to listen to what he had to say, she'd dug her heels in once again.

Graham had known she wouldn't understand, but he knew he had to try to convince her anyway. He wasn't exactly certain why he felt that way, he just did. Maybe because he felt that any woman who'd been worthy to spend time with—hell, she'd even booted him out on his ass—had to be intelligent enough to understand what he was saying. "Emily, listen to me—"

"No, you listen. What you're proposing has already been done. There was a time, even before the colonization of Tau Ceti, when the whole planet was obsessed with living inside simulated environments. Environments that allowed you to be whoever you wanted and do whatever you wanted. People used it to escape from daily realities, but it was more than that. They'd get obsessed. The police would find people dead of starvation, but still plugged into their simulated worlds. And worse, all research into new technology stopped, except for technology aimed at improving the simulations. It was the only product being consumed in any quantities other than stuff that was necessary to survive! That's why the colonists left in the first place—to get away from a world that had stagnated to the point where the universe outside the simulations had ceased to be of any interest to humanity. The economy collapsed and millions died of hunger."

Graham knew that what she was saying was perfectly accurate. He'd seen the sealed files even before they had, but continued to play dumb. "Where did you get this? It sounds absolutely ludicrous!"

"I got it from some top secret buried files."

"Why would anyone bury the files? And anyhow, it doesn't seem all that relevant—our cyberworld is perfectly stable; we won't starve."

Emily gave him a look that told him that she definitely didn't believe he was completely ignorant, but went on. "Yes, and it has been since the beginning. But did you know that the rules were originally much less strict? That the cyberworld originally allowed people to be and do almost anything they wanted, except return to their bodies?"

Graham knew. "So? What's wrong with that? Sounds a whole lot better than living all cooped up in these bodies. If we were going to throw off the chains of corporeal existence, isn't it better to go all the way?"

"Turns out it wasn't. The human brain just can't cope. By the time they managed to get the rules in place, they'd lost a staggering number to dementia. That's why you need to stop. We can't deal with it!"

"That was five hundred years ago! We've been living as nothing more than electrons in a grid forever. We were born that way. I think we can deal with it now."

But she was adamant. "Haven't you been listening to anything I said? The whole point of the rules was to keep us within the set parameters—our brains haven't had to adjust to anything new over the last five hundred years. If anything, we've become even less adaptable since life has lost most of the unpredictability of surface existence. If you took the rules out now, we'd all go nuts!"

"Are you really that limited? Do you really believe that?"

"Ever since those goddamned black walls came up, I've been feeling that the world is getting more and more insane every day. I could swear that I can feel my reality teetering underfoot. All I want is to feel that something is real, that it won't change because of some programmer's whim or a glitch in the system or because some assholes who haven't been on Earth for five-hundred years decide to disconnect us."

He softened a little, but not because he sympathized with her feelings—he pitied her. He couldn't believe that this milksop was the woman he'd felt he could count on to give his dreams backbone. She was just like the rest of them. She was a sheep.

"Then you'd better think about reviving your physical body," he said, "because things in the cyberworld are going to be changing very, very soon."

He gave her one last, sad look and willed himself away.

He blinked, and he was in a city street halfway around the world, facing Jarrien, who seemed completely unsurprised to see him.

"Hello, Graham," she said calmly.

"Hello," he replied. "I see you've stopped running." He looked her over and noticed she looked a lot better. The harried expression that she'd sported the few times he'd managed to catch a glimpse of her had vanished. "You led me on a merry chase."

She smiled. "I actually stopped running two days ago. I thought you'd find me sooner than this. I guess I must have had you more bewildered than I thought. Maybe I should have kept running."

Now it was his turn to smile. "You're good, but you're not that good. I stopped coming after I realized that I could catch up with you in short order anytime I wanted to. No, the reason I let you off the hook these past couple of days is that I had to use all my resources for research purposes. I was trying to understand a little bit more about this world we live in. It's unbelievable how much history they don't teach us. Immoral, if you ask me. We seem to live in the most heavily censored era of all time." He decided not to tell her that she hadn't been his first choice when choosing a partner for what was to come.

"There might be a good reason," Jarrien said, her expression guarded. She seemed to be debating whether to tell him something.

"What could possibly justify this monstrosity?" Graham raged. But he hadn't come to give her a history lesson. "Anyway, that's not what I came here for. I've discovered a few things about the cyberworld."

"I know. I've been monitoring you. You've found out that the safeguards are all gone, that we can program whatever we want into the simulation. That any individual who knows how can rule the world as a demigod."

"Exactly. We don't need to be locked in the chains of bodily existence. We can be free! For the first time in history, humanity can fulfill its potential, limited only by our own imaginations."

She looked doubtful.

"I know," Graham said. "You think the governments will stop us. Well, that's what I've been looking into these past couple of days. They have neither the personnel nor the expertise to mount any kind of resistance. By the time they react, we'll be firmly in control, and we'll have created a new set of less-restrictive rules. But rules that, nevertheless, will keep them from turning everything back the way it was."

"It's not that," she said. "I'm not worried about the government—remember I've been walking around with shiny blue hair for years and no one has tried to stop me or even investigated how I do it."

"What, then?"

She shook her head. "You've found out a lot of stuff, but there's still one thing you don't know. Something so massive that either the records really were erased this time, or it was never recorded in the first place. And it might change your mind about what you're thinking of doing."

"What?"

"No. This is something you have to see for yourself. Follow me."

***

Rome looked out over the abandoned remains of what had once been humanity's most important city. Signs of recent human habitation could be seen all around the ship: the *Unity*'s crew had been delighted at the balmy temperature and clear skies and had spent most of their time outdoors, leaving wrappers and bottles strewn carelessly across the grass. Rome could understand that at least. If he didn't have an entire world at his fingertips, ready to be plugged into his brain, he would also have spent as little time as possible on board. He'd had enough of the ship on the passage to Earth to want to stay there now. And besides, there wouldn't be summer nights like these on Tau Ceti II for centuries.

The grass had been crushed and flattened by human activity—when they'd arrived, it had been nearly chest-high. They'd selected this particular landing site because it was free of both buildings and trees; their maps of the city that had once stood here marked the area as the reservoir. It had apparently held a small lake back then.

Rome knew he should be working. He knew that there was still a huge amount of knowledge to be gathered about human life on Earth. Customs, interactions, how people could live and prosper within the confines of a computer simulation. There was no record of any similar society anywhere in the ship's data banks, which was logical enough, considering that no society in human history had ever renounced physical existence on such a scale.

And yet he sat on the grass, staring into the sunset over the ruined buildings and procrastinating.

The problem was Emily. Ever since Dr. Unameya had mentioned the possibility of liberating Emily from the bowels of the simulation, Rome had been able to do nothing other than think about it.

He was intelligent enough to realize that the good doctor hadn't brought it up out of sheer concern for Rome's love life. She was probably climbing the walls hoping that he would convince her to leave her comfortable little cocoon. And, at first, Emily would be hers. She'd have months of physical therapy and conditioning to go through before she could even walk on her own. In the meantime, Rome had no doubts whatsoever that the biologist would get as many tissue and DNA samples as she could to study the makeup of a current Earth-dweller's body. And run antibody tests. And who knew what else.

But after that—even during the time spent with the doctor—he would be her companion. And that was a sobering thought. He was accustomed to the way she looked inside the simulation. But, although she believed that the way she looked in there was the way her actual body looked inside its buried birthing chamber, he had his doubts. How could a body that had never moved or been out in sunlight look healthy? He imagined flaccid rolls of death-white flesh.

Was he really so superficial? Maybe Stell was right after all and the only people who could truly appreciate another human being on anything more than a physical level were the asexuals.

He chuckled. Here he was, faced with the possibility of having the most fascinating companion in the settled galaxy, and he was worried that she might be a little out of shape. He was ridiculous. Instead of worrying about unimportant things, he should be shouting his joy at having finally found a woman with whom he could sit down and talk about their differences but in a way that made him feel they were twin souls at the end of the day. He often felt that, had their roles been reversed, both would have acted exactly the same.

There was the crux. How was he supposed to know if Emily was interested in the possibility? The woman was impossible; she would tease him mercilessly until the end of time if he let her. And he still wouldn't have a clear yes or no answer at the end of it unless he went straight out and asked her.

That was what he was trying to avoid, sitting on the hillock. He knew that getting to work inside the simulation would mean running into Emily. And that, in turn, would mean having to ask her. It could be put off until tomorrow, but not much longer.

Eventually, a cold wind sprang up out of the east and, despite being much warmer than the winds from his home, drove him back inside.

∗∗∗

Emily was shaken. She'd seen madness in Graham's eyes. And not even the madness she usually associated with him: that carefree look that said that no matter what the world chose to do to him, he could roll with it. No, this was a deeper, darker look. Harder. More determined.

Over the past month—had it already been a month since the madness took over her life?—she'd learned not to underestimate Graham's capacity to get things done. Where she'd once seen him as a bit of a joke, it had become obvious that he wasn't. It had just taken the right kind of motivation to get him off his ass and working to do things that could actually be appreciated by others.

It was too bad that the things that motivated Graham seemed to be driven by the same irresponsible impulses as everything else he did.

He'd essentially admitted that he was planning to use his knowledge of the various systems to try to take over the cyberworld—or at the very least to make large, sweeping changes that would affect every single person on Earth—and she was debating whether her loyalty to him as a friend meant that she had to stay quiet about it, or whether she should run to the mayor of New York and let him deal with it. She suspected, however, that either choice would lead to the same result: Graham would do whatever it was he was already planning to do. She doubted if anyone else would have the knowledge needed to stop him. He'd been in this from the beginning and had had more than enough time to plan whatever it was he would do next.

But the question that nagged her most wasn't whether she should tell the government to stop Graham, but whether Graham should be stopped at all. The past weeks had completely destroyed her conviction that the cyberworld society was fine the way it was.

Even before those forbidding black walls had sprung up, she'd felt that her life was stagnating, that she was caught in an eternal holding pattern, that nothing could change and nothing would. And yet, she had been secure in the knowledge that the rules were set in stone.

But most of all, she had known that everyone else was content. If she felt any differently, the problem had to be hers.

Now she'd been shown just how unstable and fragile society really was. The thin veneer of civilization and rules of conduct barely concealed the fact that the entire simulation could be easily subverted by anyone who had the knowledge. And it had been subverted—for long periods of time—in the past. Was it really the best solution for everyone involved? The colonists had feared having it spread to their worlds so much that they'd pushed that draconian treaty down the planet's throat.

"Why the long face?"

The unexpected voice caused her to start, nearly spilling her coffee. She realized that she'd completely lost track of the time and that it was time for her to meet with Rome, who'd sent her a strange message on the texter they'd set up for quick and dirty communication between the *Unity* and the Earth-based technicians.

"Hi Rome," she said, smiling weakly as he sat down on the vacant chair beside her in what had become 'their' coffee shop. "What is it you needed to tell me?"

His avatar, which Emily had seen improving day-by-day, seemed to smile at her, although it might have been a painful grimace—Rome obviously still had a ways to go in getting the avatar perfect. "No fair answering a question with another question! I asked you first."

She frowned, not appreciating the runaround, but answered. "No reason in particular. I was just wondering if my life would ever go back to the way it was. It was boring and predictable, but you have no idea what I would give for everything to be boring and predictable again."

"Oh," he said. He began to speak once more and stopped. Then started again before lapsing into silence. A silence that fitted Emily's mood well enough that she didn't break it, even long after it had grown uncomfortable.

Finally, Rome seemed to pull himself together. "I need to ask you something."

"I know. I got your text."

"Oh. Yes, of course." The silence resumed, but this time he recovered faster. His avatar seemed to take a deep breath—although it only mimicked the movement and didn't actually take a breath. "I wanted to know if you'd consider coming back to Tau Ceti with us."

"What? You mean a copy in the computer memory?"

"No. I mean physically. We could release your body from the birthing chamber and you could come back with us. In real life."

Now, it was her turn to be silent. What he was proposing seemed to fit so well with what she'd been thinking that it was as though he'd read her thoughts. "You want me to leave the only home I've ever known? I'm not certain I can do that."

"I know it wouldn't be easy, but just imagine—you'll be able to go places where no person born on Earth has been in half a millennium. Your concerns about boredom will be a thing of the past. And not to mention that you'll immediately become the biggest celebrity in the colonies as soon as you set foot on our ship—you'll be treated like royalty!"

Emily laughed. "The biggest freak is more like it. Will it even be possible for me to walk again?"

Rome paused. "In theory, yes. Our medical staff has looked over the blueprints of the birthing chamber, and, hopefully, your body should be fit enough to make a complete recovery."

"It's going to hurt, isn't it?"

Again, Rome paused. It was a longer silence this time. "Yes, I think it will."

"What's it like?"

"What's what like?"

"Pain. How does it feel? The simulation shields us from all sharp pain. I've been thinking about it, and I think that's why no one wants to leave the cyberworld. We're afraid of the pain of living in a physical body."

"Not too good. It depends on what's causing the pain. I

assume the pain from the physical therapy is going to be sharp at first, and then subside to a dull throb. But there's one thing that you can't really deny: you will know what it's like to be alive for the first time in your life."

"Are you saying I'm not alive now?"

"Well… Yes! That's exactly what I mean! You're locked inside a computer simulation, for God's sake! Do you really mean to look me in the eyes and tell me you're really alive? Your body is buried somewhere, being kept functional by fluid drips!"

Emily felt tears welling up. Somewhere deep inside, she knew that Rome was right. "It's the only life I've ever known," she whispered.

Rome's avatar immediately leaned back, giving her space. "I'm sorry," he said, his voice transmitting genuine contrition. "I shouldn't have said that. It's just that I realized that I'd really like you to come back with us. You are, by far, the most interesting person I've had the chance to interact with in my life."

Emily favored him with a watery smile. "You're sweet. But the decision I'd have to take is much too huge to give you an answer now. I'll have to think about it. All right?"

"All right. But I reserve the right to bug you about it," Rome replied as his avatar gave another horrendous rictus that was meant to be a smile.

***

The Prophet grimaced. There were only six people in the room, a far cry from when his rallies had managed to bring hundreds of dissatisfied individuals together. Even the room itself was worse for the wear. Sheer necessity had forced him to move out of his basement quarters: the press, which had originally ridiculed him, and then, when he'd been proven right, had made him famous, was back to ridicule after he proclaimed his new doctrine. Now that he was a bigger target, the press went to considerably more lengths to ridicule him. His house was permanently staked out. His followers had deserted him in droves.

But that was to be expected. After all, they'd been drawn from the ranks of the most vocal of the people who'd wanted to return to surface life. That wasn't exactly true—his original followers had wanted change, any change, and he'd given them the answer.

They'd felt betrayed when he announced the new doctrine, and his heart had bled for them. But he could take no other path, and he definitely couldn't tell them why he'd changed his mind. That way lay chaos and anarchy.

"The objective of our protest is to force the government to break off the talks with the offworlders and send them back to their own planet as soon as possible. They've already shown a complete disregard for our way of life and damaged our society in irreparable ways. How can we even sit and speak to people whose idea of a suitable greeting is to destroy the infrastructure of the people they're trying to talk to?"

His few followers murmured a half-hearted assent. He winked at them. "I know what you're thinking: what can we do against a whole planet that seems to be fascinated with the offworlders? Well, you might be surprised to learn that the planet doesn't care about them as much as we think. Lately, the Mindnet ratings have, after their initial spike, fallen off completely. The only place where people still follow the diplomacy is in New York, and that's under local news." Seeing that they still looked doubtful, he played his trump card. "And since there's no central decision-making body, the situation is being managed by the mayor, who has assured me that he will give us his full support. You know what that means?"

Confused murmurs indicated that they had no idea what that meant, but the Prophet remained unfazed. He'd started out alone and had built up a numerous following despite general ridicule. He could do it again.

"It means that we will finally return to respectability. It means that we will be seen as champions for the general good. And, most importantly, it will mean that these offworlders will be gone and that this sick fascination with the idea of what it's like to be outside will eventually wane, the way all fads and fashions do. We'll be striking a blow for the continuation of our way of life. A way of life that has served us so well for five hundred years."

A flicker of enthusiasm jumped between a few members of his audience. He knew that was enough. That, eventually, he could kindle a fire from those embers. It would take time, but, he suspected, time was something he would have plenty of—it was just a question of tweaking the simulation a little.

Chapter 17

If Ashur Nartiya had been a little surprised by the chilly reception they'd gotten from the diplomats, it was nothing compared to her shock when a group of sign-toting demonstrators had irrupted into the meeting room and demanded that the *Unity* return to Tau Ceti immediately and never return.

It caught everyone completely off guard—nothing whatsoever had indicated that the Tau delegation's presence was resented beyond what was normal, considering the havoc they'd wreaked upon arrival. The Earth delegation had, so far, been content to prattle blandly. It almost seemed that they really didn't care what happened to the planet with regards to its relation to the colonies, one way or the other, but were satisfied with the possibility of talking about it.

But when the unruly mob broke in, the mayor suddenly stood firm. He took the position that the people were speaking and that, as mayor, it was his responsibility to investigate what the will of the people actually was and that the meetings would be adjourned until the investigations were concluded.

Nartiya could do nothing but hide her amusement—it made it much easier to laugh things off when there was no actual physical contact between the delegations, and when only one side, hers, had the means to commit violence against the other. If it weren't for the importance the meetings had on a galactic scale, she would have laughed. Of course, the Earth delegation wouldn't have seen her, but she would damn well have made certain they heard her.

But she held her peace. It was obvious that the Earthers had staged the demonstration to interrupt the meetings. The question now was whether they had any intention of resuming them at some future point. She suspected they didn't. Once they'd shut down their presence in the cyberworld, she turned to Rome. "So, Mr. Permek, what do you think?"

"They're going to send us back, aren't they?"

"Probably. Any idea why?" She knew Rome had had the most contact with the Earth people, both with the techs and with this Emily person the entire crew was gossiping about. He might have an idea what this was about.

But Rome seemed reluctant to talk about it. "Not really. I've only spoken with the people who originally found us. Their attitude is generally more one of curiosity than anything else. They definitely aren't hostile towards us."

"Take a guess, then."

"All right. If I had to guess, I'd say that the problem is that our arrival has stirred things up on Earth. They're starting to question things that haven't been questioned in the past five hundred years. It seems to everyone that things are going to change. And most people don't like change and will argue and even demonstrate against it if they see it coming."

He is probably right, Nartiya thought. Which meant that the government, if she was any judge of character, would break off the meetings in short order. She could, of course, simply land near any other mainframe and begin negotiations with another mayor, but she had the nagging suspicion that it would only end the same way. Despite each region being autonomous, the planet had been completely apathetic to their arrival. She suspected most places wouldn't want to have their peace disrupted any more than Manhattan had.

Which was strange, all things considered. Their arrival had to be the biggest thing to happen in anyone's lifetime, and yet, they didn't seem to care. It seemed unnatural, somehow. Could human nature have changed so much in five hundred years? Or maybe it was just a question of having lived in a controlled environment for so long—their minds just couldn't cope with anything too different.

"I think we're going to be leaving here sooner rather than later," she told Rome. "We won't be welcome here much longer."

He paled a little. *So, the stories are true, he is in love with the cyber girl,* she thought. The thought brought a smile to her lips. She could be magnanimous this once. "If you can convince her to come, she's welcome aboard," she said.

The look on Rome's face made the added expense worth it. As understanding set in, confusion gradually gave way to a cross between amazement and glee, mixed with horror that the aloof captain would know about it.

"Thank you, captain," he stammered.

"You're welcome. And you should also thank Dr. Unameya. She'd have killed me if I hadn't allowed it."

***

"We'll be leaving soon," Rome said. "I know I promised not to pressure you regarding your decision to stay on Earth or leave with us, but we don't have much time."

"I haven't decided yet," Emily replied. She looked terrible, dark circles under her eyes indicated that she hadn't gotten much sleep since their last conversation.

Rome briefly wondered how they'd programmed the simulation to give her dark circles when she didn't sleep. He'd gotten as far as laying out some rudimentary algorithms in his head that could allow him to do the trick with a few lines of code when he remembered where he was. "I don't need you to decide now. But I think we should discuss what to do if you do decide to come with us."

"I suppose you just have to get to my body and revive it. I think a doctor would be more help in that than I am."

He smiled. "We've got that part of the operation well planned. We've studied plans of the birthing chambers, and there's no medical reason to expect difficulties in the revival process. We even have the facilities to give your body the same treatment on board the *Unity*—the same nutrients injected the same way and all that."

"You don't need me, then. It's not like I can go outside and help in the extraction process," she said.

"That's true. All we really need is to know where your body is located."

She stared silently at him for a long moment, and then she laughed. "You know, I have absolutely no idea where my body is."

He stared at her. "What? How can you not know that?"

"It's not something we need to know. Try to remember that we never use our bodies. Ever. I know it must be hard for you to imagine, but everything around us," Emily gestured with her hands, "has been put together so that our entire lives take place inside the simulation. Why would we want to go out and get our bodies?"

"But surely you have some record of where it's kept? Some paperwork?"

"Again, what possible use could it be?" Emily asked. She paused, thinking. "I guess there's probably some kind of government record somewhere deep inside the system—they need that information for things like making certain the right sperm goes to the right mother, for example. But I've never heard of anyone knowing where their body was."

"We need to investigate that before you can come. Even

if you don't decide until the day we're scheduled to leave, we need to have the information available."

She looked doubtful. "I don't think we'll be able to access that kind of information from any terminal. It's probably hidden behind a whole lot of security, shielded against misuse."

"You've got access to secure information from the mayor's office."

"But my body is somewhere below Denver—hopefully far from the crater you made when you arrived. I don't know if those records will be available here in New York. And I wouldn't know the first thing about how to retrieve them, either."

Rome paused. He was beginning to get a feel for the way the simulation kept information in its simulated systems—enough to know that they were all interconnected and that everything could be accessed from any point—but he was still far from being an expert in the subject. He might be able to find the data they needed, but he wouldn't be able to do it quickly enough. They would need help.

"Do you think any of the techs would help us get the location out of the system?"

"Kate would," Emily replied without hesitation. "She's been waiting to try something new now that she's got unlimited access. She's a rebel at heart. And she's very, very good at what she does."

Rome nodded. He'd gotten the same impression. "All right. Now, all we need is to get her to meet us at City Hall after everyone else is gone."

Emily pulled out her comm.

***

Once more, Rome marveled at how complete the

simulation programming had been. Not a single detail had been left to chance, not one omitted. The huge, darkened City Hall echoed eerily as he and Emily walked toward the room that housed the terminals. The soft sound of water dripping somewhere in the distance caused him to shake his head in admiration. This simulation must have taken countless programmers years to get just right.

It was understandable. After all, the people who'd created the cyberworld believed that it represented the pinnacle of human achievement and the answer to all the social problems that had plagued mankind since its first ancestors came down from the trees. He'd read articles from the time that described the move as 'a return to the Garden of Eden'. No effort had been spared in making it perfect.

The control room was dimly lit and Kate was waiting for them at one of the monitors. Despite what must have been a long day—Emily had assured Rome that Kate had told her she'd wait after regular office hours, using a large workload as her excuse—Kate gave them a bright smile. Her face showed none of the exhaustion she had to be feeling. "Hi Emily, hi Rome. I've been doing a little preparation for our search. I've already logged in with highest level clearance."

"But I haven't even told you what we're doing, yet!"

Kate laughed. "Oh, come on! You call me, all mysterious-like, and ask me to meet you here after hours when no one's around. It doesn't take a genius to realize that you're after something you can't get with a regular public-access terminal. So tell me—what kind of sordid and illegal research are we going to be conducting today?" She made a show of stretching her arms and cracking her fingers.

"Nothing illegal, I think," Emily replied. "Just a little research that's somewhat off the beaten track. Think you're up to it?"

Kate pouted theatrically, making both Rome and Emily

smile. "I thought it would be something more exciting—something the government is hiding from us because it would undermine their power! Oh, well, you take life as it comes. What can I do for you?"

"I need to find out where my birthing chamber is located," Emily said.

The other woman's face registered surprise as the implications of the request became clear. Then she brightened. "Ooh, that's so naughty. I like it." She turned back to the console and began to navigate the labyrinthine maze of interconnections among the various government systems. "Planning a little vacation, are we?"

Emily and Rome exchanged a look. "I haven't decided yet," Emily replied. "Right now, we're just doing due diligence in case I need the information in a hurry later on."

"Okay. Tell me where you were born."

"Denver I," Emily said without hesitation.

The tech turned around and gave her a hard look. "You're kidding, right?"

"Why would I kid about something like that?"

Kate sighed. "That's going to make it a hell of a lot harder. You see, each mainframe has records of all the births that occur within its birthing chambers. From here, I can access almost all the data with no problems, as long as the mainframe itself is online."

"So you can't do it?" Rome interjected.

"I didn't say that. But it's going to be harder. I need to find out if there are any copies of those records anywhere outside the mainframe."

"How are you going to do that?"

"I'll need to use a test case. Once I find out where that person's birthing chamber is located, I'll put a search in the rest of the system using the location of the chamber in conjunction with the person's name as the search parameters.

If anything pops up, that will show us where the birthing chamber locations are stored. Then I'll search for you on that database."

"Why don't you just type a birthing chamber location without a name associated to it?"

"Because I have no idea how the chambers are labeled. If they're numbers, searching for it will just bring up every case in which the number appears. And we don't know whether they're numbers. It might be alphanumerical or coded some other way. We need to do a little digging first."

Rome nodded. "Sounds logical," he said. "So who are you going to use for your test case?"

"Kate Lysak," she replied.

"Who's Kate… oh," Emily said.

Kate winked at her. "As you pointed out, you never know when the information might come in handy in an emergency." She turned back to the screen. "Let's see. The first thing I need to do is to call up my home mainframe. Here we are: Des Moines."

Rome watched as she quickly flashed through various subdirectories until she found one entitled 'Population Statistics and Control' which seemed to be the right place to look for the information they needed.

Kate began to dig a little deeper, trying to unlock the information, but, while the database seemed to hold plenty of data regarding the current location and health data of each of the people in Des Moines's care, it showed no information regarding the location of their physical bodies.

Over the next couple of hours, Kate systematically went through all the likely archive segments while Rome, on a second terminal they activated beside her, assisted. Not being quite as familiar with the logic of the Earth systems, Rome could only check about one area while she went through three or four—but it was Rome who, completely by accident, found what they were looking for.

"Infrastructure?" Kate exclaimed, waking Emily who'd been dozing on another chair behind them. "Why would this be classified under infrastructure?"

"Who knows," Rome agreed. "But since I wasn't sure where to look, I just took my assigned databases in order, and it turned up here. There you are: Katherine Lysak. You're listed as being in birthing chamber USIODESM 00642370. Seems we have our search parameters."

"Yup, and I'm willing to bet that the Denver I code is USCODENI. You see: country then state and then mainframe name. Of course, we no longer have country or state divisions, but I suppose they were important when the system was first set up."

Emily could hardly contain her excitement. "So now you can use this information to look for the backup, right?"

Kate nodded. "Let's hope it exists," she said as she punched some more commands into the system. She was immediately rewarded by a stream of data scrolling onto the screen. "Looks like there are multiple backups. There's even something called a birth register, which keeps all your vital statistics. Wow. It looks like it holds data about everyone in the world. Look at this one: SUZUZURI. I wonder where that is?" She chuckled. "If we'd known this was here when we started, it would have saved us a hell of a lot of trouble. Don't you think it's strange that no one has any idea about this?"

Rome gave her a grin and a shrug. "Hey, I'm from fourteen light-years away. Why are you asking me?"

Kate rolled her eyes. "All right then, Miss Plair, let's get you localized." She punched a final key. "There you are. USCODENV 03010788. Now all you have to do is to figure out where in the city it's localized."

They both looked at her.

She sighed. "Oh, all right," she said, and typed up a

maintenance map of Denver's birthing chambers.

***

Emily seemed oddly calm to Rome. At first, she'd been really excited, nervously writing down the address of her birthing chamber and darting around the room, chattering about 'visiting herself'. But she'd calmed down nearly immediately and had offered to buy both of them a cup of stimcaff—at which Rome had smiled and reminded her that his avatar, despite the improvements he'd made to it, still couldn't handle liquids.

Emily said she didn't care, that she had to have stimcaff. They'd popped off to 'their' café, which was open all night, although the crowd was completely different: young kids who laughed too loud and lone men with vacant stares had replaced the well-dressed afternoon patrons. The reddish neon lighting also made it seem more intimate. Rome found himself wishing that Kate were anywhere but there with them.

"So," Rome said, "when do you want me to go look for your body?"

Emily looked surprised. "I don't. I'm going to take the maintenance robot we modified and find it myself."

"There's no way I'm letting you do this alone."

"I don't think you're really in a position to let me do anything." Emily made quote marks in the air around the word 'let'. "I'm a big girl now."

Rome was about to speak, but she interrupted him again. "Listen, Rome. I know you feel responsible for my well-being, but if I decide to return to Tau Ceti with you, you need to know that I won't feel that you owe me anything. It will be my decision, and I can take whatever results from it. So I don't want you holding yourself responsible for me. By the same token, I really don't want you to think that I owe you anything for liberating me from the cyberworld. I've already explained that this is our life, and we aren't confined here against our will or anything. I don't need a knight in shining armor to save me, okay?"

Rome nodded, a bit cowed.

"Good. Of course, you can come along while I search for the right room. You can walk beside the robot and make yourself useful by opening doors and pushing buttons, which is easier to do with a body than with a robot. Are you coming, Kate?"

"You bet your ass. I wouldn't miss this for the world."

"It's settled then," Emily said. She proceeded to turn the conversation to other topics.

But Rome felt that nothing was settled. While he was perfectly willing to accept Emily's conditions—the mere fact that she was raising that kind of objections meant that she was ever closer to taking a positive decision with regards to the voyage—he wasn't certain what to make of her reaction to the information itself. Here she was, in possession of something that no one else on the planet had except for Kate, and her excitement lasted all of five minutes. After that, she just sat there, calmly dissecting potential problems and warning him off possible misbehavior.

Rome suspected that the dampers he'd found were making their mark on her personality, keeping any emotion that exceeded their strictly-defined parameters in check. But he was at a loss to imagine how the system worked. After all, the personality itself was input from the body—the body might be dormant, but the brain was active at all times, which is why the cyberworlders needed to sleep. The only way to damp her behavior would seem to be through drugs injected into the body at the command of the simulation.

While this was probably one of the big reasons the

cyberworld had remained stable for so long—after all, anger was only possible for a short period of time—it also represented a problem he hadn't been aware of previously: what would the effects of unhooking Emily's body from the birthing chamber be?

In the first place, there was the possibility of withdrawal. Would she suffer the effects of not having access to the drugs? Could her body even survive something like that? Rome worried about it but was certain the medical team would be able to solve it in relatively short order.

The second problem was, in his mind, much more serious. Even if they managed to get Emily to the ship, she would be faced with months of physical therapy. Painful physical therapy. She would be exposed to innumerable new sensations, most of them unpleasant. She would feel real pain for the first time in her life. And she would be unfettered, free to get as angry at the pain as she liked. Her frustration could run wild. She would not only be physically miserable—her mind would encounter extremes it had never been permitted to inhabit before.

So even if her body held out, there was no guarantee that her mind would. A long-lasting depression in someone who'd never had one could be more serious than the withdrawal symptoms.

So, as Emily and Kate speculated as to what had become of Graham, both of them perfectly calm despite the huge decision that they would have to make within the next couple of days, Rome was a nervous wreck. The fact that all he'd be doing is taking another long, boring space journey was no calming influence at all.

Chapter 18

The day had dawned gloomy and drizzly, and Senni had made her unhappiness known to him from the moment they'd left the protected confines of the flyer.

"You are aware that we could have followed the whole thing from the robot's cameras, right?"

Rome gave her a sour look. "Hey, you were the one who insisted on coming along. You can go back, you know. We don't need you along right now—this is just a scouting run. Once we find the chambers, you can study them to your heart's content."

She returned his sour look with interest but shut up. There was no way in the world she was going to miss this expedition, and he knew it. And she knew he knew.

The captain had allowed them access to one of the ship's flyers in order to return to the Denver mainframe area. They'd landed next to the crater the *Unity*'s overzealousness had caused—Emily, whose sense of humor seemed to tend towards the dark, vengeful type, had merely said, "Let's meet by the crater. It's a big hole, you can't miss it. Oh, and maybe you've got the coordinates in your ship's archives." His blood ran cold to think how close the explosion had come to the birthing chambers that housed millions of innocent people.

The fact that they were early allowed them to look around, observing the decayed, vegetation-covered buildings that fronted the twisted metal bordering the crater. The buildings were, perhaps, worse for wear than the ones in Manhattan, but it was only a question of degree. The big difference was that he'd been warned by the people studying the ecology that the mountains around Denver abounded with large wildlife—bears and mountain lions at the very least, and these were animals that hadn't learned that humans were dangerous.

So, in addition to the equipment that allowed him to see into the cyberworld and communicate with Emily, which consisted of an eyepiece and an earpiece, he was also carrying a beam projector that, the military people had assured him, was strong enough to blow a hole through a concrete wall. He felt like a complete fool carrying that kind of ordnance around just to deter a few animals, but the ship had nothing less powerful in stock. They explained that shooting at an opponent clad in modern armor with anything less would get you killed in a hurry.

Rome doubted the bears would be wearing armor, and any sensible animal would be sitting in a warm den out of this miserable rain, but toted the thing anyway.

His link to the cyberworld informed him that Emily had returned to Denver. She'd explained that she absolutely hated to teleport and got upset when Rome asked her why. It seemed to him that teleporting would be a much better way to move around in a simulated environment than actual physical locomotion, but he'd kept this opinion to himself.

Anyhow, she'd made it to Denver bright and early so, having no access to ballistic flyers, he assumed she'd teleported despite her objections—yet another indication that she was seriously considering the possibility of embarking on the *Unity*.

Her voice came through his earpiece. "I've got the maintenance robot back online. It's a little battered from a run-in with an unfriendly miniature blimp, but it should be all right. I'll be there in fifteen minutes."

"All right, we'll wait," he replied.

"We?" Emily asked.

"I brought our medical expert with me. Her name is Dr. Unameya."

"Why? I haven't decided if I'm even coming along, yet." Emily sounded extremely nervous, so Rome activated the eyepiece to have a look at her. She was pale and wore a frightened expression. It was obvious that she was frightened that Rome and Senni might take the decision without consulting her.

"I know," he replied soothingly. "She isn't going to touch anything, but she wanted to have a look at the birthing chamber technology."

"All right," she said, sounding unconvinced.

"Emily, I need you to trust me. I would never do anything against your will. And Dr. Unameya isn't a monster, she's just curious. Don't worry." And besides, Rome thought to himself, all the good doctor wants is a subject. Kate will do as well as Emily in that case. And it seems like Kate will be easy enough to convince.

"I trust you," she replied, with a little more conviction. "Now stop pestering me, and I'll be there shortly." She signed off.

He grinned. That was more like the Emily he knew.

Ten minutes later, a soft rustling in the long grass told them that something was approaching. Rome tensed and raised the weapon, but was relieved to see a metallic head appear. "Hello Emily," he said.

"Hello, Rome, welcome to my home town." Emily's voice came through the earpiece, as this particular robot hadn't been fitted with communications gear or speakers. It was, after all, just a maintenance robot whose only important conversations had been conducted in binary with control modules. "I'm sorry it's a bit of a mess, but I didn't have any time to clean up."

Rome chucked. "I'd like to introduce you to Dr. Senni Unameya. She's the head of the biologists on board the *Unity* and is also our top human medical expert. Senni, this is Emily Plair."

The robot inclined its torso clumsily in Senni's direction. "Can she hear us?" Emily said.

The doctor replied for herself. "Loud and clear. I can also see what's going on in the simulation, so there's no need to give me a running commentary—I'll ask if there's anything I don't understand. Oh, and by the way, I'm very pleased to meet you, Emily." She grinned sheepishly at her slip even though only Rome could see her.

"Same here, so long as you don't go around disconnecting me without my permission," Emily replied.

This earned Rome a set of raised eyebrows, in the face of which he just shrugged. "Of course not. I just want to see how they work."

"Good. Let's get moving, then. This robot is really slow going over rubble."

Despite Emily's warning, they made good time through the tall grass and occasional debris. They'd chosen their meeting point partly because it was easy to find, but mainly because of its proximity to the place the maps had indicated was the entrance to the underground complex in which Emily's birthing chamber was located.

Despite the ease of travel, Rome was nervous. He could have sworn he saw something moving out of the corner of his eye. Something too ponderous to be a bird. But every time he turned to look at the motion, there was nothing to be seen.

He shook his head, water droplets flying from his hair, and walked on. It must have been a trick of the light.

***

Graham breathed a sigh of relief. It had been a close call, but he was certain that the offworlder hadn't actually seen them. Beside him, Jarrien did likewise.

It wasn't strictly necessary for them to follow the physical progress of the small party. There were many alternatives. Graham could easily have hacked into the data stream and followed everything from Emily's point of view. Or they could just have waited for them at the entrance to the complex. After all, they knew where it was located and didn't have to go overland.

But Graham wanted to be safe. The secret they were protecting was much too important to take anything for granted. So they'd dusted off Jarrien's remote-control airship and followed the group's progress, hiding in darkened windows, flitting behind buildings. Trying to see without being seen.

They'd been moderately successful—only Rome seemed to have caught glimpses of them as they trailed them through the remains old Denver. This surprised him a good deal because the airship, as it weaved in and out of the openings in the ruined buildings, seemed to disturb a great number of nesting birds, who would flutter around. He couldn't tell if they were making a large amount of noise, since the airship wasn't wired for sound, but it sure looked that way. Fortunately, they didn't fly off either, content to watch the airship depart once they had convinced themselves that it posed no threat.

After Rome spotted them, Graham had guided the airship into a hollow formed between two semi-collapsed brick walls. They could no longer risk following the group with the airship—they would be looking for anything unusual now—so their best bet seemed to be to make a beeline over the buildings and beat the group to the entrance to the chambers.

He turned to Jarrien. "How's the program coming along?"

"It's been done for a while—since the last time you asked, in fact. Trust me on this, I've been doing this kind of thing much longer than you have," Jarrien replied.

He grunted and concentrated on flying the airship. He would have preferred to create the jamming program himself, but he still couldn't manage to have two different copies of himself doing things that required concentration. He was getting better every day but still wasn't at the point where he could write complex code and pilot an airship at the same time. He heard a chuckle; she knew exactly what he was thinking.

"You're sure they won't be able to track us?"

"Of course. The backtrail has a self-perpetuating randomizer. It will look as though it was generated in twenty places at once."

She'd done the same thing to him when he was chasing her. It hadn't worked. He told her so.

She gave him a hard look. "You cheated. They still respect society's rules, and, for that reason, they'll get farther away from the real source with every passing day."

"Wimps," Graham said, grinning. "All right, now we can see how effective it is against them."

They turned their attention to the monitor. The blimp had arrived at the entrance to the birthing chambers and was waiting for the arrival of the two offworlders and the robot. Swaying grass in the distance was the only sign of life among the desolation.

As the figures approached the entrance, Graham could make out the robot's ungainly stride. He snickered, realizing that Emily obviously hadn't been able to plug in to its fine control centers. Now that he'd thrown off the shackles of conventional behavior, he realized just how easy doing so would be. It was a pity that Emily wouldn't come over to his point of view. That meant that he needed to stop her from acting until his plans were ready.

"Okay, start jamming them," he told Jarrien.

On the monitor, the two offworlders continued walking forward, but the robot suddenly stopped in its tracks. As Rome and Dr. Unameya turned back to see what was holding the robot up, Graham toggled the audio from their communications. Since they were communicating over the Mindnet, listening in was child's play.

"What's wrong?" a man's voice asked. *Must be Rome,* Graham thought, a slight, unexpected surge of jealousy coursing through him.

"I'm not sure. The robot suddenly won't respond to any of my commands. And I'm getting an error message saying that it's not permitted to advance any farther."

"Maybe it's a security thing. They didn't want the robots in the birthing chambers."

"That's ridiculous," Emily replied. "These are maintenance robots. They need to be inside the birthing chambers all the time. Otherwise, if anything breaks, who's going to repair or replace it? No. This must be something else, and the only thing I can think of is that someone knows that I'm aboard the robot."

"Why would anyone care?"

"How should I know? So now what? Do you think you might be able to disconnect the camera from the robot? That way, we can go ahead and see the chambers even if you have to carry me in."

Graham fidgeted as Rome studied the robot on his monitor. This was a critical moment. He was well aware that the blimp was nowhere near powerful enough to physically stop the group from entering the birthing chambers. Even if they managed to detach the camera, he'd have to block the Mindnet access to the outside world completely. That would make them stand up and take notice, and the backtrail would be impossible to hide. He'd have to rush into action.

The offworlder stepped back. "I can't do it. The power for the camera comes from the robot's solar array and battery. I need tools, and they're back on the *Unity*. We'll have to try it tomorrow."

Dr. Unameya spoke up. "I'm not certain the captain is going to agree to that, Rome. I heard something about a meeting today. She thinks the Earth government is going to ask us to leave right now."

"I'll talk to her," Rome replied.

"We can't risk it. If she says no, we'll never have another chance to study these chambers. We need to go in now."

"No!" Emily cried. "Please don't do that! I really want to be there when you go in. Please! I'm begging you."

"I'll convince Nartiya," Rome said firmly. He turned back and began to walk the way they'd come.

The doctor, furious, stood beside the entrance before she, too, walked back towards the flyer.

Graham sighed, releasing the tension he'd been feeling. He'd gotten a day at the very least. A day he needed to continue laying the groundwork. By this time tomorrow, Emily's actions might be inconsequential enough that he'd be able to ignore them. There were many things he could prepare in twenty-four hours. No one would be preparing counter measures—no one had even the faintest idea of what he was thinking, or what he was planning.

That wasn't quite true. One person most certainly knew what he was thinking, and why. And he was someone who would stop at nothing to keep Graham from achieving his goals. That person would have to be dealt with right away.

***

The Prophet was feeling extremely good about himself.

The meeting had gone perfectly, the mayor had delivered the ultimatum, and the offworlders had promised to remove themselves in twenty-four hours. Now, as the details of the situation began to leak, he once again found himself at the center of a group of journalists—a position he should never have lost in the first place.

Telling them why he'd acted to restore the cyberworld's isolation was out of the question, of course. There were some truths that humanity was not yet ready to face. But, at least, it seemed the journalists were ready to take him at face value when he explained that he had truly changed his mind and was now as fervently against returning to physical bodies as he had been in favor before the arrival of the offworlders. The traumatic landing by the delegation from Tau Ceti—the mere existence of people on planets orbiting distant stars—had made him realize that, while his philosophy was right, he'd been misinterpreting what it meant.

Essentially, he explained, it was true that every lifeform in the universe had a place to which it naturally belonged, a place where it fit. His error had come from assuming that Earth's humans were the lone representatives of the species. It had taken the arrival of the offworlders, and their subsequent violence against the cyberworld way of life, to make him realize that there was inherent value in the simulation. Earthmen had grown to fit their niche, and this was where they belonged. They could—and should—leave the inhospitable reaches of the physical world to the men and women who belonged to it.

He'd just finished reciting this to a major Mindnet site when he realized that something was very wrong. The journalist, a young woman with big hair, seemed to be moving in slow motion while he himself existed at normal velocity. A dark, opaque cloud materialized behind her, coalescing into a black wall like the ones that limited the dead mainframes, but on a much smaller scale.

As soon as the wall finished materializing, the rest of the world blinked back into motion around him.

"…whether you think it's possible for Earth's humans never to go back outside?" the reporter said. She looked at him expectantly.

But he ignored her. All he had eyes for was the dark wall behind him, which, judging by the expressions of passersby, only he could actually see. No one else seemed to have noticed that a strange black wall had suddenly appeared in their midst. They walked right past it without so much as a second glance.

No, he suddenly understood, not a wall at all. A tunnel. A tunnel meant only for him, a tunnel that would teach him further secrets of the cyberworld. It called to him.

But what if the tunnel was a defense mechanism that the simulation had generated to keep the knowledge in his head from spreading, causing a panic? What if he was about to be removed from society forever?

But that made no sense. He'd known about this since his very first foray outside with Jarrien's airship. And ever since, he'd shown that he had no intention of divulging the secret. Why would the simulation act against him now? It would have made much more sense to have done so as soon as he returned from the trip.

Besides, the simulation wouldn't need to trap him this way. It could remove him from society without the need for any theatrics. Just sever all the lines of code that kept his avatar moving through the cyberworld, and poof, it was like he'd disappeared.

No. This had to be a test, a test to ascertain whether he would be willing to grasp the opportunity, whether he was brave enough to delve deeper into the lost lore of Earth's society. Even now, Jarrien was probably being put to the same test.

He took a step forward as the irritated journalist looked on, but stopped in his tracks. Did he really want to know more about the cyberworld than he already did? What little he'd learned made him fear for the future of the world he'd grown up in. He didn't know how it could possibly go on.

But there really was no turning back. Nothing could possibly be worse than the things he'd already learned, and he might find out a little more about the implications. New knowledge might help to assuage the dread. It might be the key to being able to sleep at night.

The Prophet took another step forward and shook off the reporter. Just three more paces took him to the entrance of the tunnel. He took a deep breath and plunged in.

There was no sensation, no strange lights as he took another step deeper, just darkness. He extended an arm to see if there were any obstacles, but encountered nothing. He turned back to look at the entrance and saw the journalist standing there, a look a slack-jawed terror on her features.

And suddenly, it felt wrong. He shouldn't be here, didn't belong here. This tunnel was not the door to enlightenment. He didn't know how he knew—he just did.

With terror rising within him, the Prophet tried to run back to the entrance. But only one step into his flight, the outside world disappeared, replaced by blackness.

There was nothing but darkness, desolate, lonely darkness all around him.

***

"Got him," Graham shouted, pumping his fist in the air. "Now, all we need is to find some way to get rid of him permanently."

"Well, you could always keep him locked inside the

box—that'll keep him out of the way," Jarrien replied.

She'd only been part of the Prophet's team because what he required challenged her programming knowledge to the utmost, never a true believer. And yet, the thought of dissolving his presence within the simulation permanently did not sit well with her. What would become of his consciousness? Would it disappear the way Graham wanted, or would it roam the cyberworld, a disembodied presence seeking revenge?

"We can't just leave him there. It's too risky. What if he manages to escape?"

Jarrien admitted that it was a real risk—unlikely, but not impossible. The cell they'd created out of the very structure of the simulation was proof against anyone who didn't really know how to manipulate the simulation itself—anyone who was content to live within the limitations and rules that the simulation imposed on its inhabitants. The Prophet had shown himself willing to break the rules and challenge the conventions—and neither Graham nor Jarrien knew whether his programming skills might not be sufficient to get out.

But the alternative—Jarrien could think of no other word for it than murder.

"Besides," Graham went on, "think of it as practice. There's going to be resistance to what we're going to do—probably a lot of resistance. And even if we know things about how this cyberworld works that essentially no one else does, how long do you think it will take the concerted effort of millions of people to catch up with us? Right now, all we have going for us is knowledge—we need some kind of coercion tool, something they can't ignore. Something that will strike terror into their hearts and crush the resistance before it gets organized. We need this."

She met his gaze. There was something fundamentally wrong with the way he was thinking. Something that, in other times, would have been called insanity, even if it was backed up by cold, hard, indisputable facts.

Those very facts made his logic irrefutable. What might have seemed insane to people who didn't have access to all the information, was, in this case, merely seizing the moment. It was an extreme, ruthless act, and its cruelty would be multiplied because it would catch the world at a particularly vulnerable time, but that was the best time to strike. All in all, Jarrien knew that for the foreseeable future, it would be much better to be with him than against him.

But what worried her most was that, deep down inside, she felt he might actually be right. About this and about everything.

"All right," she said. "What do we need to do?"

"We need to find a way to dissolve his physical presence in the simulation. To do that, we need to go much deeper into the base code than I've ever dared to go before. I assume you haven't done that much cutting, either."

She shook her head. "There are some pretty daunting safeguards down there. And besides, I always tried to avoid detection whenever possible, and I doubt something that major would have gone unnoticed."

"Well, in a couple of days, we'll be well beyond the point where an investigation is going to bug us much, so that's no longer a concern. So let's find his source and cut it off at the root."

She nodded dumbly, fighting to keep the word 'murder' from surfacing again.

Graham gave her a satisfied smile. "Good girl," he said. "In the meantime, let's see if we can keep our prophetic friend occupied while we remove him."

She couldn't see what commands he typed into the air in front of him, but whatever it was, it made the man scream and scream. Graham turned the volume feedback down a notch.

"That should hold him," he said, and got down to business.

235

Chapter 19

Rome sat in his cabin thinking about the failed attempt to enter Emily's birthing chamber. While the message had been set up to look like a government restriction—and it would be perfectly reasonable that the government would want to limit that kind of access—there was just something that didn't feel quite right about the whole thing. It just seemed that a ruling body that would take no precautions whatsoever regarding the possibility of some talented programmer messing with the very fabric of reality as they saw it wouldn't seem to be the type of people who would set up an elaborate block to keep people from meddling in an area that, technically, they had no jurisdiction over.

But what really had him going is the fact that he was certain he'd spotted a tiny flying machine keeping pace with them as they made their way towards the entrance to the chambers. It had looked, out of the corner of his eye, like some kind of small dirigible, and he'd dismissed it at the time. He thought Emily's mention of an airship had made him paranoid. Now, he was wondering if he hadn't actually seen it after all.

His reverie was interrupted by a sudden banging on the door. He was about to call out for whoever it was to come in when the door burst open. An agitated Stell stood in the doorway. "We're leaving!" he said.

Rome sat bolt upright in his chair. "What do you mean, leaving? We can't leave yet!"

"The mayor has asked the captain to leave."

"Why? When?"

"They want us gone today, and as to why, I can't really say." Stell shrugged. "How can you use logic to try to understand a group of people content to live inside a computer simulation? Might as well try to predict the weather on this planet." The warmth of mid-summer had unexpectedly given way to a chill squall the night before, and Stell, who'd been enjoying the opportunity of being outside without layers of insulation was grumpy that he would never see the Earth sun again.

But Rome wasn't listening. He brushed past his friend towards the biology labs, registering with some alarm that the entire crew of the ship seemed to be strapping down loose equipment for takeoff.

The lab was pandemonium. Caged specimens whined as they were jostled by the biologists whose job it was to secure every piece of equipment. Techs ran this way and that under harsh lights that reflected mercilessly against the glossy white walls. Dr. Unameya stood in the middle of it all like a lighthouse in a storm. She mainly watched her people's efficiency with a satisfied smile but would sometimes order a small change in some arrangement.

"Senni," Rome panted. "I need your help."

She turned and gazed calmly at him. "I'm not sure I'm in the mood to help you," she said. "Thanks to your idealism, I'm never going to get a look at the birthing chambers, which are, as far as I can tell, the only piece of worthwhile technology on the entire planet. From the records I see, their research in every real science stopped dead even before they moved into the cyberworld. No nanotech, no space technology, their food, which gets pumped into the bodies is yeast-based. It's like they lost interest in the outside world. And the one thing they do have, I won't be able to study."

"That's why I'm here! We need to go talk to Nartiya. We

can't just leave!" Left unsaid were the words 'without Emily', but Rome suspected that the biologist was perfectly aware of Rome's thoughts.

Her eyes went wide with amazement. "You want to try to make Nartiya back out of a promise she gave as a representative of Tau Ceti to the Earth government? I think you're insane. I won't say a word, but I'll come along. This I just have to see."

Rome knew what the woman was telling him: *if she doesn't bite your head off immediately, I'll give you limited support. But if it goes badly, you're on your own.* And the only reason he'd even gotten this much was that Dr. Unameya was dying to see the inside of those chambers.

They ran to the bridge where Captain Nartiya was sitting in the command chair, a strange expression on her face. Dark circles ringed her eyes. "Ah, Rome," she smiled faintly, "I've been expecting you all day."

"I just heard about it," Rome replied, sensing that Dr. Unameya had stopped, which had the effect of leaving him alone in the captain's presence.

"I can imagine. You're here to convince me to keep the *Unity* on Earth."

Rome nodded, not quite trusting himself to speak. It was one thing to blurt random phrases at Dr. Unameya, with whom he'd created a certain rapport, but quite another to do so in front of Captain Nartiya.

Nartiya gave him a sad look. "If you have any arguments, use them now. I want to stay. I truly do. But there's no way we can do so without causing a major incident. Even as things stand now, only disgrace awaits us on our return home. We destroyed three of their largest cities, one of them well beyond repair. Do you have any idea what they'll do to me?"

Rome avoided her eyes, and the loaded question, and tried to concentrate on finding a solution that would allow him to bring Emily with them. Nartiya seemed lost in a world of her own, willing to let him stand there all day.

And then it hit him. "The mayor of the Manhattan mainframe has no authority anywhere but in his area. Once we leave Manhattan, provided we don't return, we'll have complied with his wishes as far as his authority extends. If the people of Denver want us to leave, let them ask. That will buy us at least some time."

"I'd really rather not have any contact with the people of Denver," Nartiya said. "They have real reasons not to like us."

"So we won't tell them we're there. I'd be willing to bet my entire fortune and every bonus I pick up from this trip that if we don't announce ourselves, no Earther will know we're there. The outside world simply isn't part of their consciousness."

Nartiya looked torn. She turned to Dr. Unameya. "I assume you want to do this as well."

"I think it would be scientifically beneficial, yes."

Nartiya sighed. "All right. They can't do more than give me a dishonorable discharge, anyway. And I've already earned that much. Let's see these birthing chambers."

Rome nodded, ecstatic, and turned to go, but Nartiya's voice stopped him at the door.

"And Rome, even if your girlfriend can't go inside, we are going in regardless."

Rome's cheeks burned at the stares the bridge crew gave him, but his happiness won out. And, more to the point, he already had a plan to deal with the jamming of Emily's robot.

****

It was still raining in Denver, but this time Rome wouldn't have to listen to Senni griping about it because she was comfortably cocooned in the *Unity*, which had settled on some buildings less than a mile from the entrance to the birthing chambers. If the Earth people ever left their simulation to have a look around, they were going to be really mad about both the landing itself and the fact that the Tau Ceti delegation had damaged even more real estate in one of their cities.

But that wasn't his problem. As far as he was aware, no one in the simulation, including Emily, was aware of what they were doing here. The reason for the secrecy was simple—Rome believed that Emily was being spied on through the simulation itself, so he planned to take a few precautions.

The first thing he had to do was to reactivate the camera on the robot. As he'd suspected, whoever had been blocking their access to the chambers had taken advantage of the robot's downtime to completely sever its connection to the simulation—Emily wouldn't be able to use it.

Unless, of course, Rome reconnected it in such a way that not only could she access the camera, but also that her own senses would be shielded against whatever was interfering with the robot's operation.

He'd been working on the code all through the previous night—it had taken much longer than he'd expected because of his lack of familiarity with the Earthers' programming language—and had a solution ready to graft in. In addition to shielding the camera from interference, he'd also written a little something to keep anyone from attempting to incapacitate Emily herself. He was appalled at how simple it would be for anyone with the necessary knowledge to simply waltz into anyone else's avatar code and blind them, deafen them, or otherwise incapacitate them. Hell, it would have been child's play for Rome himself, and he was under no illusions as to the level of his own knowledge.

And what was worse, the nagging feeling he had that

whoever was thwarting them had absolutely nothing to do with the government was getting stronger. Even if the powers-that-be wanted them to stay out of the birthing chambers, why would they incapacitate the robot when no one was looking? Any number of more logical government reactions presented themselves. The government could have shut off the robot as soon as the message appeared. Or it could have left it alone once they realized that Emily was going to heed the order.

No. It was definitely someone else. And while Rome expected that whoever it was would have more knowledge of the simulation than he did, he'd worked a pair of tricks into his safeguards that should buy them a couple of hours at least.

The camera was off the robot, and Rome used a multimeter he'd brought along for precisely that purpose to get a reading on the type of battery he was dealing with. The result made him blink a few times—the battery was an archaic twelve-volt direct current model of a type that was so ancient it had never even been taken to the colonies.

Nevertheless, his power pack could easily cope with it, once it was programmed to do so. In no time at all, he had the camera feeding images into a tiny cyberworld he'd simulated for the purpose—a cyberworld with no connections to the one in which any unseen watchers resided.

Satisfied that the camera was working and transmitting correctly, he shut it off. There was no need for Emily to see anything on the surface, so he would alert her and activate the feed when he got to the entrance. Despite his safeguards, they would need all the time they could get.

He soon arrived at the entrance and informed Dr. Unameya that the preparations were finished and that she should come meet him. He also sent Emily a message asking her to get to her home console urgently, that he would be in contact again in ten minutes' time.

While he waited for the contact and the doctor, Rome studied the entrance, which was quite gloomy beyond the reinforced concrete frame of the doorway. In the darkness, he could see a tunnel that led into the bowels of the Earth at a gentle angle. The soft curvature of the walls made it impossible to see more than a few dozen yards ahead. So he just fidgeted and waited for the rest of his party to arrive.

When ten minutes had passed, he toggled his connection to the cyberworld and activated the camera and the programming that would allow it to feed images directly to Emily's home console. The familiar setting of Emily's living room was fed to him through his eyepiece. She was waiting in front of the monitor.

"Thank God you decided to listen to my summons. I was afraid you'd ignore me."

Emily stood up quickly when he appeared—actually crossing the room to hug his avatar. "Rome, I… I thought you were gone forever."

"No. But we need to hurry. We've got one last shot to get inside the chamber. I've pulled the camera off the robot, so you'll be along for the ride. Have you decided what you want yet?"

"I want to go back to Tau Ceti with you. Nothing seems at all real here anymore." Tears welled in her eyes. "I'm scared. I don't think it was the government that stopped us yesterday."

"Neither do I." But Rome wasn't frightened. He was ecstatic. It was as if a weight he'd been carrying around without even realizing it had suddenly been lifted from his shoulders. He understood how important it was for him that Emily come with them.

A flutter of movement seen by the eye without the eyepiece announced the arrival of Dr. Unameya. "Talking to yourself again, are you?" she asked, holding out one hand.

Rome dropped the spare eyepiece and earpiece into her

palm and waited for her to put them on. "All right," he said, "let's get moving."

After the first thirty yards or so, it was dark enough in the tunnel that they had to use their flashlights.

It quickly became apparent that the chamber they were heading for was located somewhere in the ground directly beneath the entrance—a conclusion they reached because the tunnel spiraled around an axis, and one that was quickly confirmed by their position readings.

Some minutes later, the tunnel leveled off, and they encountered their first choice of possible destinations. The main corridor continued off to their right but, directly in front of them, they encountered a door that loomed a darker shade of grey in the yellowish beams of their flashlights. They stopped to consult their map as the echo of their footsteps rebounded down the gloomy, invisible depths of the corridor.

"The diagram says that this is one of the mixing rooms," Senni said. "This is where the nutrients are created for the bodies in the chambers."

"Do we need to stop here?" Rome asked. He was worried that they might not have enough time to free Emily from her chamber.

But the doctor seemed unperturbed. "This is the place where the magic happens, Rome. From what I've seen of the birthing chambers, they're just full of tubes. If anything happens that needs action from the central computer, the chemicals are mixed in the room behind this door and pumped into the birthing chambers. The only thing in the chambers are the bodies—and I've seen plenty of bodies in my life. So go on and find the chamber holding your girlfriend. I'll catch up with you in plenty of time." Dr. Unameya pushed the door open—she struggled briefly, long-unused hinges protesting with every inch of the way—and disappeared into the gloom beyond. Her voice could still be heard, however.

"Go on, I'll be there in a little while."

Rome peered down the darkened corridor. He wasn't at all enthusiastic about the idea of walking down the corridor on his own, but he also knew that there was nothing down there that could harm him unless some wild animal had made the tunnel its lair. But, despite smelling musty and stale, the tunnel had no animal odors. It was probably kept clean by the maintenance robots.

"So," he asked Emily through the comm link, "what do you think? Should we forge on ahead or wait for our learned colleague?"

"You know what I think," she replied. He noticed that down here in the bowels of the Earth, both the sound and image quality from within the cyberworld were patchier than on the surface—still strong enough to be intelligible, but patchy. Rome thought it was unusual that an installation of this sort wouldn't be well stocked with antennae, but he didn't spend much time on the thought. He would have traded any number of antennas to know the location of the central light switch.

"All right then," he replied, "let's move on." Two people followed the echoes of one body's footsteps down a long, gloomy corridor towards the body of the other.

***

"Oh shit," Senni Unameya said to herself.

It had taken her only ten minutes to realize exactly what had gone wrong, and most of that time had been spent going down fifteen flights of metallic stairs in the dark to reach the machinery. But she knew that those ten minutes were more than enough time for Rome to get a tremendous head start. She tried to reach him on the comm but got only static—unlike Rome, she was completely unsurprised by the fact that there were no working antennas in the complex. And she was much farther underground than he was.

She retraced her steps, sprinting up the stairs as fast as her legs and lungs permitted, knowing she was losing ground with each step, pushing herself harder and cursing the sedentary ship-board lifestyle. She had to warn him, had to stop him before Emily saw what she feared they would find.

The stairs seemed to go on forever, but she finally reached the top, and the doorway beyond. Thankful for the flat surface, she set off down the corridor behind after Rome and, much more importantly, after the version of Emily he carried around with him. Her heavy breathing filled the enclosed space like a presence. She hoped Rome would hear her, wait for her, but knew there was little hope of that.

Like the stairs, the corridor seemed to go on forever. The air was slightly musty with the humidity that must have seeped through fissures in the bedrock and through the surrounding concrete over the centuries. The smell of decay and neglect that reminded her that she had to hurry to catch Rome, and she redoubled the pace. She called his name, tried the comm again—all to no avail. The worst part of it all was not knowing where the hall ended; the weak flashlight beam would, in the best of cases, illuminate as far as the next bend in the zigzagging walkway.

She was ready to give up, turn back, when her beam illuminated a wall in her path, making her panic. Had she gotten turned around? Did this corridor dead-end? Maybe there had been a branch that she'd missed. Maybe Rome was miles away.

On coming to a stop in front of the wall, however, she saw her error. She noticed a faint breeze coming from her right—a breeze that she assumed had been there all along, but that had been ignored in her mad headlong flight.

But as Senni turned the final corner, her hopes were

dashed. She immediately saw that she was too late. The corridor opened suddenly into a huge, cavernous chamber, blacker than the darkest pit of hell. Rome's flashlight was on the floor, still emitting a light even after having fallen from his nerveless fingers. Rome himself was standing crouched over, weeping silently into the hands covering his face.

So he knows, Senni thought.

***

The day before had been an exhausting one, trying one avenue, one torture after another. Graham grinned anyway. He knew that no matter how exhausting the previous twenty-four hours might have been for him, they'd been immeasurably worse for the poor bugger in the sensory deprivation chamber.

The Prophet was looking quite the worse for wear. Initially, Graham had attempted to destroy him simply by erasing his physical body. But it had been no use. The code that made up his personality and thinking was still present. Most frustratingly, there seemed no way to sever them and thus remove the irritating presence from the cyberworld forever.

Graham spent his first few hours of work on the Prophet trying to find a way to cut this data stream but became increasingly frustrated to learn that it was simply impossible. It wasn't so much that the information was protected by firewalls or security programs because Graham could have made short work of either. The problem was that he couldn't quite pin down the stream itself. It felt like trying to get a grip on a bar of soap in a bathtub, as if the simulation itself would not allow anyone inside to access this particular data set. He'd identified and isolated it more times than he could count, but modifying it was like trying to shape fog.

So he'd brought the Prophet's body back, minus some bits. He brought him back without arms or a mouth and with a couple of large holes in his thorax.

Graham was honest enough with himself to know that he'd done it out of sheer frustration, to try to make the Prophet feel some of his anger. The results, however, had astounded him.

As soon as the Prophet realized his situation, his stress levels had shot off the charts, even though Graham was causing him no pain. Pain, Graham knew, would only reach the threshold allowed by the system, making torture completely ineffective. But, even as Graham watched the readings, he realized that some kind of damping system had kicked in almost immediately. The stress levels were soon reduced to those caused by mild distress, and the Prophet's expression, even mouthless, was easily readable. It was almost an expression of calm unconcern.

Graham had focused on the dampers then. Unlike the data stream associated to the individual consciousness, these had been easy to find—actual programs added onto the basic structure of the simulation, and quite obvious if you knew what you were looking for. He quickly isolated them and studied their use.

He couldn't believe what he found. Other than the truth about the birthing chambers, the dampers might be the most important secret held by the cyberworld. He'd always known that pain was limited within the simulation, and, though he'd never thought about it, a damper seemed a logical way to achieve this. But even in the wildest speculations, no one had ever postulated a battery of dampers such as these. There were carefully established and rigorously policed parameters on nearly every emotional variable in existence. And while the benefits of keeping pain to a reasonable limit were apparent, and putting a limit on anger was probably justified by the social theories of the time, and he'd just observed the usefulness of the damper that kept stress in check, he couldn't understand why anyone would limit the amount of happiness in the system. Or love. Or excitement.

He wondered idly what sex must have been like before the "correct" pleasure parameters had been found and resolved to have the experience sans artificial limits as soon as he had time.

At that moment, however, he'd had much more pressing work to do. Disabling the dampers for the entire cyberworld would have been the work of a moment. But he'd discarded that option—it was much too soon to take any action that would throw the entire society on Earth into utter chaos. In order to be recognized as the absolute leader of the planet, he needed to leave the framework in place. If people's worlds were falling apart, they would be too preoccupied to care what the new order was preaching.

But that still left him with the problem of finding a coercion tool. He needed a way to remove dissident voices, and he'd already found that making them disappear wasn't as easy as he would have wanted. And with the dampers in place, he couldn't just make everyone hurt until they did what he wanted.

He realized that he needed a scalpel instead of a sledgehammer. He had to find some way to interfere with the dampers so that pain could be administered on an individual level.

Which was what he'd spent the last few hours doing. Little by little, he'd constructed blocks, using the Prophet as a guinea pig to see where the blocks would do the dampers most harm. At first, the dampers kept a high level of effectiveness but eventually, the man's screams grew longer and more desperate. Knowing about the dampers, Graham wasn't surprised that he was only able to feel a limited amount of compassion towards his victim. He smirked.

But it wasn't just the fact that he'd found a way to make other inhabitants of the cyberworld feel excruciating pain that gave him satisfaction. It was the effects he'd been observing on the data that represented the Prophet's conscience. At first, the slippery nature of the information made it difficult to be certain, but it soon became apparent that the stream was becoming less cohesive. Tiny strands of data could be found leading nowhere, and in Graham's highly sensitive mind, he envisioned the data as a rope—a rope that was slowly but surely unraveling under the stress he was applying.

By the time he looked around, Graham knew that the Prophet's mind, his consciousness, his very existence was hanging from a single metaphorical strand. What would happen when the line broke? Would the man go mad? Would he become inert? Or would he simply disappear from the cyberworld as if he'd never existed?

Graham didn't know, but he intended to find out. He commanded the system to hit the Prophet with a jolt of pain at the highest level it could manage. More than enough to snap a tiny data little stream like this one.

The entire strand disappeared, taking any physical evidence of the Prophet with it forever. The armless, mouthless thing in the deprivation chamber winked out of existence, and Graham felt the warm sense of satisfaction flow over him. But it wasn't for the death of the Prophet that he exulted.

Graham rejoiced because he had the tool he needed. Nothing could stop him now.

Chapter 20

Jarrien found Graham sitting at the main console, a look of profound satisfaction on his face. The monitor, which had been showing the Prophet for the last few hours, was a featureless black rectangle.

"Did you let him go?" she asked, surprise and fear mingling in her voice. She would have been surprised if he had, but she was afraid of the answer. If he'd found a way to remove the Prophet, his dreams would probably come true. And while she thought that following him was the right thing to do, she couldn't be sure.

Graham smiled. "Yes. I freed him from his shackles," he replied with a beatific smile.

Jarrien's stomach dropped and she swallowed. Only chance had saved her from sharing the Prophet's fate—after all, she'd once been his top lieutenant. While it was true that she hadn't been a true believer, it was also true that she was the only other member of his movement who'd known the secret of the birthing chambers. She considered leaving Graham, running as far as she could and trying to fend off his attacks. But he'd catch her in the end, and that then, she would share the Prophet's fate.

She dreaded telling him the news she had. He wasn't going to take it well at all. She swallowed. "There are Outsiders in the birthing chambers."

He was surprised, but not angry. "Outsiders? I thought they'd gone back to their miserable little planet." He paused.

"Was Emily with them?"

She nodded, knowing that the explosion would come now.

But it didn't. Graham just nodded somberly. "It seems we need to move up our schedule a bit, then."

Gesturing for her to follow, he left the apartment and headed for the street.

She followed after a short inner debate. Short enough that she was ashamed of herself.

****

When Dr. Unameya reached him, Rome simply put his arms around her. He didn't care that the doctor was one of the least approachable human beings he knew, didn't care that in the miniature world of the *Unity* her rank made her a demigod to his peasant. He just needed someone to comfort him.

He needed to feel that something was real, now that he knew for certain that Emily wasn't.

What Rome could see of the immense underground space that had been divided by low walls to contain the myriad birthing chambers was a shamble. In the gloom to his right, a panel had collapsed and lay haphazardly over one of the walls.

Silence reigned—he'd expected to encounter the sound of fluids being pumped into constantly feeding bodies, the hum of electrical equipment, flashing lights. Instead, they'd found silence. No flashing lights, no monitoring equipment. Nothing but a thick coat of dust and a collection of metallic tubes. Tubes large enough to hold a full-grown human filled the chamber, their outline softened by the copious dust. Some of the tubes were cracked like eggshells, jagged breaks marring the smooth surface.

Rome had immediately realized that these were the birthing chambers, but, despite the atrocious condition of everything in the room, he'd simply dismissed the broken tubes as surplus chambers—the population of the cyberworld had, after all, fallen considerably since its creation and many of the chambers would have lain fallow at any given time.

Hope lasted until he reached the nearest chamber, one that seemed to be in better shape than most of its neighbors. He knew from the blueprints he'd studied that the chambers had a small rectangular piece of transparent plastic at the head, which allowed someone standing outside to look into the chamber. He wiped away the dust with his jacket and pointed his flashlight into the tube.

The eye sockets of a human skull stared emptily back at him. He jumped away, heart in his mouth.

At first, he thought he must have had the bad luck to encounter a failed chamber. But then his brain kicked in, overcoming his denial. If anybody had been inside the chamber for that amount of time, it meant that the maintenance robots had not cleaned it in... how long did it take for a body to decompose completely? Years? Decades? However long it took, all the evidence pointed to the fact that there had been no maintenance in this sector for a long, long time. Which, considering the complexity of the machinery—he could see multiple tubes, leads, and wires entering each individual chamber—meant that he wouldn't find any working chambers.

And the significance of that was staggering.

Refusing to give up, he'd doggedly, hopelessly looked for the birthing chamber containing Emily. Once he'd understood the way the chambers were organized—a simple alphanumerical grid—it had been the work of a moment to locate the address corresponding to Emily's chamber.

It was broken in half. Empty save for a couple of old bones.

He'd returned to the entrance to wait for Dr. Unameya in a trance. Emily had been silent from the moment they'd seen the state of the chambers. He knew she was still there—he could hear her moving around through the microphone pickup—but she was silent, save for an occasional sob. What he didn't know was what she was.

There were many possible explanations for what they'd found here, of course. This might be just an unused facility that had a similar name to the one they were looking for, or the inhabitants of the cyberworld might have been transferred elsewhere, but the records kept unaltered.

But deep inside, Rome knew that none of the alternatives would pan out. He was certain that there were no more humans on Earth and that the people he'd been interacting with were no more than complex computer programs—certainly not alive and probably only mimicking intelligence. They hadn't thought to run consciousness tests on anyone, simply taking what they'd been told at face value.

One thing he tried hard not to think about was the emotions he'd seen among the people of the cyberworld. It had to be a simulation, of course, but they'd all seemed so genuine. When Emily had looked at him with hope in her eyes, it was as if all her dreams lent strength to that gaze.

He shook his head. It was an illusion—a cleverly put together hoax, but a hoax all the same. And he'd fallen for it as completely as it was possible, letting his own desires overcome any misgivings he might have felt about a whole planet-full of people living inside a huge computer simulation. It was ridiculous, and he should have known a lot better.

Senni shifted slightly, bringing Rome back to the here and now. With a muttered apology, he quickly disengaged and took a step back. Expecting a reproach, he found that her look held a surprising amount of compassion. "I tried to warn you," she said, "but you had a huge head start. I'm sorry." Whether she was sorry about not being able to catch him, about the fact that Emily was nothing more than a computer construct, or about the fact that he was feeling betrayed by the entire universe was unclear. What was clear was that she truly felt for him and wasn't judging him or writing up his court-martial in her head.

She also seemed to have something on her mind and was anxiously waiting for him to get a hold of himself before mentioning it. "What?" he said.

She smiled sheepishly at the fact that he'd been able to see through her. "I'm sorry, it's just that I can't help wondering what happened here."

A consummate professional to the bitter end, he thought. "I think it's obvious. The Earthlings decided to leave, probably packed their entire population into colony ships, and waltzed off. After all, they had five hundred years of privacy in which to do it."

She shook her head. "It doesn't add up. If so, why would they have left the bones in the birthing chambers?"

He shrugged. He was far beyond caring. "Maybe they left everyone too old to withstand the physical therapy behind. All I know is that they tricked us for reasons of their own—they're probably out there somewhere laughing at us at this very moment."

Dr. Unameya nodded but looked far from convinced.

***

René Simon was a simple man. He was perfectly content with his job as an assistant buyer at one of Paris's most important supermarkets. He didn't ask much from life, just to be left alone to enjoy his family in some measure of comfort.

So he was shocked and angered when a winged man, of all things, landed in the path in front of him. He quickly realized that he was in the presence of some lunatic who had been playing with the base code of the simulation to give himself huge feathered wings and a golden sheen to his skin—which seemed to behave like any normal human's flesh, but looked like mirror-polished metal.

His first response was indignation. Who did this imbecile think he was to hack into the code? He would alert the authorities. He would make certain that his programming privileges were revoked. Lost in thought, he wasn't prepared to answer when the winged being spoke to him.

"Excuse me?" René replied, flustered. The words, clear as they'd been, had seemed strange, somehow.

"I asked if you thought that was a nice way to behave towards a visitor to your city," the winged man repeated.

And René immediately understood what was wrong—the other man's lips weren't moving. The voice was being projected straight into his head.

"Exactly," the winged atrocity said with a smile that didn't move. "And I also know that you're about to report me, and I can't let you do that." Then he paused. "As a matter of fact, I can, it would make no difference. But I won't. I've decided I don't like the way you think. So bye. Anyhow, you should feel honored—you will forever be remembered as the first dissident put down by the new order."

René was outraged at the sheer cheek. He was astounded at the fact that the simulation would allow itself to be subverted to the point where telepathy was possible. He was energized by these feelings.

It never occurred to him to be afraid. Which was perhaps a mercy, since the waves of pain that unraveled the data stream that defined his existence were bad enough without having fearful anticipation to make it worse.

His pain lasted much less than the Prophet's had. Graham was refining his technique.

***

Senni would have much preferred to have Rome with her when debriefing the captain, but he'd locked himself in his cabin and was refusing to see anyone—and she didn't have the heart to force him out.

Sadly, this meant giving Nartiya some very unsettling news with no backup whatsoever. As she entered the bridge, the captain turned from the main display.

"So tell me," Nartiya said. "What did you find?"

Senni swallowed. "After studying the birthing chambers, my only conclusion is that there's no one alive on this planet except for us."

"What?" Even a jaded starship captain who was looking forward to nothing better than an indifferent welcome—and possibly even a severe reprimand—after the trip thanks to the diplomatic setbacks they'd suffered earlier was shocked by the news. "What are you talking about?"

"The birthing chambers aren't functional. As far as I can tell, they haven't been working for the past couple of hundred years at least. The maintenance robots don't even go in there to dust."

Ashur Nartiya dropped onto one of the navigator's chairs. "But what about the people?"

"I'm not really sure since Rome has taken this rather badly. But I had one of the other computer experts look into it, and he says that, as far as he can tell, the people are simulated. They're programs."

Nartiya looked shocked. "But that can't be. I was there. I talked to them. There's no way they could be simulated personalities. Just looking into their eyes was enough. The people in there have emotions. No simulation could be that complete."

Senni said nothing. She'd done her duty, told her captain

how things were as far as science could determine. She just watched her captain think about the news for a few minutes.

"Where are the people, then?"

"We don't really know. Rome believes they got up and left, leaving the simulation behind to fool anyone who came for a visit into thinking the planet was still inhabited."

Nartiya studied her for a moment. "And what do you think?" she asked.

"I think they died. I believe the system that controlled the chambers failed catastrophically somehow, and they woke up in their metal coffins. The lucky ones might have managed to get out and die on the surface—although I saw no evidence of that. I suppose the rest were too weak to move and starved in their chambers."

An ashen Nartiya insisted. "Wouldn't the ones who got out have helped the others?"

"You don't understand. These people are not like you and me. They were kept from birth inside a tube. Since no one was supposed to leave the tube during their lifetime for any reason, no provisions were made to maintain muscle tone in any part of the body except for cardiovascular systems. To make things worse, all sensation and emotion was kept in check through a series of drugs. They never felt extreme pain or anger."

Senni, noticing the captain's faraway look, paused. Nartiya nodded for her to go on. "Imagine that you suddenly wake up, weak as a baby, trying to make your body obey you—after it has never moved in its life. Trust me, the only thing most of them would be thinking about was the pain as their muscles tore from the strain. And then, once the drugs wore off, the panic would set in. Panic like they'd never experienced before. The last thing they'd be able to do is to rescue other people."

"Oh my god," the captain said.

***

"I am alive. I just know it!" Emily insisted.

Even as his impassive avatar spoke to her, Rome could feel the tears running down the face of his real body, seated in his cabin on the *Unity*. She looked so sincere. He had to remind himself of the empty, desolate birthing chambers every few minutes to avoid getting sucked in all over again.

While most of his mind was enveloped in the roiling anger and desperation of this massive betrayal, a tiny part of him grudgingly admired the design of the simulated people. The reactions, the expressions, the emotions, were beyond anything he'd ever seen. And, considering the fact that development must have stopped when humanity left Earth, it was simply amazing that the personalities were so advanced.

He pushed that down, concentrated on the anger. There was nothing to be gained by going down that road again.

In that case, what was he doing here, talking to Emily?

"You believe me, don't you?" Her pleading voice was a travesty, a siren song seducing him from the path of sanity. "Rome, I know what I am! I can feel things, I am not just some program!"

So she'd figured out the corollary—if she wasn't alive and well inside her birthing chamber, then that could only mean she was a product of the simulation. And how could a simulation have feelings?

He opened his mouth to tell her—to tell it!—that he didn't, wouldn't ever, believe her, but was unable to go through with it. It wasn't that he believed her—that would have been too much—as much as that he wanted to believe her. He had too many emotions invested in Emily to let them go that easily. The siren song had to have something to hold on to, after all. Heartstrings to pull.

"I don't know," he said.

She looked stricken, and he went on hastily. "I mean, how can it be possible? You know what I saw. How can you expect me to just forget that? If you're alive, if you're an actual sentient being, then where are you?"

"I…" She paused, trying to compose herself, lower lip quivering as her eyes filled with tears. Rome's cynical side admired the beauty of the programming. "I don't know," she said finally. "What if we're not anywhere, physically? What if we're alive inside the circuits of the simulation?"

"Do you really think that's possible?"

"How could I know?" she screamed. "All I know is that I feel as human as I've always felt and that the world is falling apart and that Graham is destroying everything—it's on the news. I'm scared. I don't want to die." Emily broke down completely.

He reacted the only way he could: even though his avatar was unwieldy, he moved to her side and put his arm around her and held her until the sobbing subsided.

She looked into his eyes, and he saw there what he would have seen in a human woman: fear, despair, the feeling that she was alone against forces she didn't understand. "Please help me," she begged.

"What can I do? I can't change reality."

She pulled back as if struck. "I know that. But at least don't leave me here with Graham. Please."

He nodded. He could do that. And maybe a little bit more, as well.

***

At first, there had been shock when he came to a city and announced his intentions.

He'd started with Washington, just for the theatrical nature of taking the city that had once controlled the most powerful military on the planet. He'd told the mayor that he was coming and then entered the city at the head of a Roman Triumph. He'd chosen to enter the city as a winged god driving a golden chariot and had twisted all the streets in the city so that they converged on one spot: his parade.

The mayor had rushed out of the White House—that symbol of ancient power—to demand that he cease and desist.

Graham had made him dance with pain as all the man's citizens watched aghast. Then he told them what he wanted from them.

Many of them said no. He made examples of the people of Washington, and he made certain that the major news networks carried it live.

He'd moved along at a good clip. By speeding up his clock speed so that he could process at five, ten, a thousand times the speed of other people in the cyberwold, he skipped from symbolic city to symbolic city. Moscow, London, Beijing, Berlin. All fell, and after what they'd seen from Washington, the majority fell without an argument, shocked and confused as to what, exactly, would happen next.

Even in that advanced hour, though, the human spirit seemed to have survived. Graham encountered unexpected pockets of resistance—half-hearted and extremely measured resistance, but resistance nonetheless. He'd crushed it ruthlessly, wondering at the simple truth of what he'd discovered as he went: most people simply didn't care what he did, as long as he left them to themselves. He soon realized that only a few of the Earth's inhabitants were willing to change, willing to adopt the incredible power at their disposal for their own use.

The rest? Well, he'd come to think of them as drones. They'd do whatever the law told them to do.

When he first encountered these individuals, he'd considered removing their dampers, letting every tiny sensation, every emotion run wild. And yet he'd held back; he wanted that moment to be an occasion, and that meant having an audience.

There wouldn't be long to wait—the last of the mainframes he really wanted was about five seconds away from falling.

He watched as Jarrien, laughing with the power of it, ratcheted the pain on the maharajah of Bombay beyond what he would have been able to survive without the dampers, then, with a theatrical twist in empty air removed the dampers. The man screamed. But only for an instant. Then he was gone.

Graham favored her with a smile. "Good work, Jarrien. It seems you've just eliminated the mayor of the last major metropolis on the planet. Your name will go down in history."

She nodded silently.

He went on. "Now, all that remains is to tell the world what we want—to give them the freedom they deserve, the freedom that should have been theirs even before their bodies died off and gave birth to a much greater species. Give me all channels." He was being theatrical, of course. He could have shunted himself into every single comm and Mindnet channel on the planet simply by willing it, but what good was being the supreme leader of everything if you didn't have lackeys to do things for you?

Jarrien had to concentrate a little to get it done—Graham exulted at how far he'd come from the days when Jarrien's willingness to bend a few rules set her apart from any other programmer he'd ever met—but soon enough, every monitor in the mayor's office was showing a picture of Graham's face. He spread his wings for dramatic effect and was delighted to see his image, repeated ten times around the room, do the same. He cut an impressive figure.

"Greetings, people of Earth. I suppose all of you know who

I am by now—I've been on the news quite a bit these past few hours. But for those who don't, my name is Graham Johnson, and I come bearing good news."

He paused to let that sink in, to let his audience mutter among themselves and wonder how a new absolute ruler could bring them good news.

"I've come to free you from the things you think are true. For example, how many of you believe that you are just projections in the simulation of a personality that resides in a body in a birthing chamber? There's no need for a show of hands." He smiled at his little joke. "I already know that all of you think this. Hell, I used to think exactly the same thing until I went outside and had a look for myself. What you are about to see are images of our supposed birthing chambers."

He stood silently as every single screen on the entire planet showed images of the dusty, broken remains of the underground facility in Denver as Graham talked them through it. "These are the Denver birthing chambers. As you can see, they don't look functional, and, from the level of dust and cobwebs, I doubt they've been functional for years—or even centuries.

"I can guess what you're thinking. You're all thinking: 'I'm not from Denver. Why should I worry about this?'" He smiled again. "Well, I think you should worry. After discovering the situation in Denver, I decided to investigate the simulation a bit further, and discovered that three hundred and twenty years ago, the first string of birthing chamber malfunctions took place. They were easy to spot: all of a sudden, data streams from the chambers stopped flowing. The mainframes, which had, by that time, had a couple of centuries to examine human thought patterns, simply replaced this feed with a simulated version of the human thought experience. It wasn't quite the same, of course, but it was close enough to create living creatures who have never been able to tell that they weren't human—until now. Welcome to your post-humanity, my friends. You are the future."

"I imagine what you're feeling. Interest. Or perhaps a small measure of anxiety. Logic tells you that you should be feeling something stronger, but you just can't seem to work up enough interest, and you know that this will have blown over by tomorrow. I can explain that, too. The original design of the cyberworld was modified to keep our emotions in check—even before our ancestors' bodies died out. When the physical bodies were still present, this was achieved through a mixture of drugs injected into each and every one of us without our consent, without our knowledge, even."

He paused to let this sink in. It was irrelevant, of course, and had been for centuries, but it would feed the sense of outrage. "After we left fleshly concerns behind, the method used to keep our emotions under control was much more direct—feedback dampers that act directly on our simulated personas.

"That's why modern people can't really feel anger or true love or any strong feelings. The negative emotions are damped more firmly than the positive ones, true, but all are limited beyond what would have been natural in physical humans. Sometimes, the negative emotions are necessary, too. It would be unfair to tell you all of this without giving you the means to feel the necessary outrage, the necessary fear. So as of this moment, the dampers are…" He signaled to Jarrien, who nodded back to him. "Gone. Enjoy your newfound emotions, my friends."

He signed off, not knowing where his actions would lead, but certain that whatever came of it would be better than the sanitized, plain-vanilla lie they'd been living until now.

Chapter 21

Pandemonium ruled in the ship's main meeting room. The news had spread like wildfire, and the captain had immediately called a meeting of all the senior personnel to discuss what actions, if any, would be appropriate under the circumstances.

Nartiya tried to gauge the climate and found that the prevailing emotion was that of confusion, which was understandable. But below that was an undercurrent of something a little bit deeper, a little less pleasant. Perhaps outrage, perhaps embarrassment. Whatever it was, it was her job to bring it to the surface, understand why it was there and, most importantly, keep the emotions from guiding the decision-making process. Now, as never before, cooler heads must prevail.

She smiled inwardly at the irony. Here she was getting her thoughts organized to create an atmosphere of logic and reason while just a few minutes earlier, she'd had Rome dragged from his cabin to attend the meeting. She would have preferred to let him be, but he would also be necessary for what was to come—no one understood the cyberworld like he did.

She rapped on the table smartly. Once, twice. By the third rap, the room had quieted enough to allow her to speak, and she had to suppress a smile. It wasn't always easy to maintain the image of the aloof, disciplinarian starship captain, and this crew was well enough trained for it to be mostly unnecessary.

But not wholly unnecessary—there were times when a healthy respect for authority came in very handy.

"I guess you've all heard the news," she said. "What you might not know is that, just to be on the safe side, I sent out a pair of shuttles on scouting missions to investigate the situation on other continents." This was news to most of them, and the second mission had returned just minutes prior to the meeting. "They've confirmed what we suspected. Every birthing chamber they visited was empty except for a few bones. We've been completely unable to find the least evidence of living humans on the planet."

The room greeted this in stunned silence. They'd suspected that this was the case, but mere suspicion of something of this magnitude was very different from having one's worst fears confirmed. The eyes of all the ship's senior officers, both military and civilian, were trained on her—expecting wisdom, solutions, decisions.

Not yet—she needed their input on the matter first. "Before I decide where to go from here, I'd like to hear your thoughts on the matter. Dr. Unameya, you were part of the team that made the initial discovery. What do you think?"

Unameya surprised her by ignoring the main issue and moving to what, in the future, was absolutely certain to become the main issue. "Well," she said. "The planet is perfect for human habitation. My recommendation is to recolonize at once. Imagine, no terraforming needed. We'd have a temperate planet capable of sustaining a population of billions ready to receive us. There's no other planet we've been to as suitable as this one, with a perfectly balanced ecology that has, we have to admit, benefitted from the absence of population. I would even advocate leaving a team of volunteers as a startup colony in some suitably temperate location. We can spare the supplies with ease."

Three others immediately tried to shout her down.

Nartiya was unsurprised to see that Rome was among them. She rapped for order once again and pointed to the head of her diplomatic analysis team, who'd been one of the others.

"Erich, I assume you have a reason to be against this?"

He looked startled at having been singled out, but rallied quickly. "Of course. I need to point out that we have a treaty with Earth's society. We can't just ignore it and recolonize the planet."

Holding up a hand for silence, Nartiya followed up. "There are no people here who could possibly be offended at the breach."

"But there is a society. It might be difficult for us to understand, but until our computer experts prove otherwise, we have to assume that they consider themselves to be the true masters of the planet."

Senni snorted. "Masters of the planet? It's just a big computer program—I probably have better personality simulators in the game system in my cabin. And besides, they have no claim on the surface—the only reason any of them has visited in the past five hundred years is because we blew up one of their computers."

"Still, the planet is theirs. We don't live in the oceans on Tau Ceti II, yet I don't think that anyone would welcome an alien colony among us."

"They wouldn't even know we're here! Even granting them consciousness, which I don't for a moment, they've displayed all the curiosity of a damp rag. Empires could rise and fall on the surface and they'd be none the wiser."

Rome broke in. "That may be changing," he said. "One of them has been eliminating the system dampers and creating a completely new society. I was monitoring it when you dragged me down here." He glared at the assembled party. "For the record, I do believe they've achieved some degree of sense of self. It might be limited, but they think that they're alive, no matter what the doctor here says. It would be as much of a crime to break our treaty with them as it would be with any other human planet. That's all I have to say on this topic."

He turned to leave, and one of the security people who'd escorted him down glanced Nartiya's way for instructions. She shook her head, and Rome was allowed to leave the room unmolested.

Silence reigned once more, although the legalistic Erich and the pragmatic Senni still glared at each other. Fortunately, the decision they wanted to make right now was something well above their pay grade—and Nartiya's as well. Cooler heads, with the benefit of time to think, would take it. The meeting had mainly served to get the grievances out into the open. The captain was enormously satisfied that none of the individuals present had mentioned the one thing she was afraid of—that someone might decide that the cyberworld was an abomination and that the punishment for being played for fools should be annihilation, the complete destruction of every mainframe.

"I see only one course of action," she said before anyone could mention it. "We need to survey the landscape, finish the biological and mineral survey of the planet that we started, but with a wider scope—with views to possible colonization. Then we return to Tau Ceti and let them take a decision."

"No colonists, then?" Senni didn't look too pleased with the decision.

"No. And you've got a week to get the survey completed before we leave."

Senni looked decidedly unhappy now, but Nartiya didn't dare take any more time—the crew was mad at the cyberworlders, and she didn't want to give them any chance to stage an 'accident'.

***

Back in his cabin, Rome considered his options. He was well aware that the logical thing to do would be to simply shut down his connection to the cyberworld and forget about it forever. After all, there was nothing real in the simulation. But he just couldn't bring himself to do it.

Almost without thinking about it, Rome found himself connected to the cyberworld. He hadn't arranged any meetings. This allowed him to explore alone, which was a good thing since he was unsure of what would be waiting for him when he got there.

Graham, he knew from the monitoring he'd done, had wasted no time at all in changing every rule in the simulation that he could get his fingers into. The dampers had been removed—except for those keeping Graham himself from feeling pain or anxiety or anything else that might weaken his hold over the rest of the cyberworld. Others, 'liberated' by the changes, had begun to experiment with their own forms, creating fantastic monsters or copying their consciousness into more than one body at once. People were blinking in and out of existence all over Rome's monitors as they teleported from one mainframe to another.

Rome resisted the urge to do the same. The less attention he called to himself, the better—and he was extremely thankful that Graham hadn't seen fit to monitor unauthorized entry into the simulation; he was probably too busy trying to consolidate his power and had temporarily forgotten about the Outsiders. Once he'd done what he came here to do, Rome would make certain that he regretted this particular oversight.

Emily would be in her apartment, he thought. He'd purposely entered the simulation a few blocks away from where anyone waiting for him might be stationed, so he had a five-minute walk to her quarters. The day was fine—a slight breeze blew in from the plains—but he became more and more unsettled as he walked. The people of Denver were reveling in their newfound freedom from the rules of the simulation. First, the sky turned yellow, then purple, before settling on a mottled green and purple design. Then, a building to Rome's right rearranged itself, the blocky brick structure being replaced by an organic and bubbling green monstrosity. He increased his pace.

Emily's building, he was relieved to see, was unaffected by the high spirits. It stood unscathed, blocky and ugly as ever. He pushed the door open and entered, surprised not to find anyone guarding the door. Graham had evidently decided she was no longer worth wasting his time on, now that he'd destroyed the old order.

He trudged up the stairs—the elevator had been hacked by some prankster and only offered to take him to the left or to the right—and knocked on her door. No answer was forthcoming. He knocked again, feeling ridiculous at having to knock on a virtual door in a virtual world.

He was just about to turn away when Emily's face appeared in the doorcomm. She had the pale expression of someone who, dreading that her world was coming apart around her, had seen her fears come to pass. But there was more than the dull look of sadness in her eyes. Rome thought he could detect a more immediate fear, something out of sync with what he'd been expecting.

"Hello, Rome," she said dully.

"Can I come in?"

"No." Forcefully. Vehemently. Too much so.

"Why not."

Her eyes shifted. "I just don't feel like seeing anyone right now," she lied.

Something was wrong. "All right," he replied. He turned

to go, walked a few steps down the hall, and waited for the doorcomm to go dark.

Then he teleported himself into Emily's apartment, throwing caution to the wind.

The first thing he noticed was that he and Emily were not alone. A hulking figure dominated most of one half of the living room, and Emily was huddled at the opposite wall, as far away from the thing as possible. Her face showed fear and revulsion, with only a small measure of relief when she saw Rome appear in their midst.

"Hello, Graham," Rome said looking up at the giant's face. "You seem to have grown since our last meeting. I suppose congratulations are in order. You seem to have climbed the social ladder rather quickly—the last time I saw you, you were just a small-time lackey for the mayor of Denver who'd been dumped by a woman he thought wasn't good enough for him and look at you now. Absolute ruler of the entire world! About as sane as—well, I was going to say a Chihuahua on acid, but I haven't seen any dogs here, so it would be lost on you, I guess. Let's just say you're mad as a hatter and leave it at that."

"Rome," Graham grunted. "You're not welcome here. Go away."

"Not happening. I think Emily wants me to stay, and it is her apartment after all."

"That might be true, but you're forgetting it's still my world." Graham closed his eyes for an instant. Soon, however, the look on his faced went from one of absolute relaxation to one of concentration. Then confusion, followed by frustration.

Rome waited patiently until the other man's eyes opened again before speaking. "Having trouble getting rid of me? It seems that there's some advantage to being connected to this system via a cable—namely that I'm hardwired in. It almost makes up for how clumsy my avatar is. Also, I took the precaution of shielding my data stream against anything from inside the simulation. You'd be very surprised at how many administrator privileges you can't reach from inside. Hell, you can't even see them."

Graham glared at him, a slight flicker of uncertainty visible in his pale eyes. "It doesn't matter," he said. "I don't need to get rid of you. There are other options." He closed his eyes once more.

"But you don't have any more options," Rome said. Back in his cabin, Rome punched a key that set off a preprogrammed sequence of commands. Even as Graham attempted to attack the reality around them, his defenses were stripped and his face suddenly clouded.

"What? What's happening to me?" he asked. Tears began streaming down his cheeks. "Why do I feel this way?"

Rome looked at him levelly, the only expression his avatar was capable of. "Your dampers are gone, and you're being pumped full of sadness. It's on a feedback loop, getting worse and worse as time goes on. Right now, you're still coherent, but soon the grief will keep you from moving. If I were you, I'd find somewhere safe to hide—I'm sure this little coup of yours has been anything but gentle. I'd hate to think what others would do to you if they suddenly found you in a weakened state."

"Screw you," Graham spat among the sobs. "I'm going to stay right here. You can't stay here forever. Your ship has to return to Tau Ceti. And when you leave, I assure you that my revenge will be taken out in full on this little bitch here." He broke down as another wave of grief washed over him. Graham curled into a ball, covering himself with the wings he'd created.

"I don't think so," Rome replied. He turned to Emily. Her already pale face was absolutely white. How could Dr.

Unameya dare to tell him that she wasn't alive, that she didn't have feelings every bit as strong as his or hers? He tried to speak gently. "Emily, I need to know something. Did you mean it when you said that you'd come with me?"

Her pallid cheeks turned red with anger. "You know I did. But you also know it's impossible. Did you come here to tease me?"

He stayed calm. There was no way she could know. "Of course not. I came to ask you if you still felt the same. Would you come with me if there was a way?"

"Of course I would," she replied flatly. "More so, now. Do you remember when I told you that I felt the world coming apart around me? Well, here's what I meant. I'm not even real, for God's sake. How much more unraveling can my world take? Of course I want to get out and never come back." She glared at him with as much hatred as Graham had. "There, are you happy? The stupid little simulated girl would give up everything to go back with the big bad space man."

"Oh, Emily," Rome whispered, wishing that his avatar could show the pained expression on his face. "If I told you there was a way, would you believe me? Would you trust me?"

She shrugged, but there was little hope in her eyes. "I don't have many options, do I?"

"I'll make the options. I love you, Emily."

She laughed humorously. "It sounds like I'm not the only one unraveling then. I'm not real, Rome."

"But do you trust me?"

She nodded. Without further ado, he clicked another command, and she disappeared.

***

He knew that he did it out of nothing nobler than pure spite, but the guy deserved it. As he left Emily's building, he told the first passer-by that he spotted about Graham's condition, hoping to spark the vengeful attacks he'd predicted.

The man looked thoughtful for a second, but then shook his head. "I hate him for telling us the truth, but I can't really fault him. At least we're not living a lie anymore." The guy walked off in the opposite direction from Emily's building.

Rome shrugged and prepared to disengage from the cyberworld when he heard a soft chuckle behind him.

"It's a little late to put the genie back in its bottle, don't you think?"

Rome turned to find a young, pretty woman with shining hair looking at him levelly.

"And you are?" he asked.

"The name's Jarrien. And I guess you could say that all of this is my fault, although I'm more inclined to think that it was inevitable as soon as you people showed up and started blowing some things up and investigating others. It was certain that someone on the inside would have found out the truth, someone willing to tell others. The end result would probably have been the same."

"So this is a good thing?"

She shrugged. "How should I know? Maybe we'll all go nuts in the next few years and this will become hell. Maybe some power-hungry bastard will kill everyone else and the Mindnet will become an empty shell inhabited by a single cybernetic entity. Or maybe we can build a society on the ashes of what was here before. I don't know. What I do know is that the people of Earth are finally going to move beyond the dead-end society we've been trapped in for the past five hundred years."

"So you'll let Graham do exactly what he wants."

She smiled coldly. "Oh, no. Graham is much too dangerous to let him live. Remember the power-hungry bastard I was alluding to? Well, right now the most likely candidate for that honor is our friend Mr. Johnson. I was just popping in to put him out of his misery."

"So you were listening in on us? How come Graham didn't catch you at it?"

She winked. "I taught him most of what he knows, whether he wanted to admit it or not. He used the things I showed him in abusive ways, and that ruthlessness made him powerful. But I didn't think it was safe to teach him everything I knew. Seems I was right."

Rome nodded his respect.

She smiled. "Have a safe trip back to Tau. Try to make them understand that we really are alive. And, most of all, try to keep them from bombing us when they come back. Who knows, by that time, things might have settled down sufficiently for us to get our defenses back online." She turned to go.

Rome disconnected the avatar for the last time.

Chapter 22

Stell looked at him with a gaze that was almost approving. "Are you finally seeing the light?" he asked.

"What? Oh, her? Don't read too much into that—I'm nowhere near turning asexual yet." Henriette had seemed confused that, despite sitting right beside him, almost on top of him, and turning on the heat in ways that only a woman who looked like she did could, he had basically ignored her all through lunch. She'd eventually left in a huff without even waiting for coffee. Rome hadn't even glanced admiringly when she left.

Stell grinned at him. "That's what they all say, right until the moment they suddenly realize that life is a lot simpler that way." Then he turned serious. "It's that cyberworld girl, isn't it?"

Rome nodded.

"Come on! It's been a month since you found out that she wasn't even real. How could you possibly still be thinking about her? I'm just glad we got off that planet—I mean, how can a population of billions just disappear? Every light year we get farther from them is a light year better for my peace of mind."

Rome shrugged. "Maybe I just need some time to get over it. I don't know, she seemed real to me. Just as real as you and me, and much more real than the little bits," he gestured in the direction Henriette had gone, "that only want a little bit of on-board entertainment. Emily cared."

"Look, Rome, you need to get this into your head. Emily was a program. She didn't care any more than the binary machines that run this ship care whether there are people on it or not. She didn't care any more than my calculator would. All you saw were simulated emotions, programmed into a huge game. None of it was real."

"You know, I had the same conversation with Unameya. Almost word for word. She's convinced that life can't exist in a computer. She said, and I quote, 'Computers are fine for games, but you can't create life out of code. Life is, by its very nature, unpredictable, uncoded.'"

"Sounds about right," Stell replied.

"But don't you see? That was the beauty of this simulation: it had a chaotic, random factor programmed right in. It wasn't perfect, which is why they needed dampers to keep it from going into a feedback loop, but it was close to perfect."

"Did you tell her that?"

"Of course. I also told her that the data included in the simulation of each person on that mainframe was more complex than anything built out of mere DNA. If anything, they are more alive and capable of more emotion and consciousness—and therefore deserving of more respect. She didn't believe me at first, but then I showed her the numbers, showed her some analytics I'd pulled. That opened her eyes, and she went away with my research."

"She'll come back and tell you you miscalculated somewhere."

"I didn't miscalculate. It really is that big. But that's not the main reason I think Emily was alive and her world was real."

"So you admit that science isn't what is driving you? Then what? What evidence can you point to?"

"No evidence. It just seemed real to me. I can't get that feeling out of my head," Rome replied. "Just give me time. I'm going to get some rest."

Stell nodded, real worry showing in his eyes.

As Rome walked back to his cabin, he reflected that he needed the time, but not for what Stell thought. While his friend believed that he was using the time to get over his experiences and the strangeness of Earth's cyberworld, what he really needed the time for was to decide. A risky decision that could, if taken incorrectly, cost him his freedom.

But it wasn't a decision he had to take now. He tried to think about other things as he traversed the corridors, but hadn't succeeded in doing so by the time he arrived at his cabin.

He'd been spending nearly all his time in this small, cluttered room. Captain Nartiya had 'rewarded' him for his role in the exploration of Earth's cyberworld by curtailing his shifts and allowing him to spend most of his time as he saw fit. One of the things he now saw fit to do, which was a departure from his usual practice, was to lock the door—he knew the electronic lock would not deter anyone with access to the ship's security system, but at least it had been effective in discouraging casual interruptions.

Once he'd secured the door, he began his day-to-day ritual—a series of precautions to ensure that he wasn't caught. The first thing he did was to make certain that the supercomputer running every system on the ship was in perfect condition, both with regards to operation and to software integrity. Once satisfied that this was the case, he checked the two primary backups. These mainframes were identical to the main computer, were essentially powered-down versions of the primary. They were actually connected in parallel to the ship's brain and held exactly the same programming and memories, albeit dormant. Rome, as one of the ship's binarists, had ready access to both. He quickly ascertained that they, too, were in perfect running order.

This left the delta unit. Yet another large, bulky backup

unit, it had some differences from the first three. Although physically identical to the others, its memory was in a pristine state except for such programming as the original computers held at the beginning of the mission—it hadn't hooked up to any of the networks and was still wrapped in plastic sheets in a hold. None of the mission's data had entered its massive memory banks. This was a failsafe in case some kind of computer virus overcame the massed defenses of three supercomputers. It had never happened, but one didn't take chances with interstellar spacecraft.

Unbeknownst to anyone else on board, this computer's once empty memory systems and dormant processing capacity were being used for a specific purpose. A keen-eyed observer would have seen a data cable running out of the plastic sheeting. A cable that ended at a transmitter with an antenna just behind the computer.

Had anyone noticed or checked the frequency of the transmitter, and then gone through the entire ship looking for the receptor tuned to that frequency, they would have found that only the receptor in Rome's chambers was tuned there.

But no one paid attention to this machine—the first three were working perfectly.

Rome powered up his link to the delta unit. As his data came online, he thought about the decision he had to make, and about the likely repercussions if he chose the wrong people to confide in.

In the first place, his use of the fourth mainframe for personal reasons, if discovered, could be grounds for some major jail time. The computer was there for a reason: to keep the lives of everyone on this ship safe if there were an unexpected major malfunction that took out the three redundant primaries. Tampering with safety devices on a military mission was a big no-no.

That, however, brought up another problem. What could

he do with his data after the ship landed? There was no way in the world the authorities were simply going to allow him to download everything onto Tau's network. Every bit of information coming off this ship was going to be passed through a million checks before any of it was allowed to enter a single computer connected to the planet's web. This would be particularly true for this particular mission, considering the nature of the contact they'd had with Earth—one hundred percent digital.

So he had to get someone to authorize the data removal and convince the captain to sanction what he'd done. There was no way he'd be able to pull that off on his own. He needed someone higher up in the food chain.

The only person he could think of was Senni Unameya. She'd be fascinated by the prospect of testing the pattern he'd brought back for intelligence and would likely insist on creating a truly human body for the matrix to inhabit, Tau Ceti's first android. He knew her well enough that, if presented with a fait accompli that harmed no one, she would go along with it, even though—or perhaps exactly because—she was a soulless bitch who'd put her research ahead of anything else.

The fact that he'd gotten mad at her in the final meeting wouldn't help matters, but he doubted the good doctor would make much of a fuss—after all, the same calculating logic that had made her such a formidable opponent should work in his favor this time.

Quite another problem, however, was the issue of when to tell her. He most certainly couldn't tell her now; she'd report him to Nartiya immediately, and the delta's memory would probably be wiped. The only question would be whether they'd erase his data before or after they tossed him out the nearest airlock. He assumed they'd space him first.

No. He needed to tell her when it was impossible that

the computer would be needed—thereby saving his data and insuring that he would not have put the crew in jeopardy—but before they landed and were invaded by the army of decontamination and debriefing personnel.

The nature of the mission gave him a small window. Since it had been a major endeavor, and the debriefing team had to be massive, the ship would land on the surface of Tau Ceti II instead of remaining in orbit. The reentry, as always, was the one point in which the fourth computer was nothing but useless weight—if the first three failed, there would be no time whatsoever to plug the final backup into place. The ship would irrevocably crash into the planet.

But there was an upside to this. It also meant that, no matter what happened to the ship, once reentry began, it could no longer be his fault. So what he had to do was to time his conversation with Unameya for just prior to reentry. It should be relatively simple to do since there were always mission countdown clocks telling everyone just how much time remained until any important milestone.

By the time he'd finished, Unameya would have no time to repair the damage—and, he suspected, no inclination. They'd be able to get Nartiya on board before the landing. If Unameya told her something was scientifically valuable, the captain would accept it as true.

They might still throw Rome in jail as soon as they landed, but that was a price he was willing to pay to keep his most important promise.

His terminal showed a pretty decent approximation to the city of Denver as it appeared on Earth's cyberworld. It took up most of the delta unit's memory, but even then, he'd had to cut a few corners. Some shops had no merchandise; most of the apartments in the city had no interiors. But the important data, the data he'd had to trace back to the very root of the mainframe system, had been transplanted whole.

He watched the lone figure approaching down the deserted street. He noticed that she walked slowly, as if enjoying the play of the simulated sunlight on her pale skin. Her strawberry-blond hair moved gently in the breeze. She was as beautiful as the day he'd first seen her, but now had an expression of calm he'd never seen before.

"Hello Emily," he said.

She smiled. "Hello, Rome. I see you're still having trouble getting that avatar working right."

"I need to save memory space to run your personality."

"Hah. I assume we're streaking through space at obscene velocities."

He nodded. "How do you feel about that?"

She pondered for a second before answering. "You know, it's strange. For the first time in years, I feel like my life actually has some meaning. And for the first time in weeks, I feel safe."

Rome smiled and said nothing. It was still a long shot, but he might be able to keep her safe after all.

The End.

Gustavo Bondoni is an Argentine writer with over a hundred stories published in fourteen countries, in seven languages, and is a winner in the National Space Society's "Return to Luna" Contest and the Marooned Award for Flash Fiction (2008). His fiction has appeared in the Texas STAAR English Test cycle, *The Rose & Thorn*, *Albedo One*, *The Best of Every Day Fiction* and many others.

His debut SF novel, *Siege*, was published in 2016, and he has also recently published an ebook novella entitled *Branch*. His short fiction is collected in *Tenth Orbit and Other Faraway Places* (2010) and *Virtuoso and Other Stories* (2011). *The Curse of El Bastardo* (2010) is a short fantasy novel.

He is always delighted to welcome visitors to his website, so drop him a note at: www.gustavobondoni.com